BRAVED

A Cade Ranch Novel

GRETA ROSE WEST

eBook ISBN: 978-1-955633-06-2
Print book ISBN: 978-1-955633-07-9

ALSO BY GRETA ROSE WEST

Wild Heart: Welcome to Wisper A Short Story

Join the newsletter for this short introduction into the Cade Ranch world and for extra goodies and scenes. Sign up on my website.

gretarosewest.com

BURNED: A Cade Ranch Novel

BROKEN: A Cade Ranch Novel

BUSTED: A Cade Ranch Novel

BRAVED: A Cade Ranch Novel

BLINDED: A Cade Ranch Novel

Coming Spring 2022

ACKNOWLEDGMENTS

As always, this book would still be the quiet, wallflower baby brother without so many fantabulous people.

Wyatt and Sean. I love you. Thank you. Have I said that lately? Wyatt, thank you for taking me to the concert of my life, for humoring your silly old mama, and for supporting everything I do. I think I might've raised you right! <3

All the thanks and hugs to Peter Senftleben, my editor. I don't know how we got to book four, but I'm thankful for you every day, even if I disappear into my writing cave and you don't hear from me for months. I see your tweets!

M, thank you for your LOUD but fair BETA comments. At one point, I thought you might set the book on fire, or me. "Say it louder for the BASIC B in the back!" Also, thanks for the gift of Lord CH pics. Finding them in our DMs first thing when I wake up in the morning gets me a goin'! Ohhhhh, how they make my day! *tongue falls out of mouth like a horny puppy*

Tracy, thank you for loving my shy, quiet, beta cowboy. Jay loves you too, and he feels seen by you since so many people love the alphas more. Love you, Sistah!

The Cade Ranch Series is slowly catching air, and I couldn't have done it without some amazing support from my beautiful ARC readers and bookstagrammers. Thank you all for reading, reviewing, and sharing. World domination, one hot cowboy at a time, is not a one-man-band kind of show!

Laaawd, Nikki and Dianna! Even if my tik toks are basic and poorly made, you still like them. You like everything I post or email, and I cannot even express in words how much that means to me. Thanks for always tooting my horn. I did not mean that in a kinky way. ;)

Now… onto Finn's book!

TRIGGER WARNINGS

All of my books deal with heavy themes and issues, such as physical abuse, PTSD, and loss, but this book especially deals with two very serious subjects: sexual abuse and suicide. Please know before reading that if you have dealt with either of these subjects in your life, you may be triggered by this book. There is of course a happy ending, and I don't go into details about either issue—nothing happens on the page—but they are discussed, and these issues have affected the character's lives deeply.

If you are in crisis, please know there is help out there. Contact The American Foundation for Suicide Prevention. Call 1-800-273-8255, text TALK to 741741, or go to https://www.afsp.org

Survivors of sexual assault and abuse can find help through RAINN. In the US, please call 1-800-656-HOPE or go to https://www.rainn.org

You are NOT alone.

To Petunia
You were never alone.
You just didn't know it till now.

DEAR READER

Dear Reader,

I met Billie toward the end of writing Jack's book, Burned, and she was instantly my worst nightmare, yelling at me inside my head. She wanted her story told, and she was relentless. But getting to know Billie better allowed me to know and fall in love with Jay. He was so shy and quiet, even in my imagination, so much that I barely noticed him. Until I did, and then I couldn't get him out! And because he fell in love with Billie, I did too. They are very proud of each other and they love each other fiercely.

Their love story deals with some of the most serious issues plaguing our society today, and they are both subjects that have affected my life. They are heavy subjects, and I know they can be hard to read about, but I love you for pushing through and reading this book! People may pick up a romance novel for the hot guy on the cover, but we romance readers know better. We know they can be so much more than that.

I'm loving getting to know you as The Cade Ranch Series makes its way out in the world. If you haven't yet, email me!

Tell me why you love reading, tell me where you live, what you love. My readers inspire me, and I like to think we are a little cowboy-lovin' family.

After Braved, get ready for Finn's book… Wait. Can one *truly* prepare for Finn? I'm thinkin' no. ;)

love always,
greta
greta@gretarosewest.com

PROLOGUE
JAY

Ten Months Ago

"Jay!"

Jack yelled across the arena from the office doorway. It was a cold Monday mornin' in November. The day had just gotten started, and already, I was freezin' and miserable, workin' harder than I ever wanted to on my family's horse ranch. Every day, I had to convince myself I didn't hate bein' a horse rancher. Well, more like a shit shoveler. I'd never had the knack for horses, not like my brothers.

"Yeah?"

"C'mere for a sec."

Uh… okay. It wasn't very often my oldest brother, Jack, called me into the office. I kinda felt like I'd been summoned to the principal's office even though I claimed part ownership of said office just like the rest of my brothers.

I stopped what I was doin', set my shovel against a stall door, and headed over to where my brother had disappeared behind his big desk.

Knockin' on the doorframe, I looked in at him standin' there, waitin' for me.

"Jesus, Jay. You don't have to knock. This is your office too."

"Right." I stepped in, claspin' my hands behind my back.

"Well, sit down."

Like I said, called to the principal's office.

Jack sat in the computer chair behind the old dinged and weathered wooden desk, and I sat in the hard-backed chair opposite him. If I ran this office, the first thing I'd do would be to upgrade all this mish-mosh furniture. You can't have a respectable business without respectable surroundin's.

"We talked about your ideas for the ranch."

"Yeah?" I sat straighter in my chair. Really? He'd actually listened to me? He'd actually thought about my idea to grow our business and, hopefully, increase our profits? I couldn't believe it. Every time I'd brought it up, he dismissed it. Or me. Or just slammed a door in my face.

"You mentioned a dude ranch."

"Yeah?"

"Like I said, we ain't doin' that."

"Oh. Right."

I was sure he could read the disappointment on my face even though I tried hard not to show it. I hated showin' weakness in front of my oldest brother or any of my brothers—they were all older than me—but I knew I possessed the skills to make our business great. It was what I had gone to school for, but... I just couldn't find the courage to stand my ground.

Jack had held our business, and our family, together through thick and thin, bringin' it back from the brink of death more than once. How arrogant would it be for me to disregard all that?

"But..."

"But?"

"But I been thinkin' about what Mr. Williams said, about them therapy animals they got over in Jackson. A dude ranch just ain't us, Jay. Buncha rich people hangin' around the ranch, payin' us money to clean up after 'em and teach 'em how to ride for five minutes? Sure, we'd make money but we'd be miserable. I think we're better than that. I think we could do somethin' to make a little money and help people at the same time."

"Yeah. That's—yeah," I said, noddin'.

"You look surprised."

"No, I mean, I just didn't think you—"

"I looked it up. There's a shit-ton of information about it all, many different kinds of therapy we could provide. But we couldn't do it by ourselves. We'd need therapists, doctors, equipment. We'd have to train the horses specifically for it. But"—he waved his hand at the computer screen on the desk—"it's all makin' my head hurt. So, you do it. Research it. Come up with a plan. Talk to whoever you need to. I dunno. Whoever. Do whatever it is we paid all that money to send you to that fancy school for."

"Really?"

"Yep."

"Okay," I said, shakin' my head in utter disbelief. "I'm on it. I'll start now." I jumped up and turned toward the door, ready to go. I already had a million ideas runnin' through my mind.

"But Jay?"

I turned back around. "Yeah?"

"I still expect you to do your work every day. You ain't gettin' off the hook. We still need your help around here."

"Right. I know. I'll work on this in the evenin's." *Ughhh.*

More horse shit. Didn't my honors degree in business mean anything to my family?

"If you need time off to, I dunno, meet with people or whatever, schedule it. Just like you would any other job. I need to be able to depend on you bein' here."

"Right. Okay."

"Here," he said, holdin' out a stack of papers. "This is everything I found. It's not much, but I printed it all out."

Huh. I hadn't thought Jack even knew how to use a printer.

"Thanks." I took the papers from him. "Can I ask, what changed your mind? I've been buggin' you about this for a while."

"Yeah, you have." He squinted, considerin' me. "I ain't adverse to makin' money, Jay, but the whole dude ranch thing just don't sit right with me. This does. And, I guess, Evvie."

"Evvie?" The woman who stole my brother's heart in a heartbeat.

"Yeah. She says I'm bein' a dick and I oughta give you a chance. I should trust you."

"Oh, well..." I laughed. "Okay."

"Go on then," he said, wavin' me off with a flick of his wrist and a nod.

I turned and headed toward the door but stopped at the threshold. "Jack?"

Sighin', he looked up from his messy desktop. "What?"

"Thanks. Thanks for trustin' me. I won't let you down."

"I know you won't," he said, and he actually smiled.

Walkin' slowly from the office, I tried not to grin like an idiot and to look professional, but as soon as I cleared his eyeline, I ran to find Evvie. She was standin' in the stall closest to the arena entrance, brushin' a horse and cooin' to her about fairy princesses in big country castles. I had no idea what in the world she was talkin' about.

"Evvie?"

"Oh!" Both she and Fancy jumped a little. "You scared me, Jay."

"Sorry." I stepped in front of her and reached out to pull her into a hug, careful not to squeeze too hard. She still had stitches, her whole body bruised and sore. She'd been through absolute hell, but still, here she was, workin' as best she could to help Jack. To help us all 'cause she loved him. She loved us.

"What's that for?"

"Just… for lovin' my brother. Thank you."

She giggled and hugged me back. "No thanks necessary. I couldn't stop if I wanted to."

Steppin' back, I leaned in to kiss her cheek. "Yeah, but still, thank you."

CHAPTER ONE

BILLIE

"JESUSMOTHEREVERLOVINGCRAP! WHAT THE F—"

"Billie! Wake up. I've been callin' you for an hour. Dammit, answer your phone." Thick cowboy twang pulled me out of sleep, yelling at me in a tinny voice.

I ripped my boxy, faux-wood, 1980s answering machine off my nightstand and dropped it to the floor, then yanked my landline phone so hard, it came off the wall. Yeah, I was a tech geek, but old shit couldn't be hacked.

"What! Who is this?"

"It's Carey. You awake?" *Oh, the twang. I should've known.*

"I am now," I growled. "I'll call you back on my cell. I'm too tired to hold the damn phone."

"Fine. Be quick about it."

"Carey," I croaked in my thick, sleepy voice, "I know you've checked out my ass. 'Member how big it is? Plenty of room for you to find a place to stick your lips and kiss it."

"Nice to hear your voice too. Call me back. I need your help."

I'd just been having the best dream about endless amounts

of RAM and motherboards made of gold. My undies were
still a little wet, if I was honest.

Ughhh.

I noticed my machine on the floor, blinking with
messages probably from my mother, but I ignored them and
rose from my bed like a gothic zombie. I threw on my holey
sweats under my Slayer T-shirt, then pulled my red and black,
kimono-style robe over it all, but took it off. What did it
matter? It wouldn't keep me warm anyway. And no one could
see me. No one would care.

What could Carey Michaels possibly want at midnight on
a freaking Wednesday? *Wait, Wednesday? Thursday?
Whatever.*

The sheriff of Teton County—in freaking Wyoming—
needed to find a tech master much closer to home. I lived
eleven hours away, in Bend, Oregon. The further away from
my guilt-seeking mother who sometimes lived on the East
Coast, the better. She wanted me to feel guilty because I was
the only daughter she had left. Little did she know, or maybe
she knew all too well, that I hated her *because* I was her only
living child. She couldn't make me feel guilty on her
best day.

What the hell did Carey want now? He called me for
everything. "Billie, can you look somethin' up for me? Billie,
can you find someone for me? Billie, hack this, hack that.
Billie, save the world." His requests were abundant and
annoying.

But he was a good guy. And he'd been there for me when
no one else was. So, fine.

I popped a pod in my one-cup coffee maker and called
him back. "What now, Carey? Wait. Let me guess, you want
me to embezzle money from the sleazy douchebag in the
Oval Office. I'm not sure that guy ever really had any of his

own money to begin with, but I'll give 'er my best shot," I said, imitating his Wyoming accent.

"No, Billie. I need you to do your thing. I need you to find someone."

"Who is it this time? Don't tell me—Finn Cade fell in love with an aged Spice Girl and her famous soccer husband kidnapped Finnie Frances since he's so much hotter."

"What in the world are you talkin' about?"

I sighed. "You're no fun. Nothing. Who am I looking for?"

"Theodore Burroughs."

"Wait. Isn't that the dude I did research on last year for Jack Cade and his hot band of merry country bumpkins?"

"Jack Ca—? Jesus, Billie. Yeah. That's the guy. He's gone missin'. His sister's freakin' out. She thinks he's been kidnapped or killed or I dunno. But he left her a note and she received a weird text message. It's all a bit suspicious, and it's... complicated."

I found a rice cake left over from my last diet attempt shoved into the door of my fridge. It didn't look moldy. I took a bite.

"Why's it complicated?" Putting my phone on speaker, I set it on the counter and crunched my question. "The guy got a computer? I can hack it remotely."

"I'm guessin' he does. I'm at their hotel right now. He and his sister checked into a B&B in Jackson a couple days ago. But, Billie, she says he *never* leaves her like this. Can you just come here? I could really use some female backup right now."

"Don't you have a female deputy? Abby, Abey, Obie, whatever."

"Abey. A-bee. The first two letters of the damn alphabet. It ain't hard. Yeah, but Abey's outta town, so that leaves me with Frank. He's not what you'd call super feminine. The sister's name is Aislinn Burroughs. You remember her from your research?"

"Yeah. She's my age—twenty-six. Beautiful. She was in the car accident that killed her parents. She's visually impaired, right?"

"Yeah. She's… difficult, and she's not handlin' her brother bein' gone very well. Will you just come help me? I need your skills anyway, and if you're here, you can get more outta her for your searches."

Trying not to smile because I knew he'd hear it in my voice, I said, "So, let me get this straight. You wake me up, screaming into my answering machine, and then you tell me you need my help. Again. You haven't offered to pay me, by the way. You know, I charge quite a bit of money to do what you're asking me to do. Then you get snotty with me, and now you want me to book my own flight and fly out to the middle of nowhere in the middle of the night? Why would I do that, Carey?" I wouldn't tell him, but I was already going through my closet in my head. What to wear?

I liked being around Carey and the merry bumpkins. Online friends were still friends, sure, but actually interacting with other human beings in person occasionally felt good. And Carey and the Cades were stand-up guys. Their accents were stupid, but they were all good people.

And Jay Cade would be there.

"Okay, got your whinin' outta the way? Now book your ticket, soonest one you can find. You know I can't pay you. This is off the books, but there's nobody better, so I need you. I'll pay for your ticket from my own damn pocket if it matters so much."

"Please, don't insult me. I'm not taking your money." Besides, it wasn't like I couldn't afford it. And I would do almost anything for Carey. He knew about my past. I'd told him when we'd worked a case together a few years ago. It was the only time I'd ever allowed myself to cry in thirteen years. Carey had listened and comforted me with his words, not his hands. He hadn't wanted sex, and he cared when no one else in the world gave a shit. I'd wanted to commit murder that night, and Carey had stopped me.

"I didn't think you would."

"So then, you were just being a dick?"

"Yep. Get to it. I'll see you when you get here."

"Fine. But, Carey, I'm gonna need a place to stay. I could really use some of that down-home Wyoming comfort. A hotel is way too stuffy. I want to stay somewhere... cozy. Somewhere authentically Wyoming. Somewhere with horses. Know what I mean?"

"Nope. Haven't a clue, as usual. Since when do you like horses?"

"Ew, I don't. The ranch! I want to stay at Cade Ranch."

"What? Why?"

Leaning on my counter, I dumped half a cup of dulce de leche creamer into my coffee in my favorite "Byte me" coffee mug. "You know why," I said in a dreamy voice.

"Billie, I'm not gonna call the guys in the middle of the night just so you can drool over Finn Cade. Stalk the guy online. You're good at that. I'm sure you can find plenty of pictures of him. He's in a band. I don't think he's there anyway. He went on some tour with his buddies."

"You called *me* in the middle of the night! And not Finn. He's a moose. Jay. Jay Cade. I'm tired of masturbating to his collegiate pic. I want the real thing."

"Jesus, Billie."

I clicked my tongue. "What? Women masturbate, Carey.

Just like men. Probably less often, but since when are you so uncomfortable with my feminine identity?"

Carey scoffed out something from the back of his throat. "Since forever. Get your butt out here."

"Fine, but you owe me." A slow, sly smile glanced across my lips. "And get me that computer."

I landed in Jackson, Wyoming eight hours later. Carey was lucky I liked him, and that I didn't have a life and could work on my paying cases from anywhere. I only had a backpack and two laptops, so I went straight to the curb and grabbed one of the probably only two ride-shares in the little town. Checking my phone, I only half-listened while Marla, my five-star driver, chatted away about tourist spots in Jackson.

Carey had left four messages already. Jeez. Did the guy ever sleep?

Pressing speaker, I played my messages, putting an end to Marla's "Hey, girl, I know we just met, but let's be besties" routine.

"I got the guy's laptop. Call me when you land."

"So, um, the sister is not at all cooperative. Ugh. Call me back."

"Jeez, Billie. Did you drive to Wyoming? Good grief. Have you landed yet? Call me."

"Billie, did you walk to Wyoming?" He snorted into the phone. *"Oh, wait, I forgot whose voicemail I'm talkin' to."* He sighed. *"Alright, you get your wish. Meet me out at Cade Ranch. Remember where it is? Route 20, south of Wisper. And call me soon as you get this."*

Before I could even hit the callback button on my phone, it rang again. Clicking speakerphone off, I answered.

"Carey. Take a pill. I'm on m—"

"Excuse me? Sorry. Hello?"

"Oh. Uh, yeah? This is Billie Acker."

"Hello, Miss Acker. My name is Melody Carnahan. I-I got your name from a friend. He said you might be able to help me find my husband." The woman sounded like she'd been crying, and she was kind of whiny.

"He's missing?"

"Yes, since Sunday night. And, well, I recently found out that he'd been... having an affair."

I rolled my eyes. "Okay, so maybe he just left you." I had to work at trying to be compassionate with these women, and usually, I failed. I'd worked tons of these stupid cheating spouse cases. They weren't my preferred way to spend my time or my considerable skills, but they paid the best.

They almost always turned out the same way. The husband found a better hole to sink his putt into. A prettier one, skinnier, richer. Whatever. I wanted to shake the women and scream, "He's gone. You're free. Take your GD life back!"

"No. He wouldn't do that. You don't know Marc. We were working it out. We just booked a trip to Aruba. We even scheduled scuba diving lessons. I've been killing myself in the gym and—" She sighed. "He didn't just leave."

Wanna bet?

"Okay, well, I'm actually working a case right now. I can refer you to—"

"No! Please? My friend, Colin, Colin Byrne? He said you're the best. I don't want some old man. You're a woman. You understand. I want you. I'll pay. Whatever the cost."

Yeah, she would. Extra. And Colin Byrne? Guy was a douchebag I knew from my failed attempt at higher educa-tion. He worked at some tech start-up in California—how original—giving hand jobs to his rich bosses, a bunch of mommy's boys trying to invent the next new app to change the world. Like Facebook. *Insert eye roll here.*

And no, I didn't understand. I never understood these women, never understood how they could give all their power away to some guy. A bully, a liar, a cheater. Whatever. If a man said he loved you but wanted you to be powerless to him, then he didn't really.

But I wouldn't argue with a paying client.

"Okay, well, um, can you send me your info? Just email it to the address on my website. Bbtatb.com. I need to know where he works, his schedule, hobbies. Send me some pics. I'm gonna need social security numbers, yours and his, banking information. There's a secure form on the site you can use. I'll text you the link. Does he have a computer or laptop that you can access?"

"Yes. I'll send you all of that. His laptop is gone, but he uses our desktop sometimes. Will that help?"

"Yeah. Okay. I just landed in Wyoming for a case. This will take me some time, but send me that stuff, and I'll get back to you with payment info. I'll need half up-front."

"Whatever it is, I'll pay. Just find him? Please? I love him."

"Okay. I'll get back to you."

I hung up, rolling my eyes, and called Carey, but he didn't answer, so I tried to relax and to look forward to the next couple of days.

"So, have you ever been to Jackson Hole before?" Marla asked with a little twinkle in her eye in the rearview mirror.

"Yep."

"Cool! Did you come for business or pleasure? Have you been downtown? We have a lovely little downtown area. The antler arches in Town Square are super cute, and there's lots of quaint restaurants and breweries. And there's so much hiking…" She droned on and on and on, and I tuned her out. I couldn't help it. It had something to do with the decibel levels of her annoyingly excited voice. My brain just couldn't compute.

And besides that, anticipation hummed through my whole body. (If I weren't me, I would've thought I was nervous. But, like, I was me and I didn't get nervous.)

I hadn't seen Jay Cade in almost a year. Gorgeous, shy, quiet Jay Cade. Carey wasn't wrong. I had stalked Jay online, but only a little. I looked up his graduation pic from Berkeley, but I didn't allow myself to look further. Why bother?

He was too perfect.

He was different from his hunky brothers though. A little shorter, less physical and muscley-delicious. And he was sexy-smart and well-read. He got nearly perfect grades at Berkeley. I'd checked.

But he was still a cowboy.

Whatever. At least I'd get to look at him for a few days while I helped Carey. Settling in for the forty-minute drive, I looked at the dirty, dusty landscape while I continued to ignore Marla and her springy curls bouncing around the front seat, which, incidentally, didn't seem to slow her down one bit.

Okay, so Wyoming was kind of pretty. All those big dark mountains and the wheat-colored fields and green trees everywhere. I rarely left my warehouse apartment, so I supposed it was good for my brain to process colors other than black, white, and gray once in a while. Oregon was just as pretty, but why go out when I had everything I needed in my bat cave? That way, I didn't have to deal with people, and that was exactly how I liked it.

People always disappointed.

They rarely did anything out of the kindness of their hearts, so why should I? The closest I'd come was helping Carey pro-bono. And I only did it because Carey was the only guy I'd ever met who kept his word. He didn't want me to change, unlike every other man I'd ever met, and occasionally, he even called just to see how I was doing. Go figure.

That was the real reason I didn't bother to "stalk" Jay for real. The reason I didn't ever bother getting involved with men.

What was the point? It always started out so well. But then it would invariably turn into, "Do you have to spend so much time on your computer? Why don't you want to go to dinner with my friends?" And then, "Are you sure you want to eat that third cupcake?" And of course, my favorite would always be, "Wouldn't *you* feel better if you lost, I don't know, twenty pounds? Maybe thirty? I mean, I just want you to be healthy. Because I love you."

Jay Cade would be no different.

I wouldn't lie to myself though. I wished he was. I'd never met another man so alluring. His quiet way. His smile. Unruly dark brown hair with sexy, wavy curls that licked his neck like sin itself. Blue eyes the color of the tropical ocean my new client's husband was probably screwing his sidepiece in.

Jay was beautiful, and just like all the others, it would most likely start out as heaven on earth. I couldn't even imagine the sex. But it would quickly turn into my usual dating nightmare. He'd expect me to be dainty, sweet, and skinny, like his brother's wife, Evvie.

It was what all guys like him expected.

As Marla turned off the highway and drove up the lane toward his house, I wondered why Jay had moved back home after he'd graduated with honors from business school at

Berkeley. Seriously, why wouldn't he go to a city? San Francisco, New York. I mean, anywhere would be more exciting to a business guy than Wisper, Wyoming. What kind of business could he conduct here? Dirt farming?

Marla pulled up in front of the Cade's ranch house and stopped her lime green Prius, and I stepped out. All I saw as I looked around were mountains, trees, and horses. This was literally the last place on earth anyone who knew me would guess I'd be. Except, not a lot of people actually knew me. I'd been on my own—alone—since I left college. Except for Carey. Which, of course, was why I found myself in the middle of nowhere, soon to be surrounded by slow-talking, gorgeous-but-gruff cowboys.

I yanked my tight black jeans up my ass, made sure my boobs were looking pert and bouncy, grabbed my rig, and stomped up the stairs to Jay Cade's house. Even if he wasn't my Ever After, I'd bet I could lure him into a couple rounds of dirty, raunchy, sweaty, hot cowboy sex. There were bound to be little nooks and crannies in the big red barn where we could get up to no good.

It might be a challenge since Jay was such a good boy, but I never backed down from a challenge.

In fact, never met one I didn't murder.

CHAPTER TWO

JAY

"CAREY, what on earth do you want me to do? I don't know anything. I don't know where Theo Burroughs is. I've never even met his sister."

"I know, Jay. Just, please?" Carey pleaded. "Do me this favor?"

"What's goin' on, Carey? Everything alright?" Jack asked, walkin' up behind me in my kitchen while Carey Michaels, our local sheriff and close family friend, begged me to look after a stranger.

"Hey, Jack. Yeah, I was just askin' Jay for some help."

"Whatever you need, man. You know that."

"Jack, you don't know what he's askin'."

Carey sighed. "Theodore Burroughs has gone missin'. His sister's sittin' in my cruiser as we speak. He left her a note, tellin' her to come to your ranch, and she hasn't heard from him since. I've been with her most the night. Can I just bring her inside? I'll explain everything. Billie's on her way. She's gonna help me look into this."

Billie?

The hacker Billie? The beautiful, snarky Billie Acker?

"Billie's comin'?" I asked, my head swimmin' with sweaty, sexy images of her naked in my bed. Imagined images, unfortunately. I'd only met her in person the one time.

"Yeah. She's good at findin' people, and this guy needs to be found. She'll be here soon."

If Billie was comin', that changed everything.

"Okay," I conceded way too easily. I hoped Jack and Carey didn't notice the desperate eagerness in my voice, but I couldn't deny the excitement I felt at seein' her again. My brothers, Jack and Kevin, followed me out to the porch while Carey helped Aislinn Burroughs out of his cruiser.

I'd lived in our ranch house all my life with my four brothers, except for my four years at business school. But recently, all but one of 'em had moved out. So it was just me and Finn in the huge house, but he was outta town, and I didn't know the first damn thing about takin' care of rich people. I'd known a few at school, but my roommates had been scholarship kids, just like me. We'd worked damn hard for our education and took nothin' for granted.

"Jay," Jack whispered, "I told Theo he and his sister were welcome here anytime."

"I know, Jack, and I agree, but you guys are all gone. Finn's outta town. It's just me. What am I s'posed to do with her?"

"We'll figure it out. Let's just see what Carey has to say."

I held the screen door open as Carey guided Aislinn Burroughs, the little sister of the man who was to invest a small fortune in Cade Ranch in a few weeks' time, as she climbed my porch stairs.

If Theo really was missin', or worse, I'd be screwed. I felt like a jerk thinkin' of money at a time like this, especially 'cause Theo's sister looked upset and scared, but I'd worked my ass off on the proposal for my family's new business venture. Theo missin' meant his money was missin', too, and all that hard work would go right down the drain.

The proposal for an equine therapy and adaptive ridin' program was my shot. A way to prove myself to my brothers, to prove to Jack we hadn't wasted a ton of money on business school. It was a way for me to prove to my family, and myself, that I wasn't just "baby Jay." The leftover kid. The afterthought.

As Carey guided Miss Burroughs into my house, another car turned onto the property, and my heart jumped. Was it Billie? But I didn't wanna be rude. I followed Carey inside, and we all sat at the kitchen table.

Miss Burroughs had lost her vision in a car accident some years ago. She gripped a long, white walkin' cane in her hand, and she wore dark sunglasses that looked way too big for her face. Theo had told my brothers and me about his sister when we first met him this past spring, but we'd never met her. I had no idea why Carey would bring her to my house.

What exactly was he expectin' me to do?

"So, guys, this is Aislinn Burroughs. Miss Burroughs, this is Jay, Jack, and Kevin Cade. They live here on the ranch and run it. They're the guys your brother's been workin' with."

"I know who they are, Sheriff," Miss Burroughs replied in a crisp, haughty voice.

A very beautiful woman with glowin' golden brown skin and dainty features set off by short, expertly tousled brown-black hair, Aislinn Burroughs was the picture of opulence and money. She sat stick-straight at my kitchen table, holdin' her body in a nervous, rigid way. Her clothes looked fine and expensive, but they were a little disheveled.

She was almost as tall as me, and even though I wished he

was here to help me, I found myself feelin' extremely relieved Finn was outta town on a small country tour with his band. He woulda gone straight for this woman. I already knew he liked how she looked; he'd told me when we'd looked her brother up when he first offered to invest in our ranch.

"Right," Carey said. "So, like I told you, Miss Burroughs' brother left her at a B&B in Jackson the night before last and hasn't returned. Jack? Jay, are you sure you haven't talked to him? You didn't know he'd be in town?"

"No," Jack said.

"Yeah, Carey," I answered, "I'm sure. I spoke to him last week. We arranged to meet two weeks from now. He was plannin' to give us the first investment check so we could get started on buildin' out the arena for the new program. We discussed the construction company we're gonna be usin', and we talked about a few smaller issues we still needed to work out. But that's it. He didn't say he'd be in town this week. I have no clue why he came now."

"I told you, Sheriff," Miss Burroughs said, "this was a last minute trip. We returned from London to Logan International and were supposed to go home, but Theo received a call from someone, then dragged me to a hotel for two days. He booked the flight to Wyoming soon after, and we arrived Monday afternoon. And then—" She cocked her head infinitesimally toward the front porch, listenin' as the other car parked in front of the house on the gravel lane outside.

"That'll probably be Billie," Carey said.

I hadn't seen Billie Acker since last October. My brothers and I had met her when Jack's wife, Evvie, was attacked and kidnapped, and Billie helped us find her. Billie was a hacker and, apparently, a bit of a private detective. Carey had worked with her in the past and said she could find anybody anywhere.

"Can you please just take me back to my hotel? I understand why you brought me here, but I would *prefer* to wait there." Miss Burroughs didn't even try to hide her contempt for the ranch, or maybe it was Wyoming in general.

"Miss Burroughs," Carey addressed her in his most professional and calming voice, but no matter how business-like he tried to sound, I still saw the scrawny red-headed teenager that hung out with my brother, Dean, ridin' horses, throwin' a football on my front lawn, and givin' me wet willies. "I really would like you to stay here. This is where your brother wanted you to be."

"Stay here, like, sleep here? You must be joking. I will not. I will not!" She stood from her chair, clenchin' her fists just as Billie threw the kitchen door open and strode into my house.

"What's up, bitches? I'm here to save your asses. Again." She planted her hands on her rounded hips, and we all just stared at her.

Immediately upon seein' her face, with her silky, straight, dark hair fallin' down around her like heavy rain, I remembered the first time I'd met her. It was silly, but back then, I'd imagined her standin' under the moon, liftin' her arms to reach for me, like some goddess in one of my books. She smiled, and her body called to mine, wantin' mine, but all too soon, clouds rolled in above us, obscurin' that mysterious moon, and a mask of shadow appeared on her face.

I tried not to laugh out loud at myself. She'd probably never thought of me since that day, when she stomped up the stairs to my front porch and commanded the attention of everyone I knew.

Once again, my sappy imagination had run wild.

She looked around the table, and her eyes landed on mine. My jeans grew tight around my groin 'cause my whole body throbbed just at the sight of her and the sound of her husky voice.

"Great." Kevin groaned.

"What, aren't you happy to see me? I thought we were BFFs?" Billie smirked at Kev and rolled her eyes. "Afraid everybody will like me better than you? I am funnier. And hotter. And just all around better than you," she mocked, and Kev sighed. I remembered this same reaction from him when we'd met her last year. And she was spot on. Kev did like bein' the center of attention. He liked to be the smartass in the room, but Billie beat him to it.

How could I have forgotten how beautiful she was? Her silver-gray eyes, sultry and surrounded by lots of charcoal makeup, were framed by thick bangs. She radiated spitfire and a deep melancholy no one else seemed to see, but she filled up the room with her sassy energy, and I wanted to swim in it.

"Thanks for comin', Billie," Carey said. "Have a seat. I was just fillin' everybody in."

"Aislinn, this is Billie Acker. She's the woman I've asked to find Theo."

"Hey, Ace."

"It's Ace-*linn*," Miss Burroughs enunciated with tight lips.

Billie rolled her eyes again. "Right. Okay then, Carey, gimme Theo's laptop. I'll get started on that while you guys chat. And I'm gonna need your phone, Aislinn. Carey said you got a weird text message?" Billie dropped her backpack on the floor next to a dinin' chair and set her messenger bag on the table, and as she sat, she looked right at me again.

"Yes, but I haven't read it. Theo left me a letter written in braille, instructing me not to trust anything else."

Billie didn't look away from me while Aislinn spoke. I didn't say anything. I couldn't speak. Apparently, the ability flew out the door when she opened it. Nothin' came to mind, and just like the last time I'd met her, any thought I did have in her presence never seemed worth sayin'. She'd just laugh at me. She was always witty and funny and blunt. Like Finn. She'd probably like him more than she'd ever like me.

"Wait just a minute. You took Theo's laptop?" Aislinn turned toward Carey. "You can't do that. It's private. There's personal and financial information on there. You can't just—"

Finally, Billie broke the spell, lookin' at Aislinn and soundin' as bored as a person could. "Do you want to find your brother?"

"Of course I do, Miss Acker, but—"

"Good, then I need to search his laptop. If we wait for law enforcement, it could be days, probably weeks or longer till they get to it."

"Theo is a very private person, Miss Acker. He wouldn't approve of you rummaging through his things."

"Tough shit. What are you afraid of? That I'll rip your brother off? Trust me, I don't need his money. And I wouldn't do that. Take a pill. And stop calling me Miss Acker. It's Bill-*lee*."

Aislinn huffed a breath but finally sat back down.

"The laptop's in my cruiser. Go grab it. Jay, would you mind helpin' Billie? There's a few bags in the back. Bring 'em in for me?"

"Sure." I was amazed I could get that out. I wiped the nervous sweat from my hands on my jeans under the table, then stood.

"You're wasting my time, Sheriff."

Billie made a face and crossed her eyes, stood, and nodded for me to follow her outside. I did, like a dutiful puppy, and when we were at the back of Carey's cruiser, she turned to face me. Her eyes were so pale gray in the mornin' sunlight that they almost looked supernatural, and they were so mesmerizing.

"So, she's staying here? In a house with five guys?"

"Uh, yeah, I guess," I said. "'Cept it's just one guy. Me."

"What do you mean?"

"Um, Jack and Evvie live in a cottage on the property." I nodded toward their little forest house. "Dean moved in with his girlfriend, Oly, in town, and Kev moved out a few months ago. He lives in town now too."

"What about Ma?"

I shuffled my feet and looked at the dirt so she wouldn't see the pain in my eyes. So she wouldn't see how much I missed the woman who'd raised my brothers and me after my own mama had left when I was just a baby. "She passed in May."

"Oh, Jay. I'm sorry."

"Thanks." I cleared my throat. "Yeah, so it's just me and Finn, but he's not here."

"So there are empty bedrooms?"

I looked up to see her squintin' against the sun, but when she noticed me starin' at her, she stared right back and smirked. There was kindness in her eyes for Ma and some of her patented sass, and I could barely hide the smile from takin' over my face at the thought of her stayin' in my house.

"Would you like to stay here too? There's plenty of room."

"Why, Jay, I thought you'd never ask." She smiled and lowered her chin, battin' her black-coated eyelashes, then straightened. "It'll be better for me to be where Aislinn is. I have a ton of questions for her. And I'm kinda thinking it might be helpful for you, too, if I stay with her."

"Oh God, thank you. I have no idea what to do with this woman."

Billie opened Carey's truck and grabbed the laptop, then stepped back to watch me grapple with Aislinn's many heavy designer suitcases. "Well, I hope you have an idea of what to do with *some* women," she quipped. "Otherwise, I might feel like I wasted the trip." And she walked away!

Was she flirtin' with me?

Oh, I knew what to do. She didn't know it, but in my dreams, I'd already done "it" to her many, *many* times.

CHAPTER THREE

BILLIE

"AISLINN, let's go over this again," Carey said. "You were sayin' you and Theo talk every day?"

"Yes. We live together in our parents' home in Boston. There hasn't been one day we haven't talked, at least once, since—"

Aislinn stopped short, and Jack, Kevin, Carey, Jay, and I all stared at her, waiting for the end of that sentence. Well, the guys stared at her. I looked, but then my eyes zoomed in on the side of Jay's face, and I fantasized licking it.

Pulling a paperback book from his back pocket, he set it on the table, and I tried to read the title—I wanted inside his head, and knowing what he liked to read would give me insight—but I couldn't tell what it said because the cover was crinkled and folded. It looked like he'd read it a thousand times. Or maybe ran over it with a truck.

"Since what?" Carey prodded Aislinn.

"Since forever! We talk every single day. Even when he's overseas. He never forgets to call me. Never." She gripped the sides of her arms so hard, the skin was turning red.

"Okay, I'm sorry. I don't mean to upset you, and I don't

think he forgot, but I need to know. Now, you're sure he didn't say anything about where he was goin'?"

"I'm not upset." She scoffed. "And no, he didn't say a thing."

"Okay. But what did he say exactly the last time you saw him?"

"Nothing!" she screeched, getting seriously agitated with Carey's questions. "How many times do I have to repeat myself?"

"He didn't say 'goodbye' or 'see ya later'?"

"Well, of course he said 'goodbye,' but he didn't say anything else."

"Okay, that's fine. But can you tell me *exactly* what he said? Doesn't matter what it was about. Anything you can remember might help."

She hung her head, yanked the sunglasses away from her eyes, and pinched the bridge of her nose between her thumb and finger.

"Please, take your time, but try to think. What exactly did your brother say before he left your hotel room?"

"This is ridiculous. What does this have to do with anything?"

"Please, just humor me," Carey said. I could tell he wanted to sigh, but he held it in. He had always been better with the hand-holding than I was.

She held her breath for ten seconds and huffed it out, then looked up. Her eyes were the most mysterious shade of light green, like see-through sage, which was striking against her dark skin. "Fine. He said, 'I have to run an errand in the morning. I won't be long, but would you stay in your room please?' to which I replied, 'Of course, where am I going to go? On a sightseeing tour of this backwards country dirt show?'"

My BFF—a.k.a. Kevin Cade—snorted but tried to cover it with a shamefully pathetic attempt at a cough. Carey turned his head to glare at him, and Kevin pressed his lips together hard, trying not to laugh.

I laughed right out loud. I was starting to like this chick.

"Okay, and why'd he want you to stay in your room?"

"I don't know. Because he's completely controlling? He thinks I can't do anything alone, but I am perfectly capable of taking care of myself. I don't need his help." Aislinn sat a little straighter in her chair, puffing her chest out, trying to look strong and unaffected. I did feel bad for her. This had to be pretty scary.

"That's all he said? Are you sure?"

"Yes."

"And when did he tell you to come to Cade Ranch? You said earlier he left instructions for you to come here."

"I don't—" She stopped short again, closing her eyes and holding her breath, then she said, "He wrote in his letter that if I found myself in trouble or needed help, I should come to the Cade Ranch. That he trusted the people there and knew if anything ever happened to him, that's what I should do because they would help me."

Leaning to the side, she lifted her ridiculously expensive leather purse from the floor, a brown one with gold "LVs" all over it, setting it demurely in her lap and searching with her fingers for something, then pulled out a piece of paper and her cell phone. "And then, late last night, I received the text and an email, but they aren't from Theo." She held the phone and paper out toward Carey, and he took them and handed them both over to me.

"Theo left this letter with the front desk, and they delivered it after he disappeared. All it said was for me to come here. He said he would be unreachable through his phone. He left me the number to this ranch and said that I shouldn't talk to anyone else. But the manager of the B&B called you because, apparently, since I'm blind, I couldn't possibly know how to operate a telephone on my own."

"Had Theo ever said anything like that to you before?" Carey asked. "I mean, had he ever warned you like that?" He looked at me with his eyebrows raised and nodded to the paper on the table.

Um, so what? Now he expected me to be able to translate braille out of thin air? Well, when in doubt… I pulled out my phone. Ha! A photo translator app. Thank you, internetland. I downloaded the app, snapped a photo and uploaded it, and waited for results. But the letter was a bust. It said almost exactly what Aislinn had: Don't leave your room, don't talk to anyone, and call the Cades at Cade Ranch. I caught Carey's eye, shook my head, and shrugged.

"Warned me? No." She scrunched her face in thought. "But until recently, we had staff I could call if I ever needed anything."

"Oh? What happened to change that? Why can't you call 'em anymore?"

"I can. I did. I called Theo's driver, Tim McCullough. He's back in Boston, but he hasn't answered my calls or texts. And I tried Louise, but she's not answering either."

"Who's Louise?"

"Louise Gross. She's my maid, my—she stays with me when Theo goes out of town sometimes or has a long meeting. She's my cook, my…" Aislinn sighed. "I haven't seen or spoken to her in two weeks. Theo said he gave the staff some time off. I didn't really understand that decision because we'd just come back from a trip, so they already had time off. But he told me not to worry about it, so I didn't. But it's odd that she hasn't called or texted me. She works for us, but we're… close. She's been with me since our parents died."

"I'm sorry for your loss, Miss Burroughs."

She huffed again and shook her head. "How is this helpful? I don't need your sympathy, Mr. Michaels. I need your skills. *If* you have any."

Kevin sniggered. "Oh, shit."

"Okay." Carey threw my BFF a look but pushed on. He wouldn't let a little attitude deter him. I'd always admired that about him. We'd worked several cases together a few years ago, and each time, I'd become more and more impressed with his people skills. Like I'd said, mine were pretty much nonexistent. "Okay, tell me again what you and Theo did when you arrived here on Monday."

"You've asked me this three times already. How is this helpful?"

"Just bear with me. It's helpful 'cause every time I ask, you remember more."

"We arrived at the local airport and went straight to the inn. We were supposed to leave this morning. That's what my return plane ticket says."

A black and white cat padded toward Aislinn from the living room, and she tilted her head to the side, listening to the tiny noise. The cat sat next to Aislinn's chair and purred. I heard it all the way across the table. Aislinn turned her head one millimeter more in its direction, and a smile tried to form on her lips.

"Did your brother act out of the ordinary in any way? Do you remember anything weird or outta sorts?"

"What?" She focused back on Carey. "'Outta sorts'? No. But Theo's always on his phone, how would I have any —but…"

"But what?"

"He did get a call at the airport. As soon as we got off the plane. I remember thinking he seemed nervous somehow before he answered."

"See? You remembered something new. Nervous how?"

"No, Sheriff. I don't 'see.' Whoever he spoke to was loud, and I put my earbuds in and ignored Theo. We left the airport and checked into the B&B, and Theo was in and out all afternoon, but I have no idea what he was doing. He seemed really busy, so I stayed out of his way. I stayed in my room until he brought dinner. I wanted to go to a restaurant so I could get out of that awful motel, but Theo said no. I have no idea what his intention was in coming to Wyoming. All he ever says is, 'It's business.' He booked the hotel. He made all of the arrangements and dragged me along. He treats me like a child."

"How soon after you got off the plane?"

"What?"

"The phone call. Exactly when did your brother receive that call?"

Aislinn scoffed. "I don't know."

"Think. It could be important."

"I don't know. We hadn't gotten to baggage claim yet."

"Hm. Right. Okay."

Carey stood, his chair squeaking across the linoleum floor, and Aislinn scrunched her face up again, like she'd eaten something sour. "Wait a minute. Were you planning to just leave me here?"

"Uh, actually, yes," Carey said, pushing his chair in and taking a step back. He put his hands on his hips. "This is where your brother wanted you to go. And I'll know if you're here, you'll be safe. Billie's gonna stay here so she can get some more information from you, and Jack and his wife, Evvie, are less than a mile away."

Aislinn turned her head in my direction and made a face. I didn't think she was too excited to be dumped on me. I wasn't over the moon about it either.

"I don't need a babysitter. I can take care of myself."

"Miss Burroughs, there's obviously somethin' goin' on with Theo, and it most likely isn't anything good. Is there anyone else you can call? A family member, friend?"

"No. There's no one. Not until I can reach Tim or Louise. But I don't have my clothing or even a toothbrush."

"You do. It's all in your bags. I had the hotel pack it up for you."

"You—you just took my things? Without asking me?"

Carey looked at me and begged with his eyes. *Help.*

I rolled mine and stood. "Can someone take Aislinn's bags to one of the empty bedrooms and we'll try to relax a little? Aislinn, you hungry? I'm starving. What do you guys have to eat around here?"

"Uh," Jack hedged, "actually, I'm pickin' Evvie up in town here in a few minutes. Why don't I grab somethin' from the diner? I bet José already has a batch of chili warmed up or they have good sandwiches."

"A diner? Chili?" Ace shook her head. "No, thank you. I'm fine."

"How about a salad? Do they have good salads?" I asked, trying to help Jack out a little. Had he even looked at Aislinn? She was skinny as a rail. I doubted she made a habit of hogging down on good ol' country cookin'.

"A salad would be fine," she said. "I don't eat meat."

Bingo. I raised my eyebrows at Jack, and he nodded and smiled. "Yeah, they do. They have a great house salad, actually. José makes the dressin' himself. I'll get some of that. You know what, I'll just get a buncha stuff, and you guys can pick and choose. I'll call Daisy and have her throw some stuff together."

"Good plan," I said, watching Jay drag two of Aislinn's bags, which, of course, matched her purse, through the living room to a bedroom at the end of a little hallway. "Okay, Ace —" She scoffed. "Sorry. *Aislinn*. Let's go take a breather, and I'll see what I can find on your phone." She planted her hands on her hips, but I walked around the table and took one hand gently, then dragged her to the bedroom.

See? I could be compassionate.

"Okay. Let's get you changed, huh? Looks like you've been in those clothes a while," I said while Jay deposited Aislinn's third bag on the bed in the downstairs bedroom and quietly left the room. He shut the door behind him but not before grimacing at me first, and I tried not to watch his ass in his tight jeans when he walked away. Okay, so maybe I didn't try very *hard*.

"What?" She smoothed her hands down her wrinkled silk shirt. She looked so… lost. "Do I look awful?"

"No, no, that's not what I meant." *Way to go, Billie.* "You just look a little uncomfortable. Do you have some sweats or comfy jeans or something?"

"No. I don't wear sweats." She sighed. "I have linen trousers, I think." She took one tiny step toward the bed, then stopped. "I d-don't have any idea where I am, Miss Acker. Please," she whispered. "Please help me." She stood tall and took a deep breath, trying to cover the crack in her armor she'd just exposed.

"That's why I'm here, Ace. Don't worry."

Ace fell asleep on the bed while I searched her phone. From my research months earlier, I knew she was close to my age. Actually, she was only a few months younger, but I saw her as older. Maybe because she was so much taller. Or maybe it was her air of privilege or her disdain for ordinary things. Like sweatpants.

Maybe it was because she'd been through so much. Both her parents had been killed instantly in a car accident several years ago when Ace was just a teenager, and she had been blinded by damage to her optic nerves from countless injuries.

In the blink of her eye, everything she'd ever known had been taken away.

Her only sibling, Theo, had stepped in. He'd been away at college, but he took over raising her, and finished college, and then grad school. Before that, and since, Aislinn had never wanted for anything materially.

She was as lacking and sheltered as a person could be otherwise.

Her brother did everything for her. Managed her life. Provided, advocated, decided, and determined for her. Short of actually living and breathing for her, he did everything.

Setting my rig up to search for Theo, I spent most of the rest of the afternoon going through his computer. I didn't expect quick results since I didn't have much to go on yet. And I hadn't found much on Ace's phone, but it didn't surprise me.

There was an email in Aislinn's inbox that she hadn't opened. It had been routed through a dozen servers it shouldn't have been. Oddly, something about the email seemed familiar to me, but I didn't know what. There was a link in the email that led to the same dummy site the text had, with a recording of what I assumed was Theo's voice, telling

her to go to Cade Ranch, but the email hadn't come from
Theo. Ace's phone had been messed with, the location
tracking turned off.

Her brother wasn't missing; he'd taken off. I had no idea
why, but from what she told Carey, it seemed obvious to me
that he was into something he most likely shouldn't have
been.

Why would he bring Aislinn all the way to Wyoming
from Boston, to a place she didn't know, and leave her
instructions to come to Cade Ranch? Why wouldn't he leave
her with someone in Boston? A friend. A co-worker. Anyone
she already knew. Why would he send her to strangers?

Theo had run, and he'd sent his sister, his only living rela-
tive, to the one place he knew she would be protected and
treated like family. I knew because it was how the Cade
family treated me. From the moment I walked in the door last
October to help Evvie, I had been respected, included, fed,
joked with, relied on, and befriended.

And, like Ace, I hadn't had that in a long time.

No one here looked at me and saw a failure. No one saw
my flaws. Well, maybe Kevin did, but I was pretty sure it was
because I was way wittier than him and it pissed him off,
which filled me with joy. I wasn't sure why his misery made
me so happy, but I enjoyed it, so I didn't search too hard for
the answer. But it was only in fun.

I'd never had brothers and only one sister, but we'd been
just like the Cade brothers were together. We joked, laughed,
fought, argued, poked and prodded each other. We'd given
each other nicknames, called each other "sissy."

My sister had been everything to me. My parents were
there, mostly, but not "there," my mother too busy methodi-
cally working her way through the small Connecticut circle of
the rich and famous, and my father well on his way to

drinking himself to death. And their absence in our lives was the reason for everything bad that had ever happened to my sister.

And then Jessie was gone, and she took the only family or home I'd ever known with her.

CHAPTER FOUR

JAY

I YANKED my shirt on when I heard Billie's voice comin' up the stairs, talkin' on her phone. Dammit. I'd just showered, but now my hands were slicked with sweat again, and my knees felt weak.

"Yes, Carey, I'm being nice to her. What did you find out? Did Theo's driver call back yet?"

Stoppin' in front of Finn's bedroom door, she listened to Carey for a minute, and I peeked out into the hallway from my room.

"The call Theo received at the airport came from a burner. I can't find anything about it other than the time and the length of the call." She bit her bottom lip between her teeth, listenin' to Carey. "Oh, well, that doesn't sound good. Okay. But it helps me. I can add that to my searches. I don't know what I'll find but—no. I won't say a word. Okay, see you when you get here. I'm gonna use Finn's computer. I can get more done if I set his up to search too."

Oh God, no.

She hung up, and I threw my door outta the way with my

fly hangin' open and my T-shirt bunched around my shoulders, my arms not yet through the arm holes.

"Don't go in there!" I ran past Billie and yanked Finn's door closed.

"Oh!" She jumped back and dropped her cell phone. "Excuse me. I have to go in there. I need the computer." She bent to pick it up and looked at me as she stood. Plantin' her hand on her hip, her gray eyes dug into mine but then slowly traveled down my chest and landed on my unbuttoned jeans. An unabashed smile spread across her face, and she looked back up.

"Sorry." I pushed my arms through my shirt and pulled it down as far as it would go, hopin' it covered the gigantic erection I'd just sprouted when she looked me over. "It's just, Finn's room is a disaster. It smells."

"Well, thanks for looking out for me, but I remember the tornado zone that is Finn's bedroom. I think I can handle the mess. My own personal cleaning lady has been on strike as of late, so I doubt I'll be too offended." She rolled her eyes but then looked at my groin again, crossed her arms over her chest, and licked her heart-shaped lips. Even with her mouth closed, they were always a little bit parted.

Shit. I buttoned my jeans, and Billie pushed Finn's door open.

"Ugh, yeah, okay. I'm so not going in there. It does smell. Like dirty socks and wet dreams. Oh my God, is Finn thirteen?" She made a show of pluggin' her nose and walked down the hall, her full hips swayin'. "This your room?"

She wore all black, just like the last time I'd seen her, but this time, her arms were exposed in a sleeveless, fitted tank top. I imagined caressin' her pearly pale skin with just the tips of my fingers. I'd bet it was soft as air.

She pushed my door open.

"Uh, yeah. Yes," I said, shufflin' my bare feet again. God, she made me nervous. Watching her approach my bedroom door did things to me. To my body. My bed was in there. Oh, the things I could do to her in my bed...

But at least there weren't dirty cups and plates, a mountain of empty water bottles and energy bar wrappers, and protozoa growin' in there.

"I'll move the computer into your room so we don't have to move it downstairs. It looks like a not-so-Quality Inn room. Perfect."

She walked in and I froze. I felt rooted to the hall floor. If I followed her in there, I didn't think I'd be able to stop myself from grabbin' those hips and yankin' 'em against mine, probably makin' a fool of myself, 'cause yeah, I was no Casanova. But it would be rude if I stayed where I was and just yelled at her from down the hallway. I walked to my door but stayed in the hall, leanin' against the door frame, tryin' to look relaxed, but my whole body felt like a block of wood.

"We can put it here. Is there an outlet?" She bent over to look under my childhood homework desk for an electrical outlet, and I groaned. *Ah shit, was that out loud?* But her ass in her skin-tight black jeans and her hair fallin' over her shoulder like... *Ugh.* I imagined her trailin' her hair all over my naked body. She looked over her shoulder at me, smilin' a little, but not with her mouth. It was in her eyes.

"I'll leave you to it then. I'll just go... I'll go check on, uh, on..." Words escaped my mouth, but I had no idea what they were, and it sounded like someone had their hand around my throat, chokin' me.

"Check on Aislinn?" Her eyebrows jumped and she flashed a coy smile.

"Uh, yeah."

Turnin', she walked to me standin' in my doorway. "She's

fine. She's still napping. I could use your help though." She stood right in front of me, gazin' up at me with wide, expectant eyes, and my breath rushed outta my body in a whoosh when she placed her hands on my hips and pulled. "Scootch a little."

"Huh? Oh." She was only tryin' to move me outta her way so she could get Finn's computer. But she didn't walk away.

As she stared up at me, her eyes slid down to my lips, and she bit the tip of her tongue between her teeth, then cleared her throat. "Carey says he still hasn't heard back from the Burroughs' staff. He thinks something's going on that maybe Aislinn doesn't know about. So, I need Finn's computer. I'll set up some searches up here so we don't have to lug it down the stairs. I can get twice the work done. Help me? The tower probably weighs a ton. That's a heavy gaming computer," she said, and she tugged me by a belt loop to Finn's room.

"Well?" Carey asked Billie when he sat at my table. Billie had woken Aislinn, and they came into the kitchen as my brothers all converged for dinner. Evvie'd made pasta. Somehow, even though they all had other homes to go to now, I still ended up with a mountain of dirty dishes most nights.

"Well what? I just got the computers running, Carey. And I think you can allow me a little time to relax. I did jump on a plane at five in the morning for you." She held a boxy-lookin' laptop in one hand and guided Aislinn to a dinin' chair with the other. "Here, Ace, sit here. Two steps to your left. Seven o'clock."

"Right," Carey said, noddin'. "Okay, well then, I'll fill everybody in, and we'll go from there."

"Great idea, Dudley Do-Right," Billie quipped, and she opened her laptop on the table and sat next to Aislinn.

Aislinn giggled. She seemed to have relaxed a bit, until my brothers all barreled into the house, with Tony the dog followin' behind. He plopped down next to Aislinn's chair, gazin' up at her and pantin', and she scooted her legs away from him and leaned toward Billie a little.

"That's Billie," Kev practically groaned, introducin' her to his boyfriend, Luuk.

"Well, hello to you, too, my long-lost BFF. And who is this?" She stood, wipin' her hands on her jeans, and extended her hand to Luuk.

"*Hoi*, Billie. Luuk. Nice to meet you," he said in his perfectly smooth Dutch accent, shakin' Billie's hand while she drooled at him. Great. If I couldn't compete with Finn, how the hell could I compete with unattainably gay, adorable Luuk? He was way more handsome than me, more mature, a hundred percent blonder, taller, and a freakin' veterinarian! "*Hallo*, you must be Aislinn. It's a pleasure to meet you." He didn't extend his hand to her, so Kevin must've told him she was blind, but she reached forward, and he clasped and shook her hand as his phone rang. Even Aislinn was charmed by Luuk. I rolled my eyes. Who wasn't?

"*Pardon*. I must take this." He excused himself to the porch but stuck his head back in the door a minute later. "I need to run down the road for a moment. Cal Johnson would like me to look at one of his new calves. I won't be long."

"Okay, see ya soon." Kevin walked over to meet Luuk at the screen door, and they kissed. It was just a quick peck on the lips, but Billie gasped.

"You're freaking gay?"

"Jesus, Billie." Carey shook his head, embarrassed at Billie's lack of filter.

"What? Oh, I'm sorry. Did I offend your sensitive manly feelings? Please. Besides, I think I just creamed my undies a little. That was hot."

"Oh my God, Billie," Evvie squeaked, but she smiled, pressin' her lips together to keep any sound from comin' out.

Luuk rolled his eyes and backed out the door. "*Tot later, schatje.*"

Tony raced to follow Luuk, and Jack scolded him. The damn dog loved Luuk almost as much as he loved Jack, which was hilarious since Jack pretended he couldn't stand Tony. Secretly, I was sure Jack adored him.

"What? Jealous?" Kevin boasted a little, and his chest puffed up with pride as he walked back toward the table.

"Damn straight. Also, I think I like you now. You're better gay."

Kevin's face turned pink, but he said, "Bite me," and sat in the chair next to Billie.

"I'd rather watch Luuk do it," she said, and Dean, Jack, and Carey groaned. "And props for landing someone *not* from the hoedown."

Aislinn laughed, a real, actual laugh, but caught herself and clammed right back up.

"Okay, enough shenanigans, Billie," Carey said. "Eat and get to work."

"Fine, but Carey, 'shenanigans'? Really? And what exactly am I looking for? I can find Theo easy as pie, but finding *why* he ran is another story. I have my searches going, but without more to go on, I don't expect detailed results too quickly."

"Anything you can find. I dunno. Emails, financial transactions, text messages. We don't have his phone, but I have a feelin' that ain't gonna stop you."

"No, it won't. Child's play, but I already did all that," she said, flickin' her long hair over her shoulder. I woulda given anything to pull my fingers through it.

"Aislinn, I wasn't sure if you ate shrimp," Evvie said, carryin' a huge bowl over to the table, "so I made plain pasta too. I've got mushroom spaghetti sauce, and we have veggies I can add, if you like. And there's lots of garlic toast. I'm sorry. If Finn were here, you'd probably have better vege-tarian options."

"Plain pasta and red sauce is fine."

"This is really cute," Billie said. "Do you guys eat dinner together every night like this? You're like a Norman Rock-well painting, except instead of professional-looking people dressed in their 1930s Sunday best and cute kids in red hats and mittens, you're all brooding cowboys in dirty boots and flannels." All three of my brothers looked down at their clothes, and Billie snorted while a car zipped up the drive outside.

"That'll be Oly," Dean said, jumpin' up from the table, hurryin' to look outside. The biggest, most moronic smile spread across his face when his girlfriend, Oly Masterson, lumbered up the porch stairs. Dean held the door for her, and she slowly appeared, her big, rounded pregnant belly precedin' the rest of her. "Hi, duck. Long day?"

"You have no idea," she said. "And on top of that, I think these kids built a condo on my bladder and moved in. I have to pee. Again." Dean tried to kiss her, but she snapped at him. "Right now, Dean. If I don't get to the bathroom in, like, three seconds, I'm seriously gonna pee my pants." He chuckled as Oly pushed past him, but then she noticed Billie and Aislinn and stopped to chat. What the hell?

I still couldn't believe my brother was gonna be a father to twins. And both girls! He and Oly had only found out a couple months ago, and I still laughed when I thought about it. They would both be princesses. Hopefully, Oly could keep 'em grounded 'cause Dean would carry 'em around on his shoulders like a human palanquin.

"Hi, Billie. It's so nice to finally meet you. And you must be Aislinn. I'm Oly. Carolyn, but everybody calls me Oly."

"Hello," Aislinn said.

"'Sup?" Billie was already at ease in my house.

"Please, excuse me. I really do need to use the restroom." She walked over to smile guiltily at Dean and kissed him, practically meltin' right there when their lips met. "Sorry, babe. And then I'm gonna need a big ol' plate of whatever it is you guys made. Who cooked? Finn's still outta town, right?"

"Evvie cooked," I said, and Jack reached up to rub Evvie's back. She stood next to him, dishin' pasta onto plates and passin' 'em around the table.

"Great. Evvie, make me a plate!" Oly called over her shoulder, disappearin' into the downstairs bathroom. She groaned so loud, we all heard her, and Dean laughed. He loved Oly bein' pregnant. He'd never been so happy. He took her prenatal abuse like a champ, even looked proud of her for it.

Oly returned a few minutes later, and by the time Luuk got back from his farm call, the whole gang sat around the table, shovin' food into their mouths. Finn was the only one missin'. And Ma.

"Oh my God, you guys are like a pack of lions snarling around a buffalo carcass."

"Sorry, Miss High-and-Mighty," Kev said through a mouth full of pasta. "We work a little harder than just punchin' some keys on a keyboard all day."

"Oh yeah, I know. All I've gotta do is go through ten

years of emails, bank records, text messages. Oh, and locate a guy clearly not wanting to be found. No big."

Someone knocked on the door, and Jack hollered for whoever it was to come in.

"Hi," my mama said, stickin' her head around the screen door. "I don't mean to interrupt. Oh, I'm sorry, you're already eating. Here, I just wanted to bring some fresh salad in case your guest wanted more. José went a little overboard trying to come up with vegetarian dishes. I have a quinoa salad with lots of fresh veggies and tofu. And I brought some coconut custard cake for your dessert."

"Please tell José thank you, Daisy," Carey said.

"We just sat down, Daisy. Please, join us," Evvie said. "There's plenty of food."

My mama looked to Jack, and he almost smiled and nodded. She didn't bother to check with me even though I was the only actual occupant of the house. She never did. No one did.

"Okay. Thank you."

Dean pulled a chair in from the porch, and she sat between Luuk and Evvie. The kitchen table hadn't been so full in months. After Ma died and my brothers moved out, there was a glarin' hole in the room any time we were all together. Finn was around usually, but it felt like everyone was gone. Everything had changed. And the awkwardness of our mama bein' back all of a sudden after bein' gone for twenty years didn't help things.

"Daisy," Evvie said, "this is Billie and Aislinn. This is the guys' mom."

"Hello, thank you for bringing the salad," Aislinn said and she smiled, but it was polite and curt.

"Oh, Daisy Lorraine Cade," Billie mumbled, her mouth full of garlic bread. It amazed me that she could be so outgoin', so bold and unapologetic around people she barely knew. "Yeah, I saw your picture when you showed up here last Christmas."

My mama smiled when Evvie handed her a plate. "My picture? You did?"

"Yeah. I find people. Well, in my heart of hearts, I'm a hacker, but I've honed my skills to use for good deeds every once in a while, to find missing people. Too bad they didn't ask me to find you. Woulda been a piece of cake." Eyebrows raised all around the table, but Billie went on. "Anyway, Carey asked me to look you up. And that cartel guy you lived with. Yeah, it's not like those guys are shy about their activities. If they'd asked me to find you a few years ago, a little facial rec search and voilà. Woulda had you."

A weird, high-pitched laugh bubbled outta my mouth. My whole life wasted without my mama, and Billie had the answer the whole time?

Billie looked at me, then her laptop made a loud bell noise.

Her eyes dropped to her screen. "Welp, Theo's in California. Told ya. Easy peasy. I'm better than even I thought." She shoved a huge bite of grilled shrimp and noodles into her mouth.

"How do you know?" Kev asked.

"Duh," she said, chewin'. "He's using a credit card."

CHAPTER FIVE

BILLIE

"A CREDIT CARD? I thought this guy was smart." Kevin laughed, and Ace stiffened in her chair.

"To his credit," I said, looking over the search results on my laptop, "it's one he opened using someone else's name. Aislinn, you ever hear the name Perry Bruchard?" I forked another bite of shrimp scampi into my mouth. Evvie was a good cook.

"Yes, that was my mother's half-brother. He lived in Canada somewhere. They weren't close. They weren't raised together. I don't think my mother knew him well at all."

"Well," I said, holding my fork to my mouth. I really wanted to inhale another bite, but I figured I should at least attempt to be civilized with everyone looking at me. "He still lives there, and Theo definitely knows who he is. This guy, Perry, he's sixty-seven, has Alzheimer's, and lives in a long-term facility in a small town in Saskatchewan.

"I found some travel receipts on your brother's computer. Seems he went up there recently. Probably where he got the idea to use Perry's name. Or maybe he went up there to make sure, if he did use it, there wouldn't be anyone to come nosing around. Perry has no family left. No one visits him."

Aislinn hung her head, sighing. "He went there because he felt guilty. If you look further, you'll probably find a large anonymous donation to the home or the town. Doing that to someone would just about kill Theo. He must really be in trouble.

"Our parents started their first company before I was born. Theo was young. They both worked two, sometimes three, jobs to scrape the money together. My father went into business with a friend, and that man took advantage of him. I don't know exactly what happened, but it destroyed my parents. He took their money, ruined their credit. They had to start all over. They never talked about it, but Theo mentioned it to me last year. So he would never steal someone's identity or take advantage of them like that unless he had a very good reason."

"That helps me. I'll see what I can find about all that. I think there's a reason Theo brought it up then. I found some large withdrawals over the last several years. The first few were only twenty thousand each, but the last one, only three months ago, was a hundred thousand dollars. That's not a ton of money for Theo, considering his net worth, but it was all done in cash. That's not the only odd thing. Theo took the money from a secondary personal account he has. There have been three cash withdrawals over the last year. Someone's blackmailing him."

Aislinn gasped. "But why? Theo's a good person. You can't tell me he did something so untoward that someone could use it against him. He's a good man." Tears fell down her face and she cried.

It wasn't the first time I was glad Carey had called me in to help. Clearly, there was some shady shit going on, and I knew I could figure it out a lot faster than probably anybody else.

The guys all cringed in their seats. Jeez. One weeping woman and they all went stiff.

"No, Aislinn. That's not what Billie mea—"

I shook my head, cutting Evvie off. "I'm not saying that, Aislinn. Maybe it has to do with your parents. They had a lot of money, were well known on the East Coast. It could be anybody doing this to your brother."

She sniffled and wiped her nose with her napkin, then folded it and placed it properly in her lap.

"Did you find any recent travel receipts other than to Canada?" Carey asked.

"No, so he must be using another alias. Or maybe he bought a car. I'm still looking. Who knows how much cash he has. If he's using it to travel, we can't track him, but he did use the credit card so that makes me think he doesn't have access to a lot of cash. That's what made me suspect he might've bought a car. If he knew he was in trouble, he would've stashed some quick cash. I would. But if he'd used it all to buy something big, like a car, then he'd have to use the card." I thought for a minute. "I mean, I can't prove any of this yet. It's just a theory."

"It makes sense," Carey said, his lips pursed. He was thinking too. "Where in California?"

"Just north of LA. He stayed at a motel there last night and paid for something at a store nearby this morning. I don't know what. But I have an idea. Maybe if I went there, I could see where he stayed. I doubt he's still there, and I've got my computer rigged to alert me if he uses the card again. But… I don't know. It might help to be closer to him? If I can figure out why he's there, maybe I could help him somehow. We still have no freaking clue *why* he ran."

"Yes!" Aislinn almost jumped in her chair, turning toward me. "That's a great idea. If we could get close enough, I could talk to him. He'll listen to me."

"No," Carey said. He tried to sound nice, soften his voice, but there could be no mistaking the authority in it.

"And why not?"

"Aislinn, there's a reason your brother wanted you here. You're safe here. Protected. We have no idea what's goin' on with him." Carey sighed. "Dammit, what have you numb-skulls gotten yourselves into this time? It's always somethin'. Remember the good ol' days? When all we did was drink beer and—"

"Sheriff, you can't tell me what to do. I'm an adult. You're not going to stop me. I'll pay for it myself."

"Please, just call me Carey. And no."

"No." Aislinn's eyebrows shot to the ceiling. "No? Just like that? Like I'm some incompetent little girl and I don't have a say in my own life? This is my brother you're all talking about." She stared right at Carey, like she could see him. I was kind of proud of her for standing her ground, but I knew it wouldn't matter.

"I know that. And yes, you are an adult. Yes, you have a say. But what if this is about you? What if your credit cards are bein' watched? You got cash? Gonna fly, hire a car service? That can all be tracked. I'm sorry, it's just not a good idea." Carey pushed his plate away and dropped his napkin on the table.

"So you're not going to do *anything*?"

"I didn't say that."

Everyone sat silent at the table, their heads bouncing back and forth between Aislinn and Carey. I knew what Carey was thinking, or at least I thought I did, and I hoped I could take Jay with me. I wanted to get my hands on that man, and if we were alone on the road, I would get the chance. I peeked and caught him staring at me, but when our eyes met, he looked down at the table in front of him.

"So, I'll go," I said, and I waited for Aislinn to throw a fit. She was used to getting her way and being catered to. Theo did whatever she wanted. She was not used to being told no.

"Wait just a minute," she argued, right on cue. "Billie gets to go? Why? She's a woman too."

Jay coughed. Yeah, I bet he agreed. I'd caught him daydreaming about my ass.

"What does bein' a woman have to do with it?" Carey said. "Billie will go 'cause she has experience with this kinda thing. She knows how to take care of herself, and she has contacts and resources she can use if she gets into trouble. What would you do if you found yourself in a sticky situation?"

"Well… I—but why can't I just go with her?"

"Technically, I can't stop you from doin' anything, but my gut tells me you need to stay here."

"He's got a good gut, Aislinn," Evvie said. "Trust him. And I'll be here. We can do all kinds of fun things while they're gone. Oly will hang out, too, when she's not working."

"Mmhm." Oly nodded, sucking a gigantic forkful of pasta into her mouth.

"We have a fun dinner party with Phil every week. It's my turn to cook, so you can help me. I need all the help I can get." Evvie laughed, and Jack smiled indulgently at her. Dude's face muscles looked weird when he smiled.

"Who is Phil?" Aislinn asked, a sour, condescending look taking over her angel face.

"Oh, you'll love Phil. She's like a weird grandma to us all. She and Daisy have been teaching me how to bake and garden," Evvie said, and Daisy smiled shyly at her. Daisy didn't exactly appear comfortable sitting at the dinner table with everyone.

"I'll leave in the morning," I said, interrupting Evvie again, knowing full well the macho, protective cowboys wouldn't let me go alone.

"Kev can go with you," Jack said.

My BFF snorted. "Yeah, I'll pass."

"Gee thanks, BFF. Way to be a helper. Like you'd be my first choice. As if," I replied in my best California valley girl impression. "It's fine. I usually work alone anyway."

"I'll go," Jay said.

"No, really, I'm fine on my own." And there it was. Jack wouldn't leave the ranch, Dean wouldn't leave his baby mama, BFF wouldn't be caught dead stuck in a car with me for days, Finn was MIA, so, three, two, one…

"No, I'm goin'. Everything I've been workin' for goes down the drain without Theo," Jay declared. He stared me down, sexy eyebrows raised. "I'm goin'."

Perfect. How easy was that?

"Um, yeah. Sure. Okay. That's fine, I guess," I said, and an itty-bitty smile played across Jay's plump, sexy lips, the ones I couldn't wait to sink my teeth into.

"Okay, now that's settled, break out that coconut custard cake," Oly said, rubbing her belly.

"Jeez, Oly, you ate a foot-high pile of pasta. Those poor kids are gonna jump outta your stomach 'fore they get strangled with linguini."

I elbowed Kevin in his ribs at the same time the hot, gay veterinarian did on his other side. "Dude. Rude much?"

"Oww! What? Both of ya?"

"Come on, big mouth. I am exhausted," the hot vet said in his weird but sexy accent. "Let's go home."

I raised my finger in the air to point out the infinite ways BFF could put that mouth to good use, but Carey speared me with his eyes, lips pressed into a hard white line, so I conceded and dropped my hand into my lap. Party pooper.

"Yeah," Kevin said, "okay. I gotta be up early anyway. Isaac will be here at the crack of fuckin' dawn." He scoffed. "Tell me again why you stuck me with the kid, Jack."

"'Cause it amuses me. And 'cause you deserve it. And 'cause it's good for you."

BFF groaned.

"Wait a minute," Dean said. "If Jay's goin', who's stayin' here with Aislinn?"

Ace crossed her arms just to be contrary, but I think she knew Carey was right and she should stay at the ranch.

"Oh, well, Jack and I can stay over here since this is where everyone hangs out anyway," Evvie said. "And you and Oly will come by in the evenings, right?"

"Yeah," Oly agreed. "It'll be fun."

King Jack nodded his approval of the plan, and after Evvie, Oly, and I demolished the coconut cake, everyone pushed away from the table, saying their goodbyes and scattering to the backwoods winds.

Aislinn, the poor thing, looked lost in all the commotion, so small and timid in her chair even though she was at least a half a foot taller than me, so I grabbed her hand. "I'll room with you tonight, Ace. We can gossip, but you might have to teach me how."

"Really?" She looked relieved. "Okay."

I hoped I could make her feel more included, and though I'd never admit it, having her company would make me feel that way too.

Yeah, yeah, I put on a big front, but who liked to be alone?

When it was just Ace, Jay, and me left in the kitchen, everyone grew really quiet. She stood silently next to me, biting the inside of her cheek, and Jay looked down at his worn, dusty work boots. I looked too, but then my eyes slowly slid up his legs and zeroed in on his zipper. Memories of my red barn fantasies filled my head, but I shook them away.

"Well, isn't this pleasantly awkward," I said, and Jay looked up. "All right, I'll check my searches now and again in the morning, and then we can leave. I'll book us tickets to LA and a rental car. I'm gonna need a few things, some gear to make myself more portable, but we can get all of that when we get to LA." He looked right into my eyes, so I put on my most seductive smile, and he ducked his head again, but I definitely saw another hint of a smile dance across the edge of his sexy AF mouth.

"Thank you."

"For what?" I asked, leading Aislinn to sit on the bed in the unoccupied downstairs bedroom. The little black and white cat followed us and jumped up onto the bed, stretching her long body, then lay down and rested her head on her white-tipped paws. Aislinn carried her cane, but she let me guide her with her hand on my forearm.

"For staying with me. I'm sure you're just trying to be nice, but I really wasn't looking forward to being by myself tonight in this house."

I snorted. "I'm not nice. I didn't want to be alone either. Besides, Finn's room is upstairs. It's disgusting. You can probably smell it from here."

Ace scoffed. "Well, if that sheriff thinks I'm just going to stay here indefinitely, he's sadly mistaken."

"Here's your bag. Grab some jammies, and let's get ready for bed. I still need to book our flight and rent a car." I hefted her biggest suitcase onto the bed, and she used the tips of her fingers to feel her way around it, pulling out pink silk pajamas.

I watched her change. I didn't mean to, and it wasn't a weird thing, but damn. Her body was perfect. She had a perfect tight ass, perfect perky breasts, perfect slim curves. She wore no bra. Perfect everything. Long legs and one of those gaps you hear women talk about. There was no gap between my thighs, that was for damn sure. You could start a fire with the amount of friction down there, roast a marshmallow, and make a fucking smore.

I shook my head and pushed my jeans down, stepped out, and grabbed my favorite ratty sweats from my bag. I pulled them up and took Aislinn's hand again.

"C'mon, I know I joke and give them a hard time, but seriously, there probably isn't a safer place for you to be. The guys are really nice. They'd do anything for you. So would Carey. I've known him a long time. I'll tell you about Evvie. You won't believe the shit she went through last year, but these men were all there for her. They fought for her. Come on."

I pulled her through the living room to the little bathroom under the stairs, and we washed our faces and brushed our teeth together like it was a sleepover and we were twelve. On our way back to the bedroom, she asked, "Who's Finn?"

"Oh, that's right, you've never met the guys before, have you? Finn is like a blond moose. He's Jay's brother."

"How many brothers are there?"

"Five," I said, looking behind me to make sure I didn't

lead Ace into any furniture. Her breasts were all but visible through the thin silk she wore, nipples hard and high. *Ugh.* Yeah, that wouldn't do in a house full of beautifully virile men. I didn't worry for her safety or her virtue, but if she wasn't careful, by the time Jay and I returned from our trip, Ace might be in some kind of polygamous reverse harem situation.

Once we were back in the quiet bedroom, she asked in a timid voice, "What do they look like?"

"Who?"

"The Cade brothers."

"Oh, well, Jay is"—I sighed—"dreamy. God, what I wouldn't give to get my hands on that tight ass. And his arms? Ugh. So freaking sexy, the way he pushes his sleeves up all the time." I sighed again loudly. I must've sounded like a rom-com betty. "Oh, and Kevin looks annoying, and Finn looks like a blond moose. I'm not kidding. He's huge."

"Do you mean he's overweight?" she asked, feeling for the edge of the bed. She crawled in, pulling the covers over her legs, and the cat climbed on top of them while she stroked her fingers through its fur absently. The purring was so loud, it reminded me of a white noise machine.

"No. He's probably the most physically fit person I've ever met. He's a moose 'cause he's tall. Like nine feet tall. He's kind of gorgeous, if you're into that perfect beauty thing." I grabbed my lite laptop from my backpack and crawled into the bed next to her, and she lifted the covers and laid them over my legs, too, just like a sister or a mom would. It felt nice. Comforting. I hadn't had a nice person in my life for a long time. Not a nice woman, anyway.

My mother, for the last half of my life, had been a self-absorbed child living on some rich guy's boat in Bali, or the south of France, or somewhere. I couldn't remember. There'd been so many guys, so many boats.

I booted up and chewed on my fingernail while I waited for the airline website to load.

"Gorgeous how?"

"Finn? Mm, I don't know. He's got charisma, you know? He's funny and kind. His hair is kind of long and angsty. And his eyes? They're sexy pools. Like the blue of the ocean in Tahiti. Have you ever been there?"

"Yes."

"You have?"

"Yes, my parents used to take my brother and me on vacations. Three or four times a year usually. They said they'd worked hard to earn their money, and we all deserved to enjoy the spoils. Tahiti, Iceland, all over Europe. Japan. It was fun when I was young but—I assume you've read all about what happened to my parents. The accident. After that, Theo tried to continue the tradition but…"

"But what?" I searched for flights from Jackson to LA, finding two seats on a nonstop flight leaving at eleven a.m., so I booked them, then pulled up the rental car website I'd used in the past.

"It's not much fun to travel when you can't see," she said, leaning back against the headboard and crossing her arms over her chest.

The contempt she had for herself, for the life she could be living, was a potent thing all around us, and it baffled me. I didn't say anything. I wasn't her life coach.

She picked at the edge of the comforter and chewed her lip. "What?"

Well, since she asked. "Okay, not that I have *any* idea what it's like to be visually impaired, but you can't have fun if you can't see? I'd think it would give you a unique point of view." I pulled up my favorite sweatpants website. Ace looked like a size small-tall, but I clicked medium so they'd be roomy.

"What do you mean?" She scoffed and shook her head, completely dismissing herself and the rest of her body because one part didn't work. I guess I was being a brat, but I'd grown up with a mother who believed she was incapable of doing anything on her own. She never tried, not once, choosing instead to wait around for someone else to do it for her, whatever "it" was and whoever "they" were. Usually a man. Usually *not* my dad. It pissed me off.

"Think about it. The last time you traveled, what did the water feel like? How was that different than how you experienced it before you lost your sight? I mean, just because you're lacking one sense doesn't mean you can't utilize the others to your benefit. You could do the things you used to love and help other people at the same time.

"You could travel and blog about it. Imagine a blog that described traveling through a blind person's perspective. The sounds, smells, the way a place feels, its vibe. The way the ocean feels on your toes, the warmth of the water, the feel of the London rain on your face. Oh, the food. You don't think other people would like to hear about that? Blind or not. Ooo, or you could be an influencer for products designed for the visually impaired."

She sat quietly and still for a few minutes while I checked my searches one last time and finished booking the rental car, then closed my laptops, setting them on the desk next to the bed. I lay down and tugged the covers a little and the cat, Iggy, meowed at me and flicked her tail in my direction.

"What's an influencer?"

"It's someone who uses their specific knowledge to test

products and then they post about it on social media. Make a video, a vlog or whatever."

She whispered, "You think *I* could do something like that?"

I yawned. "Why couldn't you?"

More quiet.

"Billie?"

"Hmm?"

"I don't want to stay here when you leave tomorrow. I don't know these people."

"Don't be nervous. They may sound a little funny, but everyone here is kind. They'll be here for you. By the way, don't wear those jammies again. They're a little too revealing. I ordered you some sweats. They'll be here in a day or two."

She touched the collar of her pajama top and caressed her fingers down to her cleavage. She laughed. "You did? Why?"

"There are way too many guys around here for PJs like those."

"Oh, please. Like anyone would be looking at me."

"Is that so hard to believe?"

"I-I mean, why would they?"

"With that body and that beautiful face, I bet people ogle you all the time. You just don't know it."

"Beautiful?" she whispered.

"Ace, you're a stunner."

She didn't say anything more, but I watched as she thought about what I'd said. I could see the feminine-power realization spread across her face and travel through her body as she sat a little straighter.

I drifted, but just before I fell asleep, she asked, "Billie?"

"Yeah?"

"Thank you."

"You keep saying that, but I haven't done anything for you I wouldn't do for anybody else."

"That's the point."

"Good night, Ace."

"Good night," she said, scooting down. She tugged the covers back her way a little, and before I could find the energy to argue, I was out.

CHAPTER SIX

JAY

"HEY, brother. Hold on, lemme step outside. It's really loud in here." I heard a door squeak open through my phone as Finn pushed through it in whatever honky tonk bar he'd found himself in. The background noise cut off. "Okay, what's up, baby Jay? What's goin' on? You miss your big bro?"

"Yeah, like I miss shovelin' horse shit," I said, and Finn laughed. "How's the tour goin'?"

"Ah, well, you know. Same shit, different dive bar every night. But I get to play music and pretend like I'm rock star. We got a little bit of a social media followin' goin', so there's pretty ladies showin' up for the show every night. That's fun." He chuckled.

"Yeah? We got 'em here too."

"Got what?"

I sighed. "Beautiful women."

"At the ranch?"

"Yeah. Remember Theo has a sister?"

"Theo? The investor?"

"Yeah. He's missin', and Carey brought his sister here to stay."

"Missin'? Missin' what? How?"

"Dunno. Billie's here, too, speakin' of beautiful women. She's been lookin' for him. She says he's in California."

"Wait, I'm confused. He's missin' or he took off?"

"Dunno. Both, I guess. But, Finn, if he doesn't come back, my proposal and the horse therapy project is dead."

"Well, Billie'll find him. She's good, right? Carey trusts her. Don't worry."

I clicked my tablet's screen, checkin' out Billie's website, bbtatb.com. What the hell did that stand for? Stickers with the website address haphazardly covered her laptop case, and I couldn't get the letters outta my head. "Yeah, I know. She and I are leavin' tomorrow mornin'. She thinks we can track him down and bring him back here."

"Ooo. A California road trip. That sounds fun. Billie's hot."

Hot? Was he kiddin'? "She's literally the most beautiful woman on the planet."

There were no pictures or personal information on her site, just an advertisement for her private eye services and links to many different domestic and sexual abuse hotlines, suicide and mental illness hotlines, and links to contact her.

Finn laughed. "Well then, a sex-fueled road trip. Even better."

"Yeah, okay." I scoffed. It would be that easy for Finn. Women swooned and dropped at his feet wherever he went. He could talk to anybody.

Not me.

"Jay. What's this about? You never call just to chitchat."

"If you ever repeat this, I will superglue your balls to your leg in your sleep, but… how do I… talk to her?"

"Jay"—he chuckled a little at my expense—"just be your-self. Do what comes natural. You're my brother, so I know you got it in you to be a heartbreaker. You're smart as shit. This is cake. You got this."

I took a deep breath, bolsterin' myself. "Okay. You're right."

"I always am. Hey, what's the sister like?"

"She's um, well, she's not real excited to stay at the ranch. I think she's used to much nicer accommodations. But she's pretty scared. She's worried about her brother. Jack and Evvie are stayin' here so she's not alone while Billie and I are gone."

"Well, maybe I oughta come home a little early. Good ol' Finn'll cheer her up. I remember her from her pic online. She's gorgeous."

I snorted. "Good luck with that. This woman would eat you alive."

He chuckled low. "Oh, baby Jay, I like me a challenge."

———

I always forgot how different California was from Wyoming, especially Southern California. The palm trees and desert scenery always felt jarring to me, like I was in another country instead of just five hours down the coast from where I'd gone to school in Berkeley.

The heat rose up from the road in a pocket of hot, wavy air all around me, dryin' out my tongue as I breathed in the weird desert-ocean air while we walked from the tech store Billie had insisted we'd needed to go to, back to our rental. I felt like a soggy, microwaved potato, sweat drippin' down my neck, wettin' my shirt in the space between my shoulders. I needed sunglasses but hadn't thought to bring any.

"Why do you always wear long-sleeved shirts?" Billie asked. "You should've worn a T-shirt or a tank."

"I don't own any sleeveless shirts. I like my button downs. You don't like 'em?" Unlockin' the rental car, I set Billie's bags of various tech gadgets on the back seat and pulled at the hem of my thick, navy blue, button-down, pushin' the sleeves further up my forearms. A nervous habit.

"I didn't say I didn't like them, did I?" She lifted her Ray Bans, eyein' my shirt. "I like them fine. In fact, they're sexy on you, but aren't you hot?"

Sexy? She ogled me often, but sometimes I felt like it wasn't in a good way. Like maybe she judged me a little. I didn't know what about, but my ego didn't care. It wanted her eyes on my body in any way she cared to look. She spent half the flight to LA turned in her seat, just studyin' me. I didn't know if she wanted to devour me or punch me for some reason.

"Let's get on the road," she said. "I'd like to find the hotel Theo stayed in. I'm sure he's moved on, but it can't hurt to check. We'll make our way north on LA's spaghetti noodle freeway system. I think we need to take the 405."

"Sure."

"Are you hungry? I'm starving. Let's hit an In-and-Out on our way."

"A what?"

"It's the best burger joint in the southwest. You didn't eat there when you were at Berkeley?"

"Oh, yeah—wait. How do you know where I went to school?"

She climbed into the passenger seat and watched me get in. I felt her eyes on me before I saw 'em. Situatin' myself, I locked my seatbelt into place before lookin' at her, but when I did, she wore a shit-eatin' grin. "How do you think?"

I didn't respond, just put the rented SUV into drive and checked my mirrors, pullin' out into the worst traffic I'd ever experienced, and we hadn't even gotten on the freeway to hell yet. But I thought about what she'd said. That meant she'd looked me up.

I liked that, and I got a hard-on just thinkin' about her sittin' behind her computer, lookin' at pictures of me. I realized that was weird and tried to discreetly rearrange myself, but she was still starin' at me, so I was sure she noticed. She didn't say anything though.

Damn, this was provin' to be a long drive, and we'd barely been in the car five minutes.

We took the 405 to the 101 and headed west. Billie said Theo had stayed at a cheap hotel off the freeway so that was where we went first. It seemed odd to me that he'd stay in some mediocre motel like normal people would, but maybe he just hadn't thought to make a reservation and couldn't find a room at a nicer hotel.

He wasn't there, of course, but it had become a kind of adventure to Billie to get more information about his stay at the Ramada Inn knockoff. She sat in the passenger seat, diligently workin' on her laptop, while I tried not to stare at her thighs flowin' outta her short, black skirt.

"So, I'm gonna need you to do something for me, but knowing what I do about you, I don't think you'll like it."

She looked up at me when I parked outside the motel that had been built to try to resemble a hacienda-style house but failed miserably. Hacienda houses were usually beautiful, painted white or some variation of a warm sunset color, with red clay roofs and big, wide airy arches all over the place. There were a lot of 'em up near Berkeley, and I'd always thought they'd be nice to live in with the arches and big open windows, lettin' all the fresh ocean air flow through all the time.

This hotel had short, fat arches and had been painted an ugly grey-beige color. They'd gotten the roof right, but it looked like it hadn't been cared for and maybe like the Niners had played a few games up there.

Turnin' to look at her, I asked, "What do you want me to do?"

"Do you see that woman at the desk?" She nodded through our windshield and through the glass doors of the hotel to the reception desk where a woman with short, curly blond hair stood, scrollin' down her phone.

"Yeah."

"She's by herself right now. We have about fifteen minutes until her relief comes in. I need to get on her computer. I just need five minutes, if that. Do you think you can distract her?"

I snorted. "Are you kiddin'? You need Finn for this. How am *I* supposed to distract her?"

"I don't know. Flirt?" She scanned my body with her sultry gray eyes. "Oh, I know, give me your shirt."

"My shirt?"

"Yes, Jay, your shirt," she said, snappin' her fingers and holdin' out her hand. "You know, that thing covering your chest?" Her eyes dropped to the buttons on my shirt and they glazed over for two seconds before she looked back up and said, "Gimme."

"Okay," I said, unbuttonin' my shirt and shruggin' my arms out.

"Hurry up, we don't have much time."

"Okay, okay." Ballin' it up, I dumped the sweaty bundle of fabric into her hand. She searched for the arms, then pulled till they tore and ripped 'em off.

"Hey! That's my favorite shirt."

"Well, now it's gonna be *my* favorite shirt. Put it on." She threw the shirt back at me, and I fumbled with it, quickly tryin' to cover myself.

She watched me dress, and the look on her face was kinda severe, her eyebrows dippin' down just a little and her mouth puckerin'. Her eyes locked onto my chest, then slowly moved down my body, and I didn't know what she could be thinkin' to look like that, like she was mad. She made me feel exposed. I rebuttoned and looked to her for direction.

"Lean in."

I did, and she ruffled my hair with her fingertips. We were face to face, two inches between us, and I smelled her sweet breath when it whispered across my face.

"Now, go like this," she instructed, scrapin' her top teeth over her bottom lip hard, and she licked it. Blood rushed to my groin, and I forgot what she wanted me to do. I just stared at her lips, imaginin' suckin' 'em and shovin' my tongue in her mouth as I—

"Jay! Jesus, come here." She wrapped her hand around my neck to pull me closer and used the fingers of her other hand to pinch my lip. "Now, lick it." I licked my lips and she groaned. "Yeah, that'll work." She released my neck and inhaled, then blew out a measured breath. "Okay, pretend we're married"—she pointed back and forth between us—"and we need a room, but I have to pee, so then you be the scumbag husband and flirt with the girl. Try to get her out here, ask for directions or something. I'll be quick."

"Oh… o-okay." I knew I sounded like an idiot, but she'd just touched my lips, and all I could think about was pinnin' her to the side of the Jeep so I could yank her cute little black skirt up and—*damn*. It was all my body could think about too. A certain persistent appendage tried to pound a hole through my jeans.

She climbed out, so I did, too, rearranged myself, and walked around to meet her on the other side. I stood there motionless, like a tool.

"Move, Jay!" She smacked my ass and twined her arm through mine, draggin' me along beside her, mumblin' something about sweaty and lickable, and I smiled. She wasn't as unaffected by me as she wanted me to believe.

Somehow, I lured the receptionist outside, and turned out, she was *very* into cowboys. I didn't figure it was obvious, but apparently, I sounded like one. I didn't have a hat, but she didn't seem to mind. She ogled my arms and my lips, so I supposed Billie knew her mark well. In fact, the lady couldn't keep her hands off my arms. She kept findin' reasons to touch 'em, so I flexed a little and licked my lips a lot like an idiot.

I pretended to be a witless country boy who didn't know east from west or air from dirt and looked out in different directions, sayin', "We came from that direction, I think, but is the ocean that'a way?" while pointin' toward the mountains to the east. I acted like Jack, sayin' ma'am every other word and noddin' instead of speakin'. I smiled and winked, and then Billie was there, loopin' her arm through mine again.

"Did you figure out where we are, baby?" she cooed.

"Uh, yeah, we're not far. The ocean's only a few miles that way," I said, pointin' west.

"Oh, well, if we're that close, let's keep going. We can get a room closer to the beach. Thank you, miss."

"Yeah, sure. Come back if you can't find anything. I'll be here again tomorrow morning at seven," the receptionist said, scannin' me up and down before she glared at Billie for a few seconds.

Billie pulled me along while I looked back at the woman,

nodded again, and said, "Thank ya, ma'am. Have a nice day now," layin' the cowboy accent on real thick, and I licked my lips again and winked. She touched her fingers to her mouth, and her eyes dropped to my ass as we walked back to the rental car.

Jeez.

"So, you are an actor. Good job. I didn't find anything too interesting, but I was able to confirm that it was Theo renting the room. He looked a little anxious on the video I found, but he checked in and then left this morning in one piece. The store where he used the credit card was a general kind of store, but he also had some bags from a clothing store.

"I think he might have bought stuff to change his appearance. Hair dye, maybe clippers to shave his head. It's just a guess since I couldn't see through the bag, but"—I opened the car door for her, and she hopped in—"I think we really should rent a room though. I need to set up some new facial recognition searches. But not here. Your new GF will want to hang around if she knows you're near." She smirked, and her eyes sparkled before she hid 'em behind her dark sunglasses.

"Okay."

"Wait. You sit here. I wanna drive this bad boy."

"Uh, sure, okay." I handed her the key fob, and she hopped back out and pushed me with her hands on my chest into the door. "Sit there and be a good boy."

I'd never driven with Billie before. If I had, I never woulda handed over that key fob. Jesus. I feared for our lives. She zoomed in and out between cars on the freeway like a getaway driver in a movie, racin' away from the scene of a crime. I felt like that frog on the old video game, jumpin' in between cars and trucks as they drove by, tryin' to cross the road and river. At any moment we were gonna go *SPLAT*. I cringed and gripped the sides of my seat. Finally, she pulled into a little, pink adobe strip mall, all but skiddin' into a parkin' spot in front of a discount store.

"Come on, let's get some provisions," she said, climbin' outta the Jeep. "I need caffeine, and you need something else to wear. You're all sweaty. I'm not gonna force you into Bermuda shorts and Hawaiian shirts, but you at least need one tank top. And sunglasses. You're gonna get a headache if you keep squinting like that."

I didn't say anything. I was still clutchin' my seat and tryin' not to hyperventilate.

───────────

We found a quaint little motel by the beach some two hours later, after maddenin' stop and start traffic, which, thankfully, I drove through so Billie could mess around on her computer.

It cost two hundred and seventy-two dollars for one night, probably 'cause it sat nearly in the water, even though it wasn't in the best of neighborhoods and had long since been considered a Ventura hot spot, but Billie didn't care.

She tried to pay for it, but I replaced her debit card with mine and slipped hers back to her. Jack would probably kill me for spendin' the money, but I couldn't let her pay for everything. She'd already paid for our airline tickets and the rental car. I didn't think she even noticed; she took it from my fingers while her eyes were glued to somethin' she saw on her cell phone. I filled out the old-school hotel registration and pushed it back across the check-in desk.

The man behind the desk looked us both up and down. "You guys remind me of the start to a bad joke. 'A cowboy and Penny Dreadful walk into a bar…'"

Billie scoffed. "Penny Dreadful? Ha ha. You're an idiot." She snatched the room key from his hand and dragged me beside her, turnin' to walk away, but stopped, looked back at the guy, and shoved her hand down the back of my jeans, squeezin' my ass while she winked and arched an eyebrow, lickin' her lips all slow and dramatic. The guy made some kinda strangled chokin' noise, and Billie laughed low and sexy.

I pulled her away, yankin' her backpack outta her hand, slingin' it over my shoulder, and steerin' her out the front doors of the ramshackle lobby.

There were no other hotel guests around, and once we were outside, surrounded by the salty ocean air, I pushed her up against the side of the buildin' and held her wrists in my hands. I'd never been so forward with a woman before, but somethin' about her attitude and rudeness made me wild. I felt a little outta control, like I didn't know what I might do.

I almost growled at her. "What'd you do that for?"

"That guy wanted you. He couldn't take his eyes off your mouth, so I thought I'd give him a little something to jerk off to later."

I looked down into her eyes, questionin' her. She had a habit of treatin' me like a piece of meat, and I was gettin' a little tired of it. I'd never been more attracted to someone, but still, that didn't mean she could treat me like her cabana boy.

"Did that piss you off? What? You don't like being treated like an object? Get over it. Imagine what every woman on the planet feels like every day of her life," she argued. "You think I don't notice you staring at my ass or my tits all the time?"

My fast-growin' erection was pressed against her stomach, and even though I was angry over her obvious possessiveness of my body, I throbbed and ached to get inside her. My hands shook. She felt it and her breath caught in her throat.

"See?" she whispered. "You're not immune. Besides, I've

wanted my hands on you since last year, Jay." She closed her eyes so I couldn't read 'em. "You're acting quiet and coy, but I know you want me too."

"I ain't actin' like anything," I said, and she peeked up at me, feelin' a little shy about what she'd just admitted, I guessed. We looked at each other for a minute in silence, and I watched as her gray eyes glowed almost silver in the wanin' light of the day. They turned from mockin' and sassy to deep and hungry.

"You don't wanna fuck me up against this wall?" she purred.

"That's beside the point."

"Is it?" She lifted up on her toes, tryin' to reach my ear with her lips, rubbin' 'em along my jaw. I felt her warm breath skate across the skin of my neck, and it raised goose-bumps all over me. My whole body ached and strained to cover hers. To be skin to skin, to feel her soft against my hard. "I think it's exactly the point. We have a room. What are you waiting for?"

CHAPTER SEVEN

BILLIE

HE HAD BEEN QUIET, but maybe it wasn't an act. Maybe he really was that shy. Or he doubted himself, though I couldn't understand why. He was the most perfect man I'd ever seen. What did *he* have to be self-conscious of?

But he stared down at me with obvious need in his eyes. It was absolutely the hottest thing I'd ever seen, and my body responded. Moisture pooled, soaking my underwear, and my nipples hardened against his chest through the fabric of my tank top.

Yanking my wrist away, I grabbed his, pushing his hand between my thighs, under my skirt, and his breath hitched. I let go and he raised his hand, cupping me and using his finger to push the thin fabric aside. Lifting his chin, his face angled up and away from mine, he peered down at me through heavy, slitted lids, sliding his finger up and back through my thick, very slick, wet heat. He watched me with the sexiest look on his face—it was pained and wild, his eyes all deep, stormy, blue ocean—and for just a second, I couldn't look away.

I moaned, and my head fell back against the white-washed wood of the old California surfer motel. I panted, and he took advantage of my distraction, tilting his head and covering my mouth with his, but he didn't kiss me. The heat from his breath washed away my own, and I gasped in another and whimpered at the intimacy. I hadn't been expecting it. I expected him to take me, not take his time with me.

I kept my eyes closed, embarrassed at not knowing how to return the intimacy he gave. I just did what I knew I was good at. "Screw foreplay, Jay. I want you."

He groaned and whispered, "Billie." I felt the grumble of his voice against my lips, and it made me wetter.

I still held the room key, so I pulled my other hand free from his grasp, dangling the little yellow wooden surfboard keychain in front of his chest, taunting him. "Take me to room eight and fuck me."

He didn't make a move. He stood still, pressed against me, his finger still torturing me between my legs, and I felt him staring at me. But still, he didn't budge. Finally, I opened my eyes (had he been waiting for that?) and he lifted me up, wrapping my legs around his waist, balancing me precariously with his hands under my ass. He squeezed, and I clawed at his body and kissed his neck and chin, bit his earlobe, and ground myself against his concrete-hard cock through his jeans.

It was a little uncoordinated, but he stomped down the outdoor corridor to room eight and, once we were outside the door, pressed me against it, taking the key from my fingers. He unlocked it and pushed inside, letting the heavy door slam shut beside us.

The lights were off inside the room, but a small glow

from a streetlight came in through a window next to the door, and I could see the strong silhouette of his face. His square jaw was clenched, his wide shoulders flexed and straining to hold me up. He walked forward, trying to find the bed, bumping his legs against it, and we fell down onto it.

From that point on, he was like a wild animal, pushing my skirt above my hips and digging and licking and scraping his teeth on my skin. He shoved my tank top up above my boobs and nuzzled his mouth between them, over my bra, and inhaled, breathing deeply, and as he traveled down, I gasped and moaned at every new touch of his mouth and tongue on my body.

Thoughts of my fat stomach and too-wide hips barely even crossed my mind when he licked between my legs, over my undies, a slow and languid lap of his tongue. He moaned, his breath hot, and the stubble on his cheeks abraded my skin when my legs squeezed his head, trying to force him to stay right there, right where I wanted him.

I was desperate for him; I'd daydreamed, night dreamed, and masturbated to thoughts of this very situation. I couldn't think. I knew I wanted to say something, something I didn't want to forget, but no matter how hard I tried, I couldn't find the thought in the swirling, boiling lava flowing through my head and down through every vein and nerve ending in my body.

I could only think about him, inside me, all over me.

He slowed and kneeled above me, trapped my legs with his on either side, and very slowly unbuttoned his shirt, then tore it off and slid his warm hands over my torso, between my breasts to my shoulders and down my arms. I watched his body, and the harsh light from the window highlighted his abs, casting deep shadows below each one. I wanted to lick them, but I was too mesmerized by his hands all over me to make my own move.

When he reached my hips, he squeezed the flesh with his fingers and hooked them under my undies, then scooted back to pull them down my legs. He dragged them off and stood to remove his jeans and boots, and I could hear his deep breathing in the dark room but could barely see him, only the outline of his body. Jesus, what an outline. He was lean but strong, and his chest tapered down into that delicious V above his cock. Oh, his cock… It was hard and huge, and I *wanted* it.

My arms reached out of their own free will for him, and as he came back down to hover above me, positioning himself to enter me, the hardness of him rubbing the soft skin of my thighs, my phone buzzed and beeped in my backpack somewhere on the floor. He rolled to the edge of the bed to find it, and I felt cold and exposed without him.

"Leave it. Come back," I begged, breathless, and my whole body turned an embarrassed shade of red even though he couldn't see me. My small voice in the dark was the only sound between us besides heavy breath, and it was intoxicating.

He did come back, hovering over me again, his arms on either side of my head, and I reached to lick a bicep. Oh, the sweat on his skin tasted so sweet, and he chased my mouth with his. He took it, moaning and invading me with his talented tongue, pressing the head of his hot cock between my wet lips again, ready to push inside, and I gasped into his mouth.

I *ached* there, deep inside. It hurt, real physical pain as the muscle contracted in on empty nothingness. As I lifted my hips to meet his, he pushed a little more, and I panted and whimpered at the need I felt for him to ram himself inside me—

And my phone pinged and buzzed *again*, vibrating against something inside my backpack, making a tinny, metal, tapping sound—my stupid water bottle.

I groaned. "That's my phone telling me Theo's using his card again."

He breathed hard, a sharp exhale. "I'll find it," he said in a distant, hollow voice, removing himself from my body carefully and kicking around the floor until he collided with something big, probably stubbing a toe. "Dammit!"

Light flooded the room when he found the switch on the wall, and the sudden illumination had me realizing what we'd just been about to do.

We'd almost had sex without a condom.

"Shit, Jay. What were we thinking?"

He'd bent to retrieve my backpack but looked up when I spoke. OMG. His body. In the light, I could see. I'd felt every inch pressed against me before, but seeing it, seeing the heat in those deep blue eyes? I wanted him. So much. I pictured him shirtless on his ranch doing some kind of manual labor and was a little ashamed of how hot I found the image, and my arms shook and throbbed to reach for him again.

Breath heaved out of his mouth, pumping his chest up and down, and tendons and veins stood out everywhere. His hair was a mess and so sexy with his deep, wavy brown curls licking at the edges of his neck.

But we needed a condom. And we needed to find this guy, Theo. Damn it. It was the whole reason we were here. I slammed my legs together, closing the pornographic chapter from the book of my dreams. If it weren't for Ace back at the ranch, vulnerable, scared, and confused, I would've ignored the alert from my phone.

I didn't dare lower my eyes any further. If I had, I was pretty sure I wouldn't have been able to stop myself from jumping him again.

"Go find something to do. I need to find this guy."

He scoffed. "'Scuse me?"

"We don't have a condom anyway. Whatever that was could have turned into the biggest mess." I peeked up at him standing naked in front of me, and the look on his face, all confused and delicious, reassured me that stopping this had been a good idea.

Something had been screaming at me since he'd pinned me to the wall outside, and now, with distance from his body, his fingers, and his soft, seductive tongue, I heard it loud and clear: getting into bed with him would be a bad idea.

He was a cowboy. A man's man.

I didn't need one of those in my life, didn't need someone telling me what to do, what to think. I'd been so completely distracted by his beautiful face and body, but I would be stupid to screw him and think I'd get away unscathed. I was too involved with him, his family, Carey. This whole situation would come back to bite me.

And I knew he was too good for me. Too kind and pure. I'd been so intent on getting him alone, but he'd want more from me than just a good fuck, and I was so not about that. Okay, fine, maybe I wasn't being entirely honest with myself, but whatever. It didn't matter.

He set my backpack on the bed, and I sat up, looking away from him and righting my clothes. I pulled my rig out and booted it up, then logged in and my fingers flew. I didn't hear him say anything more, but after a few minutes, I realized he'd left the room.

I felt bad, but I couldn't help it and didn't want to. When I worked a job and had a lead, I tended to get lost in my head. I didn't notice the world around me. It was part of what made me a great hacker—singular focus—but maybe I should have warned him about that.

Even if having sex with him was a horrible idea, I didn't want to be too rude—he was helping me.

Moving from the bed to the cheap desk in the corner, I opened my lite laptop, starting searches on it too, the concentration on the task clearing the lust from my body. I scribbled notes on a notepad next to me as I found information and searched through thousands of faces in different hotels, at least in the ones that didn't have closed systems, and stores in San Luis Obispo, California.

That was where Theo had been when he used his credit card again. I thought I'd found him in the convenience store he'd used his card in, but it was such a shitty quality of video, I couldn't be sure. If it had been him, then I'd been right, and he'd changed his appearance. The guy I saw had a buzzed head. Theo did not. At least, as of yesterday, he hadn't.

I began to feel more confident we could catch up with him because he'd just used the card again at a motel in Obispo. It seemed like he'd decided to hunker down there. I searched again through all the stuff I already had on Theo, but California never came up. Obispo must've been where he'd been instructed to meet his blackmailer.

I found a video of the man I was ninety-nine percent sure was Theo entering his motel room and set my rig to notify me with any movement. It would probably just end up waking me up all night, but the camera faced Theo's door, so I hoped there wouldn't be too many other motel guests loitering in front of it.

Was he being blackmailed? I mean, I knew he was, or I suspected because of the payments I'd found, but by who? And why? And why had he left Aislinn, and why had he told her to go to the ranch? Something wasn't adding up, and it was really starting to freaking bug me.

I decided Jay and I could stay put so I could keep looking through all the info I found. I still didn't have anything conclusive, but I'd found some old tax forms and attorney's papers from Theo and Aislinn's parents from when Theo was young, when they'd gone into business with the jerk that later ripped them off, a man named David Ormand. Theo's father had grown up with him—and oh boy, did he rip them off.

I spent the rest of the night going through all his old financial transactions and searched through as much as I could find on the guy and Theo and Aislinn's parents. But David Ormand had died ten years ago, so it couldn't be him blackmailing Theo.

Pulling up the email Aislinn had received, I studied it again. Carey hadn't yet heard back from Aislinn's staff, and I had my suspicions about what could've happened to them. Carey was still looking into it. He'd contacted Boston PD and was waiting for a call back to confer with them.

Following the email's IP addresses, I found it had been routed through many different international servers. Why? Just send a damn email. Why all the cloak and dagger? And how did Theo get involved in this? He was a regular ol' busi-nessman. From my research, I knew he wasn't into anything too tech-y.

I had a shit-ton of searches running on both laptops, and finally, I knew I'd hit a dead end for the night. I thought I heard Jay come back into the room at some point, so I turned and called out for him but had been greeted with silence. The bathroom light peeked out from under the closed door, though, and when I listened harder, I heard the shower.

I changed into my sweats and climbed onto the bed—the only bed in the room—to wait, intending to talk to Jay when he got out of the shower. I felt bad for basically blowing him off after the few intense moments we'd shared. When I thought about it, remembered his hands on my body, his kisses—God, just his breath on my skin—I got hot all over again. I stopped myself, though, pinched the inside of my arm to distract myself with pain so the horniness would fade.

And then I waited, checked my searches again, and texted Carey to update him on Theo's location and what I'd found. While I sat there waiting for Jay to get out of the shower, it dawned on me that I'd seen that email signature before. But where? It was on the tip of my tongue, but I guess I fell asleep because the next thing I knew, night had turned to day, and the alarm I'd set on my phone for six a.m. had gone off.

Jay was still asleep in the tiny chair in the corner. He looked like a drunk pretzel trying to fit his body in the chair comfortably, but it clearly hadn't worked. He would be blessed with a wicked kink in his neck for the rest of the day, I was sure.

He looked completely and maddeningly adorable, all twisted up and uncomfortable, most likely sleeping in the chair to avoid waking me when he'd come out of the bathroom last night. I wanted to crawl into his lap and kiss where his long dark eyelashes lay fringed across his cheeks, like an idiot.

Instead, I tiptoed around him, trying not to wake him on my way to the tiny bathroom, and trying to save myself a few more minutes without having to deal with the awkwardness from how things had ended between us last night.

Well, how *I'd* ended them.

His toothbrush, paste, a tiny travel box of floss, and a man's disposable razor sat on the counter. Aww, how cute was that? Jay flossed. I wiped away yesterday's face with my industrial-strength makeup-removing wipes, washed my face, brushed my teeth, used some of the floss, and took a shower (and shaved my legs with his razor, of course).

Dresses were never my go-to attire—plenty of skirts, short and tight—but not usually dresses. But something had inspired me to throw a maxi dress into my bag at the last minute when I packed back in my apartment in Oregon, and now, I was glad I had.

The California air had infected me, so I donned the dress (yes, it was a girly dress, but still black, loose, and baggy, with spaghetti straps and deep pockets on the hips). I braided my hair down the sides, all flowy So-Cal hippie, and used the motel's complimentary hair dryer to blow out my bangs, making them straight and sexy. I hadn't worn braids in years, probably since high school, but I thought they looked cute.

I contemplated going all out California and leaving my face bare, but no—I wanted to be strong and fierce. I applied my daily kohl eye makeup, thick and smudgy, mascara, Chapstick, and pinched my cheeks for a natural, sexy, earthy glow—

Wait. What? Since when did I give a shit about looking cute? Normally, applying my makeup felt like my own tribal ritual—to ward off everyone and everything. After a second thought, I covered my lips in my usual blood-red lipstick.

When I emerged from the bathroom, days later and surrounded by a cloud of wet air, Jay had disappeared. I looked outside, walked down to the motel lobby, but he was nowhere to be found. And the rental was gone. What the hell? He hadn't left a note or a text or anything.

After checking to make sure Theo hadn't left his room, I packed my gear and looked outside for Jay. Double checking my phone for a text, I sat on the stone wall overlooking the ocean, shoving it back into my backpack just as Jay pulled in, balancing a cardboard drink carrier in one hand when he stepped out.

"Here," he said, walking past me, shoving a large to-go cup in my hand.

"Thanks."

I turned to watch him march down the corridor to our room, then followed and waited when he disappeared inside. He reemerged a minute later carrying his backpack, nearly knocking me over when he stepped back out.

"Ready to go? From the sounds of your fingers clackin' away all night on all those computers, I'm sure you found somethin'. Where we headed?"

"Where'd you go last night?"

"Nowhere. To the beach behind the hotel. Went for a swim. I'm surprised you noticed. You didn't say a word when I came back in," he said, walking ahead of me toward the Jeep, mumbling, "even though I said your name, like, five times, and then we had some semblance of a conversation you probably don't remember."

"Jay, I'm sorry. I should've warned you about that. I get into a zone sometimes when I'm working. I didn't mean to be rude. Or hurt your feelings."

"You didn't hurt my feelin's, Billie."

"Then why are you mad at me?"

"I'm not." He took my backpack out of my hand and slung his over his shoulder. He was mad, but he didn't want me to know. "Ready then? I'm drivin'. I don't know how you obtained a driver's license, but you ain't drivin' anymore on this trip. You scared the shit outta me yesterday."

I laughed. "Sorry. I'm not used to having someone in the car with me. Plus, as much as I hate people, I'm usually a public transportation kind of girl."

"Here, get in." He opened both passenger side doors and

set our backpacks on the back seat. "Seems like maybe you ain't used to havin' anyone around, ever. Make yourself comfortable. I'm gonna take the key back to the front desk, and then we can be on our way."

"Wait," I said, climbing into the passenger seat, still clutching the huge latte he'd gone to find for me. Jay froze with his hand on the door, ready to push it closed. "I think we should call Theo. Maybe if he knows we're in California, he'll let us help him. Maybe he'll tell us why he's running. He checked into a motel last night, but he hasn't left there yet. He's in San Luis Obispo. He told Ace he wouldn't be 'reachable,' but maybe he just disabled his location tracking. You have his phone number, right?"

"Yeah. But whatever's goin' on with him, it seems clear he doesn't want help."

"Yeah, but maybe he didn't ask for help because he didn't know anyone *would* help him. Maybe he didn't know who he could trust. But he knows you. He trusts you. Maybe if we offer, he'll accept our help."

"Okay. You're right. It's worth a shot." Jay pulled his phone from his back pocket and clicked a few times, then held the phone to his ear.

"No. Put it on speaker. You talk, but I wanna hear what he says. Even if he brushes you off, I still might be able to get some clues from the call."

"Okay."

I chewed on my fingernail while the call connected. It rang six times, and Jay looked in my eyes the entire time. Finally, he reached out and pulled my hand down, and Theo answered.

"Jay?"

"Theo. Um, listen, your sister's at the ranch. She's worried about you."

"Oh, good. Yes. Thank you for looking out for her. I knew you would. I'm sorry to spring this on you without warning, but I-I have some business to take care of. I couldn't bring her with me, and I couldn't leave her in Boston."

"Why didn't you just call? I woulda helped."

"Right, well, I, um… Look, Jay, I can't really talk right now. Please tell her that I'll be back for her soon. Tell her not to worry."

Yeah, right. There was so much stress in his voice, it was nearly palpable through the freaking cell phone. I mouthed to Jay, "Tell him you're here." I pointed to the ground, like Jay would know the ground meant California. "Tell him you want to meet him."

"Okay, I'll tell her, Theo, but I'm in California. I can be in Obispo in a few hours. I'll meet you there. I wanna help. I dunno what's goin' on, but you can tru—"

"How do you know where I am? How do you know I'm in Obispo? Fuck. Did someone tell you that? Did someone approach—"

"No. Theo, the sheriff brought Aislinn to the ranch. He's a friend of my family. He called someone, a-a private detective, of sorts. We wanted to find you so we could help you."

"No, Jay. Thank you, but no. I have to take care of this myself. Please just go back to Wyoming. Please, look after Aislinn. I'll be in touch."

I whispered, "Tell him Aislinn is freaking out. She'd feel better if he'd let us help."

Jay closed his eyes and sighed. He didn't want to lie. It wasn't an outright lie; Aislinn was really worried, but it was still a kind of manipulation. "Theo, your sister isn't handlin' you bein' gone very well. If you'd just let us meet you, I know we can figure this out. Whatever it—"

"Who's 'us'?"

"Oh, uh, my… friend. She's the private detective. Well, she's a hacker, but she's good at findin' people. Whatever this is about, she can help you."

"Is she with you right now? Where are you?"

"I'm in Ventura. Yeah, she's right here."

"What's her name?"

I shook my head furiously, but Jay said, "It's Billie. Billie Acker." He shrugged and winced.

Face palm. Ugh. I should've warned him. Damn it.

There was silence for a whole freaking minute, and I bit my nail again.

Jay shuffled his feet. "Theo?"

"Sure, sure. Yeah, you can meet me at—there's a café on Broad Street and Pacific in Obispo. I'll meet you there at noon."

"Okay, we're leavin' Ventura now."

"Yeah, sure. Okay. I'll… I'll see you soon then," Theo said, and then he hung up.

"Damn it, Jay. I should've warned you."

"Why don't you want him to know your name?"

"It probably doesn't matter, but last night, when I was looking at the email Aislinn got, something felt familiar about it. I don't know what." I bit the inside of my lip, trying to figure out where I'd seen the routing signature of that email before. "Come on, let's get on the road. Maybe we can get there early and scope things out. Theo sounds spooked. I mean, *obvi* he's hiding something, but he sounded rattled."

"Yeah, that's for sure. That wasn't the confident business mogul I've dealt with in the past."

I took a swig of my latte. "Well, what are you waiting for? Let's go!"

The traffic wasn't so bad after we got away from Ventura, but still, it would be a couple hour's drive to Obispo. Jay didn't seem in the mood to talk, answering my questions with a "hm" or "mm" here and there, so I pulled out my laptop and checked the searches I could access in the car using my new 5G hotspot for wi-fi. I called Carey to check in, but he didn't pick up, so I called the ranch and asked to talk to Aislinn.

My BFF grumbled into the phone, "Yeah? I mean, Cade Ranch."

"It's Billie."

"Great. I'll text the mayor."

I rolled my eyes. "Just put Ace on the phone."

I heard a knock, and a minute later, a door squeaked open.

"Here. Billie's on the phone for you."

"Oh. Thank you," Ace said. "Can you tell me where the end call button is?"

"Oh, right. Sure. It's the red one."

I snorted. Classic BFF.

"Oh. Sorry," he said, sounding embarrassed. "Here, bottom right-hand corner. Yeah, you got it."

"Thank you."

I heard more grumbling, a door closed, and there were shuffling sounds.

"Billie?"

"Hey, Ace. How's it going back there?" I asked. "I'm gonna kick Kevin's ass when I get back. He could be a little nicer."

"No. It's fine. I'm fine. I still wish Sheriff Michaels would take me to a hotel though."

"Give it up. Carey won't allow it. He wants you in his sight, or in Dean and Jack's. They're treating you well?"

"Yes."

"Where are you?"

"In my room."

I laughed under my breath. Did she think Cade Ranch was like her own private rundown B&B? "Aislinn, get out of there. Go do something. I'm calling Evvie. I'm gonna have her come get you. You need some sun on your skin, or at least sit out on the porch or *something*. Don't stay stuck in that room. Promise you won't."

She sighed. "Fine. I think she's out in the kitchen already."

"Good. Go find her and live a little."

"Have you found anything yet?"

"Yes. Theo stayed in a motel in San Luis Obispo last night. We're meeting him there."

"You talked to him? Is he okay?"

"Yes, this morning. We're on our way now. He didn't say much, but I found some stuff on the guy who screwed your parents over. He's dead, though, so I don't know what it means yet. Maybe, when we catch up to him, Theo will explain."

"I hope so."

"Don't worry. I'm on it. I'll talk to you later. Now, go do something."

We hung up, and I set my phone in the center console.

"What'd Kev do?" Jay asked in a quiet voice.

"Nothing. He's grumpy."

"Hm."

"'Hm' what? That's all you've had to say all morning. 'Hm' this, 'mm' that. Is there a problem I'm not aware of?"

"No."

"So what the fuck does 'hm' mean?"

"Nothin'. Just, grumpy's not unusual for Kevin."

"Maybe not, but I hoped torrid gay sex with the hot vet had happied him up a bit." I crossed my arms over my chest and harrumphed. Yeah, okay, I realized Jay's bad mood was probably a direct effect of mine, but I felt ridiculously hurt that he would barely talk to me.

He laughed under his breath as we passed a road sign for Avila Beach.

"Turn there," I said, pointing to the sign. "I need air. I'm suffocating in this damn car."

CHAPTER EIGHT

BILLIE

"THERE'S AIR ALL AROUND YOU," Jay said.

"Ha, was that sarcasm? I didn't know you had it in you." I rolled my eyes. "Can you just get off the freeway? I need to get out of the car."

"Sure."

Turning away, I sighed and stared out my window at the coastal mountains to the east. California was really beautiful and it annoyed me.

I felt bad for hurting Jay's feelings, and it pissed me off that I felt bad about it. And it pissed me off that it hurt *my* feelings. And I couldn't stop worrying about Ace. Why? I didn't know her. I mean, sure, she was alone and kind of defenseless without her brother, but she was an adult, a smart woman. She didn't need me to fix her life, or basically live it for her like her brother did.

It wasn't like me to be so… helpful. Usually, I only helped if I was getting paid for it.

Jay followed the signs to the beach and parked right in front of the water. It was still early morning, so the sand was empty of tourists, and I only saw a few beach walkers. I didn't get out of the car though. I rolled down my window and sat there, zoning out, watching the subdued blues and oranges of the fleeting sunrise and listening to the waves crash and the seagulls call and screech over the pier.

Jay climbed out, took off his boots and socks, and rolled his jeans up to his knees. "I'm gonna take a walk, stretch my legs for a minute," he said, clearly trying to escape my attitude.

Great. I felt bad about that too.

My phone buzzed with another call from my mother. Clicking "deny call" with a little too much anger in my finger, I tossed the phone into the back seat. She'd spent years ignoring me and sweeping our family "drama" under the rug like a good little Jewish housewife, until she needed my money. But now what? All of a sudden she was Chatty Cathy?

I groaned at myself and rolled my eyes. "Jay, wait up." Hopping out of the car, I kicked off my flip flops and tossed them back through the open window, then jogged to catch up to him. He was already halfway to San Francisco. Jeez. "Your legs are too long."

He walked backwards to taunt me. "Your legs are too short." I caught up to him, finally, and he slowed his pace to match mine and faced forward.

"I'm sorry about last night."

He nodded kind of vaguely, if such a thing were possible.

I tried again. "You're right. I'm not used to being around people. Seriously, I always work alone. Usually in my apartment." I snorted. "Usually in the dark like some evil tech terrorist from a bad movie." I didn't mention our interrupted hot-and-heavy session, and neither did he.

"It's okay. S'pose I forgive ya." He squeezed his hands into fists, then shook them out and shoved them into his jeans pockets. It wasn't the first time I'd noticed him do that. "You know, I don't think I ever asked. How'd you meet Carey? Seems like you guys have known each other a while."

"A few years. I met him in Casper when he was working with the Wyoming State Police on a missing persons case. A little girl, Layla Clark, had gone missing somewhere between Casper and Idaho Falls."

"I remember that girl. Her mama was all over the TV. I felt so bad for her. We all joined the local searches. Searched the woods around Wisper. I think I was home on spring break."

"Yep. It was the end of March. Well, so a friend of mine from school recommended me to Carey. He knew I'm like a dog with a bone, and he knew I could find my way around some of the... legalities other people couldn't.

"Carey had a hunch about the case, but the asshole detective running the investigation wouldn't listen to a lowly beat cop. This was before Carey became a detective and ran for sheriff. So, he called and got me involved, and we worked together to find the girl. We did. We found her.

"But that old jerk was too worried about image. And you could tell he didn't really care about the girl or her family. They weren't rich enough or white enough to pique his interest—Layla was Arapaho, from a nearby reservation—but the governor got involved, and the case got media attention, and it was his department. The prick didn't have a choice."

I laughed. "He really didn't like me coming in. A young woman, looking the way I do. In fact, he pushed me out. It's the only job I've ever been fired from. But Carey and I kept going.

"Anyway, I guess I kind of got a reputation for those types of cases. Not kids, specifically, but just missing people. I'm not sure I could work only on children's cases. It's too hard when I can't find them." I crouched down, digging my fingers through the sand till I found a pebble, then lobbed it toward the water.

"I can't imagine. But that's really cool that you do that. I'm sure you could get a high-payin' job lots of places. It's pretty commendable you use your Jedi powers for good."

I looked up at him as he peered at the ripples my pebble made in the water. He still thought I was a sweet little girl. "Don't saint me yet. Lately, I've been taking paying cases. People looking for other people, things, whatever. The money's good."

"So then, why'd you take Aislinn's case? I can't imagine the state of Wyoming pays what you're used to."

I huffed a laugh. "Uh, no. It doesn't. It's not really a case, not technically, more like a favor. But Carey asked so…"

"You and Carey have a thing or somethin'?"

"A thing?" He side-eyed me, raising his eyebrows. "Eww. No." I made a face. "Carey's like my weird, red-headed, hillbilly step-brother. No, Carey was there for me when I… when I needed a friend. I don't have a lot of those."

"Oh." He looked at me, but I looked back at the water. I'd already said too much. I wasn't about to drone on and on about my pathetic, solitary existence. "Well, so how come you don't work for the FBI or the CIA or whatever? If your skills are as considerable as you say." He nudged me with his elbow. He was flirting with me. Shy-flirting but flirting, nonetheless.

"Oh, they are considerable. Do you doubt me?" I smirked up at him, arching an eyebrow, and he raised his hands in front of his chest in mock-surrender and shook his head, smiling. "But I don't have a degree. I dropped out of college. It wasn't for me."

"Where'd you go?"

"MIT."

"Jeez, Billie."

"Yeah, well, like I said, it wasn't for me. It made my mother happy for about five minutes though."

"Oh yeah? She got big expectations?"

I shrugged. "She never really cared about me being happy or finding a career I loved. After—well, we had some bad shit happen in our family, and she just wanted me to make her look good." I'd almost said Jessie's name. Thank God I'd caught myself. I wouldn't have been able to hide the pain in my voice if I hadn't. "I'm pretty sure she still tells people I went there. She just omits that I dropped out after one year."

"You're not close with your mama?"

I sat on a bleached-out driftwood log. "Nope."

"Your dad?"

"He's gone, died about ten years ago," I said. "What about you? How are you doing since Ma passed? I'm really sorry, Jay."

"Oh." He sighed. "Yeah. Thank you. I miss her. A lot. Man, that woman was somethin' else, you know?"

I laughed. She had been "somethin' else." Ma had been a feisty woman, and she'd done a great job raising Jay and his brothers. Their real mom had just waltzed back into their lives a little less than nine months ago after staying away twenty years. I couldn't even imagine. My mom was no angel, but at least she'd been there physically. "Yeah, she was." I giggled. "Remember how she yelled at Finn and smacked his ass for cussing? But I never heard her yell at you. Don't you ever swear?"

"No, I mean, not really. I guess I'm not loud like my brothers."

I peeked up and stared at the side of his face. I wondered if maybe he wanted to say more, gazing at the ocean with the saddest smile on his face, but he wouldn't.

"Your mom came back from the dead. How was *that*?"

He sat next to me. "This place is beautiful. I guess I forgot how different California is from Wyoming. It's like another world." He looked at my feet in the sand and reached down to toss a bunch of little stones away, and I dug my toes in. "You have cute toes," he said, raising his eyes to mine.

My vagina stomped her foot. *Get him in here!* she screamed.

"Cute toes? Oh my God, you're weird. They're short and stubby." I scrunched them, digging deeper, but my sarcastic hacker heart wrapped around his words and squeezed tight.

"They're cute." He took a deep breath and closed his eyes, breathing in the salty, beachy morning.

"So, how's it been since she came back?"

"I guess she did come back from the dead, but now that it's all over, I look back and I think, what did I really miss out on? Ma was my mama." He sighed and shrugged. "I dunno. It's not much different, really." Opening his eyes, he plastered them to the side of my face while I gazed out at the water, but I knew they were bluer than the ocean in front of me. "Were you serious the other night? Think you coulda found her?"

"Yeah. When Carey asked me to look into it this past Christmas, I found her right away. But everything I found was from the last few years, from when she was with that cartel guy. Before that, when she was in France and before, there wasn't a lot to find. You haven't talked to her about all this?"

"A little."

"Seriously? I would've demanded answers."

"Kev did. She left when we were little 'cause she lost a baby. I mean, not like a miscarriage. She gave birth to a little girl, and the baby died in her arms. She says she had post-partum depression pretty bad, and she was afraid of hurtin' us." He looked out at the water, too, watched the waves lapping and frothing. "She hasn't actually said it, but I think she means she was scared she would hurt us physically. Me, specifically. I was born after the baby."

"I've heard of that. It can cause women to do things they would never normally do."

"Yeah, so... Anyway, I guess it's good she's back. I haven't really spent much time with her. Dean has. Kev has. Jack's comin' around slowly." He chuckled. "Evvie's practi-cally shovin' Daisy down his throat. But I was pretty young when she left. I don't really know her."

"Do you want to?"

He shrugged. "Sure. Guess I do."

I looked at him then, really looked. There was so much more he wanted to say. It was written all over his face, but he didn't.

"Why are you always so quiet? What are you really thinking?"

"I dunno." He peeked at me. "C'mon, gettin' hungry yet? I'm starvin'."

"Haven't you noticed?" I asked, pulling my feet out of the sand, feeling the tiny grains rub the skin between my "cute" toes. *Really? Cute toes?* "I'm always hungry."

We found a breakfast burrito food truck around the corner from the public beach access, then hopped back on the freeway toward Obispo. My apology and the following conversation seemed to have loosened him up a bit, and now he talked freely. Well, more than he had before anyway, and I searched through my phone for some totally bitchin' road trip music to get us in the mood.

"What kind of music do you like?"

"Hm? Oh, uh, whatever's fine," he said, lowering the visor, trying to block the bright sun peeking over the mountains. He wasn't wearing the sunglasses I'd picked up for him at the Discount Mart.

"Whatever? Music is a deeply personal and spiritual choice. There is no 'whatever' when it comes to music. Come on, tell me."

"I dunno. I guess I like old stuff. Classic rock. Folk…? I like the Boss. And Tom Petty. What about you?"

"Well, my music tastes are varied and educated. But right now, I'm on an extreme metal kick."

"Extreme metal?"

"Ever heard of Meshuggah?"

He choked on a laugh. "No, I've never heard of 'em, but that makes sense." Peeking over at me, he said, "But I heard you in the shower this mornin'. That was no extreme metal. Am I right? Was that… *Celine*?" He drew the name out in a mock-French accent.

"Hey. It's bad form to make fun of someone's taste in music. And yes, it was Celine. The metal is for when I'm hacking. The tempo sets my pace and keeps me on track. But Celine, she's for when I need a little inspiration. She is the Grand Diva of *all* the divas, in my humble, or maybe not so humble, opinion. That bitch can *sing*. You can't deny it."

"Wouldn't dare."

"But right now, how about… Ah, the Peppers. We are in California." I connected to the rental's Bluetooth and hit shuffle play on the Red Hot Chili Peppers discography in my music steaming app, and "Californication" started up. Fitting.

"So, what got you into hackin'?"

"I dunno. I always liked computers. How they work. I like figuring stuff out, you know? And I'm good at it. When I left school, it was a way to support myself. I'm not like a hard-core hacker. I mean, don't get me wrong, I can get into anything. But I'm not on some kind of dramatic, 'Let's take over the world and own the internet' campaign. I just don't like barriers. When things get in my way, I bust through 'em." *Like people.* "What about you? How did you like Berkeley? How'd you end up there?"

"It was good. I liked it. I applied to all kinds of schools. Back then, I wanted nothin' more than to get away from the ranch. From my dad. I got good grades in high school, got some good scholarships."

"Then why did you go back there after graduation? You can't do a lot with your fancy business degree in Podunk, Wyoming."

"No, well, the deal was that I'd put that fancy degree to use for the ranch. That's how Jack talked my dad into lettin' me go."

"So then, why aren't you running things?"

He sighed. "I don't think Jack ever really meant for me to actually run things. He's been in charge of the ranch since I was a kid. Even when my dad was still alive, Jack was the one who got stuff done. He knows what he's doin'."

I snorted. "That makes no sense, Jay. You said he talked your dad into it, so why wouldn't he want you to use what you learned? You guys barely have a digital presence. You need social media accounts and advertising. Your website sucks. No one updates it. Why don't you?"

"It's not my place."

"That's bullshit. You're part owner of the ranch, right? Or did your dad leave it only to Jack?"

"No, he left it to us all."

He looked over at me, and I raised my eyebrows to scold him. "So?"

"Jack's just not ready yet."

"Jack's not ready or you're not?"

CHAPTER NINE

JAY

BILLIE'S SHORT-LIVED good mood degraded by the minute. San Luis Obispo had been a waste of time. Theo wasn't there.

We sat at an outdoor table in front of the coffee shop where Theo was supposed to meet us while she pitched a fit over her error in judgement after a bike messenger delivered a secret spy note from Theo. All it said was, "Don't follow me. You don't want to get involved in this. I won't let him hurt my sister." All the kid with the bike knew was that he was paid five hundred dollars in cash to wait for us to show up and then give us the note.

"Damn it. We should've known he'd run. I knew he sounded sketchy. All this fresh fucking ocean air is messing with me," she griped, slammin' her cup of coffee on the table. Slumpin' back in her chair, she huffed out a breath, blowin' the hair outta her eyes. "And you." She glared at me.

"What'd I do?"

"You're distracting me."

"How am I doin' that?"

Narrowin' her eyes, she sat forward, grumblin', "Never

mind. At least Theo doesn't know I'm tracking his credit card," and pulled her laptop closer to her from where it was loadin' up in the middle of the little wooden café table.

She ignored me while she worked, searchin' away, so I sat back and tried to relax after callin' Carey to make sure he and the guys were lookin' after Aislinn closely. The note was the first time we'd heard anything about Aislinn bein' in danger. There hadn't been any commotion back home, though, and Carey said he had it covered.

Relaxin' wasn't an easy task for me with Billie across the table, lookin' as beautiful as ever, even with the irritated scowl on her face, but here in this quiet town, near the beach with the warm salty breeze calmin' me, I closed my eyes and breathed.

She'd kinda apologized this mornin', but I still had no idea what had happened last night. I mean, yeah, her phone buzzed with an alert about Theo usin' his credit card, but her whole demeanor had changed in an instant. She became so cold. Just like that. And this mornin', she acted like nothin' had happened at all.

She'd been right about the condom. I hadn't even thought to bring any with me, but it wasn't like I couldn't think of a whole myriad of things to do that wouldn't require a condom. And it wasn't like I thought she'd just fall into my arms 'cause we were on a road trip together—far from it—but I remedied that problem anyway, first thing when I picked up her coffee this mornin'. She had every right to change her mind. If she didn't wanna be with me, I would respect that, but if she did—I mean, I wanted to be prepared.

My doubts and insecurities had been stranglin' me all day though. Had I done somethin' or said somethin' that made her wanna stop? She'd been into it. She'd told me—no, ordered me—to take her to our room to "fuck" her. I'd never had a woman say that to me before.

I liked it.

It sounded bold comin' outta her mouth. Confident. Sexy. She was the boldest, most outspoken person I'd ever met, and she intimidated the shit outta me. But last night, in the moment, I'd never felt more confident. Her sayin' the thing I wanted right to my face, her lips against my skin, her breath —she made *me* feel confident, and I took what I wanted. Or I almost did.

I wondered what had made her so strong. Had she gone through somethin' hard and come out on the other side of it knowin' she could just take what she needed from life? Or had she been born strong like that? I wanted to ask her about it, but she probably wouldn't tell me anyway.

Maybe she'd just decided she didn't want me. Maybe it was the situation we were in, or maybe I'd been right before and Finn was more her speed. Or someone smarter, cooler, someone into computer stuff. Someone who knew what the hell he was doin' with his life, like she did. She left school 'cause she already knew what she wanted. Or what she didn't. MIT. A person would have to be pretty confident about themselves to snub their nose at that.

I still had no clue. I'd bet none of my brothers ever felt inadequate or like they didn't belong on the ranch. I'd felt inferior to my larger-than-life brothers since I was a kid. Finn with his looks, humor, and charm. Kevin with his wit and ability to manipulate and woo just about anyone he came in contact with. Dean with his muscles and huge love.

And Jack. The man of our family, the leader of us all, and the brains behind the ranch. Plus, he'd taken care of me after our mama left us. He'd been more like a father to me than a brother, more so than even my own dad had been.

I could never be like Jack.

Maybe Billie wanted someone more like that.

I wouldn't blame her. I went off to college thinkin' I'd go home different. I thought I'd be stronger, more confident. I felt that way about the knowledge I'd gained from school—I knew I could put together a solid business plan, a marketing campaign, do the books, accountin' and all that—but what I still lacked was the courage to do it. The courage to walk up to Jack and say, "I got this. I'm takin' over."

I did have every right. My name was on the deed to the ranch and business just like my brothers, and it was true that it had been the motivation for me to go to college in the first place, to be able to come home and put my fancy degree to good use.

But even if I could say the words, why would he believe in me? I'd never proven myself to Jack. Sure, I put together the equine therapy proposal, but look where that got me. Nowhere. In the middle of California with a pissed off hacker who probably wanted to be anywhere other than where she was. I had no business, no investor, and no fuckin' clue.

"What are you thinking about now?"

I opened my eyes to see Billie sittin' forward with her elbow on the table and her chin in her hand, starin' at me. I couldn't see her eyes behind her black sunglasses, but I could feel 'em.

"What?"

"What were you thinking about just now? Your face got all solemn and scrunched."

"Ah, nothin'. Just wonderin' where we're headed is all. We don't have any idea where Theo went. How are we supposed to find him?"

"No. Well, there's a small regional airport here, but there haven't been any flights today. He could still be here. Or he's driving. But I don't have any clue which way he'd go. I assume he'll still head north, but will he take the PCH or the 101? I have no clue."

"PCH?"

"Pacific Coast Highway? Duh. Highway One? There are road signs everywhere. Are you sure you went to school in California?"

"Oh, right. Well, if those are our choices, I say the PCH. Probably a nicer drive, more relaxin'."

"There's a million choices, Jay. A million roads. Until he uses his card again, there's no way for me to track him. He used it once after you talked to him, at a gas station. So maybe he's driving and he filled up, but that doesn't help me know which way he went."

"Okay, then we get another room and wait. You can spread out and get your computers goin'. I'll get us some good food, and you can rest a bit."

"We're wasting time," she whined. "Maybe we should just pick a route and commit to it. If Aislinn really is in danger, we're out of time."

"And if we find out later he went a different way, how much time will we lose backtrackin'?"

She took a deep breath and sighed. "Fine."

It seemed Billie had found somethin' that made her feel better: pokin' fun at me. Little jabs here and there, like my brothers always did. Not in a mean way, just lighthearted, but still, it irked me. Made her feel better, though, so I didn't say anything.

Until she made fun of my name.

"So, baby Jay. What's for dinner? You said you'd get me

something good to eat. I need sustenance." I flinched when she added the 'baby' before Jay, and she noticed. "What? Ohh, you don't like being called baby Jay?"

"Not particularly." I unlocked the door to our new motel room, number sixteen in the Sunset Coast Motel in San Luis Obispo. I didn't know why they called it that; it faced mountains, not the ocean, and this one had two beds.

"Isn't that what your brothers call you?"

"Unfortunately."

"How about Jay Bird? Or... Ooo, I know, little Jay, a variation of baby Jay. You are the youngest of the Cade men, right?"

"Yep. I'm the youngest. But no. Just Jay."

"Jay's short for Jonathan, right?"

"Yep."

"So why do they call you Jay?"

"Dunno."

"You don't know where your nickname came from?"

"I guess from my mama. She called me JJ when I was little, but I don't remember it."

"Aww, JJ," she mocked. "That's *so* cute."

"No, it ain't."

"Hmm. How about I call you Johnny Boy." She giggled.

I snapped, "How 'bout you call me Jay."

"Okay, okay, jeez. Sensitive much?"

"What's Billie short for then? And I'm not sensitive," I said, droppin' our bags onto the motel bed and unloadin' her computers, "but my name is Jay. Or if you want somethin' different, Jonathan. Though, you'd be the only person on the planet to call me that."

She grabbed her laptop from my hands. "Fine, Jonathan. You're no fun. And Billie isn't short for anything. My name is Billie."

I didn't believe that, but I didn't push. I said, "I was named after my uncle. He was my favorite person when I was little, till he died."

"Oh."

"My uncle Jonathan, my dad's brother. We called him UJ." I was proud to be named after him. When he and Granny were killed in a car accident, I thought I'd never wanna hear that name again. But comin' outta Billie's mouth, I liked it, even with the spit and ire in her voice. I wasn't about to tell *her* that though.

"How old were you? When he died, I mean?"

"I was four maybe. He taught me to read. To love to read. He taught me you can get lost in a book, go on an adventure, escape your life." I smiled, rememberin'. "He read *The Chronicles of Narnia* to me whenever my dad wasn't around. He used to read to my mama, too, before she left. I dunno why I just remembered that." Probably 'cause she'd come back into my life in the blink of an eye. I'd been remembering all kinds of things.

The problem was, I was a little kid when she left. The memories were hazy at best, but I remembered UJ readin' to us. I remembered bein' snuggled up with my mama, listenin' to her heart beat slowly and the deep, calm sound of UJ's voice. It had been the only time in my life I hadn't felt unimportant. My brothers hadn't been there. It had just been me and my mama.

Billie set herself up in the motel room, and I took the Jeep to wander around Obispo, just drivin', lookin' for Theo, though I was sure Billie was right and he'd taken off the second he hung up the phone this mornin'.

Meanderin' downtown till I found a fresh seafood restaurant, I splurged a little and bought some grilled sea bass that smelled so good on the way back to the motel. My mouth

watered so much, I drooled like the newest member of the
Cade family, Tony the rescue pit bull, longin' for a steak just
outta his reach.

When I walked into our room, Billie sat facin' away from
me with bulky, funny-lookin' headphones on her ears and her
nose nearly stuck to a computer screen. She had two laptops
workin', some type of tablet, and her phone on some kinda
stand on top of the desk. Her leg jumped really fast to her
weird metal music, I assumed, and she gulped the last of the
coffee she'd brought back with her from the café, then tossed
the cup absently toward the garbage, but it missed the mark
and rolled to my feet. She was practically vibratin' in the
chair.

Sure she'd noticed the change in the light when I opened
the door, I picked up her cup, lobbin' it into the can, and set
the food beside her on the little desk next to a notepad with a
bunch of indecipherable scribbles on it. She jumped so high
her chair fell over, and she landed on her backside on the
floor. She knocked into the desk and her phone fell, makin' a
loud clatterin' noise when it bounced off the wood, then
thudded on the floor.

"Motherfucker!"

"Jeez, Billie. You okay?"

She launched herself at me, pummelin' my arms and chest
with her fists. "You dick! Why would you do that?"

"I'm sorry." I tried not to laugh. "I thought you noticed
me come in. You alright?" Grabbin' her wrists, I held 'em to
stop her assault, but she yanked 'em free and sat on the end of
the bed closest to her, breathin' hard. She bent at the waist,
resting her forearms on her knees, and hung her head. Her
shiny dark-brown bangs fell over her eyes like a short curtain
of silk, so I couldn't see her face.

"You scared me to death. My heart is pounding. How

would I have heard you come in, Jay? I had my headphones on."

I bent down to retrieve the wireless headphones that had fallen off her head and been kicked under the bed. When I straightened, she clutched the skirt of her dress in her fingers, up above her knees so her legs were right in my face. I felt the urge to bury myself between 'em, but didn't.

It had been a constant struggle all day not to touch her. She looked beautiful in her dress, with her hair in those adorable braids, and I kept tryin' to imagine her face without all the makeup she always wore.

"Sorry." I stood and grabbed the food. "Peace offerin'? I picked up some fresh fish and a steak in case sea bass ain't your thing. There's more coffee, though I'm thinkin' a bottle of water might be a better choice." I set it all up for her and stepped back, grabbin' a container and a plastic fork for myself.

"Thank you," she said, but she sounded distant again. This hot and cold thing was really startin' to get on my nerves.

"You're welcome." Well, I could be distant too. I sat on the other bed and snatched the TV clicker from the table in between the two, turnin' the small flat-screen on and flippin' through channels. "Find Theo yet?"

"No, Jay. I haven't *found* Theo yet. He hasn't used his card again. I'm just going through more of his old financial records. And I'm searching everything I can find about his parents and their company, and that guy. The one that ripped them off. It seems he had a son. I'm not having much luck yet finding anything on him, though, at least not anything recent."

"Hm."

"There you go again with your intensely verbose

responses. Wonderful. Here, this is a pic of the guy." Pointin'
to her laptop on the desk to show me a picture of a really tall,
well-built and fair-skinned guy in a tuxedo at some fancy gala
or ball or somethin', she glared at me. "Dude's huge."

"Well, so what's he got to do with Theo and Aislinn?"

"I said I don't know! Jesus. What, you think I'm freaking
omniscient? It's not like I'm not trying."

She griped at everything I said or didn't say, so I kept
quiet and continued to absently click through the TV channels. Finally, I turned it off and pulled my well-worn copy of
Skipped Parts from my backpack and tried to read. She still
glared at me. I could feel her scowl even though I refused to
look at her, and finally, she went back to work, eatin' a bite
here and there. She liked the sea bass. After she finished hers,
she looked around for more, but I'd eaten the other piece, so
she picked at the steak and green beans still left in the bag
from the restaurant.

I took a shower while she worked and changed into the
new pink and purple board shorts she'd bought for me,
intendin' to take a walk, maybe dip into the pool outside our
room for a swim, but I must've fallen asleep at some point. I
hadn't meant to, but I had to admit, tryin' to keep up with her
irritated, bad, and worse moods was exhaustin'.

In the mornin', I woke to somethin' rubbin' my leg. At first I
was annoyed, assumin' Finn had let Tony into my bedroom,
but then the rubbin' moved higher, toward more sensitive
places, and I woke right up, rememberin' where I was in an
instant.

Billie was snuggled up beside me, headphones still on her
head, but they'd traveled down durin' sleep and wrapped

around her neck like a collar. She lay on her side facin' me, but she was still fast asleep. Her lips were parted, and she breathed these sexy little "ahhs" with each exhale. She'd removed her makeup before fallin' asleep, and her face looked healthy, pink, and stunnin'.

I lay there, just starin' at her for the longest time. She had some freckles, not many, but damn, they were cute on the bridge of her nose and cheeks under her eyes. I had no clue why she always wore so much makeup; I'd never seen a woman more naturally beautiful. Her eyelashes were long and black, and I wanted to feel 'em with my fingertip but didn't wanna wake her.

Her nose was just a little too long, the bridge a little too bony to be considered "perfect," but I liked it. It accentuated her mouth, like a big ol' blinkin' neon sign sayin', "Look here, this is whatcha want!"

And I did want it. Her mouth, bold and dirty as it could be, was just about my favorite thing in the world. Everything comin' out or goin' in it fascinated me and/or turned me on, though I had to admit, seein' her like this, quiet, peaceful, and snark-free was a welcome treat.

Man, this woman could get under my skin, but lookin' at her now was definitive confirmation that I was helpless to deny her. It confused me. Usually, when someone was abrasive the way she could be, I avoided 'em. My personality was the opposite.

But somehow, with Billie, it was what attracted me to her. Maybe it was 'cause I knew, even though she wanted me to think of her as a fierce warrior kind of woman, deep down inside, she was just as broken as me. Maybe the mask she always wore was what she used to hide her own insecurities.

Her lips were perfection. Not too big, not too thin, but the little gap in between 'em was sin made flesh. Her upper lip looked like a long, pink bowtie, narrow in the middle with plump pillows on either side of it, and the whole thing puffed out over her bottom lip a little, the corners turnin' down just a tad, even when she smiled. I imagined slidin' my finger in there… or other things.

Well, one other thing.

I had mornin' wood, of course, but lookin' at her and listenin' to her breathe added a pain and angst to it. I had to clench my fists and lock my arms across my chest to stop from touchin' her. After about ten minutes of starin' at her like a stalker, I needed to get up. I needed the solace of the bathroom and the lock on the door.

I tried to move sideways off the bed, but she dug her fingers into my thigh and moaned. Like that helped me any. I scooted an inch at a time till she threw her leg over mine and her arm over my stomach, holdin' me tight. I tried so hard not to wake her. I didn't want her to feel embarrassed about cuddlin' up to me in the night, but there was just no way for me to get free of her, and I had to get some distance.

I didn't think I'd ever been so hard in my whole life.

"Billie," I whispered, movin' her hair away from her eyes with the tiniest swipe of my finger.

"Mmm."

"I gotta get up. I, uh, need to use the restroom."

"Mmhm."

Oh God, the gritty, moanin' sound of her voice coulda killed me right there 'cause I couldn't stop myself from imaginin' her makin' that sound with my cock buried deep inside her body. Blood *pounded* into it. Somehow, in her sleep, she noticed or felt it, and she took it in her hand through the stupid surfer shorts. My whole body stiffened and I groaned. How was I supposed to get free of her now, without comin', and did I really want to?

"*Fuck*, Billie." My dick hurt, I was so hard, and it took every single ounce of my self-control not to thrust my hips.

Snugglin' closer, buryin' her face in my neck, she squeezed her hand. A moan escaped my lips, even though I tried so hard to hold it in, and she kissed below my ear, just the softest touch of her lips to my skin, then licked it. *Oh, shit, shit, shit!*

"Billie, you gotta wake up. I don't think you realize what you're doin'."

"I know exactly what I'm doing, and you just cussed," she whispered, pushin' herself up to straddle me. She'd fallen asleep in her black dress, so she dragged it up around her thighs as her eyes opened, and she looked down into mine. Scootin' down my legs a little, she untied the tie on my shorts, loosenin' and pullin' 'em down. "I want you. Let me have you?"

Her voice was so quiet and vulnerable and sexy, and she implored me to say yes with the question in her eyes, all shy and searchin'. I'd never seen her look so open before, and she'd never been more beautiful.

I couldn't deny her.

My heart thudded behind my ribs, but I reached down beside the bed for my bag and grabbed the box of condoms I'd bought from the front pocket. I watched her as I brought it up and tore the little cardboard box, grabbin' a single packet and rippin' it open. A tiny smile glanced across her lips, and her eyes closed a little. She took the condom in one hand and used the other to pull my achin' cock from my shorts and rolled it on, then moaned so softly and lifted up on her knees to hover above me.

My whole body was hard as concrete, frozen with desperate anticipation, but I had to ask, "Billie, are you sure?

I thought you'd changed your mind." I whispered 'cause the silence in the dark room was deafenin'.

"Changed my mind? About wanting you?"

I nodded. I couldn't speak with her hand wrapped around me, positionin' me to enter her body. She shook her head, and her messy bangs fell over her eyes again. "I didn't change my mind. It's all I can think about," she whispered, and she sank down onto my ready cock, takin' me all the way.

CHAPTER TEN

BILLIE

MY HEAD FELL BACK, and Jay groaned. I clutched at his chest, trying to find something to hold onto, something to ground me. I felt like I could float away, still clinging a little to sleep, but I trembled from head to toe while he shimmied his shorts down his legs and kicked them somewhere.

Oh God. He felt so good inside me. We'd barely moved yet, and already, I felt that delicious, full, "this isn't going to take very long" feeling. Sex was still a bad idea, but I'd hit my limit. I couldn't keep my hands off of him for one minute more.

And as the seconds ticked by with him inside me, filling me and luring me to the dark side, I couldn't remember why I'd tried to convince myself I should.

Yeah, right. Like I needed to be convinced.

"Billie." Eyes rolling closed, his lashes fluttered against his cheeks, and he reached for my hips, gripping them and my dress in his tight fists. I lifted up and plunged back down, and he hissed, clenching his jaw. I rode him then, slowly and gently, watching the pleasure play across his beautiful face.

He pushed my dress up around my waist, trying to get it

off, so I took it from his fingers and pulled it over my head. Reaching behind me to unclasp my bra, I let it fall down my arms and brought them back around to plant my hands on his chest for leverage to own him between my thighs, but his T-shirt blocked my access to his skin, so I threw my bra to the floor and pushed it up, and he lifted his arms to help me. The motion messed his hair, making his wavy curls wild and even sexier, which was really saying something because I'd been having the hardest time trying not to pull my fingers through them every minute of every day we were together.

His skin was warm, and I followed the soft brown hair between his pecs with my fingers, down his stomach and that taut V between his hips, to watch him moving in and out of me. I moaned at the obscenity of it, his cock so wet, hot, hard, and huge, spreading my pussy lips and sliding into me with every delicious clench of his ass, and I ground down on him harder, taking him as deep inside me as I could.

He opened his eyes, and they traveled back and forth between my breasts and my face, until he couldn't take it anymore. He raised up, his abs flexing and making my mouth water, and took my nipple into his mouth.

Oh my God.

Breathing so loudly, I moaned and panted as he licked my breast, sucking it with his warm, wet mouth. His other hand pushed and glided over my skin, around my back, and he tangled his fingers in my hair and pulled me closer. The way his body reached to be skin to skin with mine, like we were two needy magnets, caused his pelvis and lower abdomen to rub against me in that nubby little spot and sparks ignited inside, from the tips of my nipples down, down, down, to—

Way too soon, the need to fuck the balls right off his body took over, and I increased my pace. He moved his hips with mine, but when I rolled them even faster against him, seeking more of that pressure, his breathing became ragged.

He didn't say anything. He barely made a noise, but he looked so intense. The way he watched me, stared at me, into me—he made me feel so bare. It felt good. I felt powerful and so sexy.

I felt unashamedly beautiful.

All the negative thoughts about my body loitered in the back of my mind, waiting for me to open the gates so they could rush through like a bunch of robot tweens at a K-pop concert, but I held them back. Actually, I found myself not even having to try. Nothing mattered besides him and me and our bodies, where they connected.

But he disconnected them!

One minute, I was above him, riding him to ecstasy, and the next, I was on my back with him between my legs.

He pulled out and kneeled above me, removing the elastic bands still holding my braids in, then tossed them on the bedside table and removed my headphones, combing my hair with his long fingers and spreading the kinked locks out on the pillow beside me.

He was so quiet and gentle, and it felt so viscerally private—almost uncomfortably private—but I couldn't look away from his eyes while they dragged over my hair, my neck, my face, and down my body.

Okay, so maybe a *few* of the doubts snuck past security. He looked me over thoroughly, but I didn't want him to focus on my stomach, my thighs—my fat. But there wasn't time for my embarrassment and insecurity. Grasping those thick thighs in his hands and spreading my legs, he swooped down, latching onto my clit with his tongue and lips.

Rolling my hips into his face over and over and over, scratching my thighs against the stubble on his cheeks and jaw, I grabbed fistfuls of his soft, sexy hair, whimpering and gasping for breath, as he pushed two fingers inside me and pulled them out.

He became relentless in his rhythm, still licking and sucking the little swollen nub that existed basically as click-bait for my orgasmic womb. Pressing with his tongue, he thrust his fingers so far inside my—

"Ohh, oh, oh Jay. Jay. Jay. Jay!"

An orgasm slammed into me like a freight train. My thighs squeezed his head, and the itty-bitty, teeny-weeny part of me that still held coherent thought wondered if he could still breathe. *Ohmygod.* I soared, and he continued to suck and push and pull in and out, prolonging my high, but then he dragged his fingers slowly from my body, lapping and sucking my cum like he needed it to live. I heard it, the wet smacking of his lips.

Finally, I opened my eyes to see him kneeling again between my legs. He gazed at me, his chin lifted and his eyes peering down again like outside the motel. He was the sexiest man I had ever seen. The lazy, hungry look on his face attracted me like a junkie to her fix. His lips were wet, still glistening with the proof that he was all man—there was no baby Jay here—and he licked them. I couldn't look away. I couldn't speak. All my snark and wit had disappeared, flew out the window, probably with all my brain cells when he made me come.

Oh, but the need in his eyes—there could be no misunder-standing that, even without brain cells.

Leaning over me, he touched his lips to mine, his deep ocean-blue eyes staring into mine, and with sleepy, half-closed lids, he kissed me. A chaste peck on my bottom lip. "I'm gonna fuck you now. That okay? Still want me to?"

Some strange laugh escaped me, and I felt my eyebrows

crawling up to my hairline. What did he think we'd just done? I didn't care. I wanted more. I nodded. Apparently, the orgasm he'd just given me had caused my vocal chords to stop working, much like my brain cells.

He sat back on his heels and *yanked* my body with his hands on my hips, down the bed to meet his. He wasted no time. As he pulled my pussy to his cock, he entered me, ramming into me and thrusting so hard, I felt it in my lungs. The breath rushed out of them, and I gasped more in, and an almost guttural groan tore from his throat.

Wrapping my legs around him, he grabbed my ass, using my cheeks to push and pull me on his cock. *OMFG*! His head fell back, and his mouth fell open as he breathed.

I ached just to watch him, and something inside me squeezed and clenched, but not in my vagina. In my chest. I didn't know what it was, but I knew it would be trouble. It felt so strange, and my heart sped up, pounding even faster than it already was, frantically trying to keep up with him.

Whatever it was throbbed inside me and made me want to touch him.

I lifted my hands to his chest, rubbing and caressing down his ribs, and I watched him, feeling each ridge and valley while he fucked me like I'd never been fucked before. Jesus! The passion inside him. Where had it come from? I thought he was just some quiet country boy. He never talked about himself, never gave any clue about the thoughts in his head.

Apparently, there were many, and they were deep and ardent and hot, and suddenly, I needed to know them all.

I couldn't look away. I tried. I swear I did!

Lifting up onto my elbows, I drank in the sight of him moving in and out of me. So raw and sexy and—my core clamped down on his cock, and he fell forward, eyes open, thrusting even faster.

He leaned further down, caging me between his arms, forcing me onto my back again, kissing me and sucking my ragged breath into his mouth. He pounded into me again and again, and my body just gave up.

I'd been trying to hold out until he came. He'd already given me the most amazing orgasm, but I couldn't stop it now. The muscles inside me contracted hard, like they were trying to eat him alive, and I came again.

Holy shit.

Opening my mouth to scream, no sound came out. It was *that* powerful an orgasm. But he must've been waiting for me too. He took my mouth again, almost brutally, shoving his tongue inside, but he felt too good riding me through my orgasm—the hard, wet slide of his cock inside me, rubbing and driving into me over and over and over—and I couldn't concentrate on kissing, so I just sucked his bottom lip into my mouth, holding him captive as he rammed into me once more and came.

Ass cheeks hard as granite under my greedy fingers, his whole body shuddered and shook, but he didn't make a sound.

We stayed like that for about a minute, still connected, slick with sweat, panting, hearts pounding, and then he removed himself from my body and climbed off the bed.

He almost jumped away from me. *Umm… okay?* It felt so jarring. After the way we'd just connected—I mean, I didn't expect a marriage proposal but, like, I guess I expected conversation, or… something. *IDFK.*

I couldn't say I'd ever been a warm and fuzzy "hold me?" kind of person either, but come on. He just came literally, like, sixty seconds ago. I felt like some naggy bubblegum idiot. I'd never felt so discarded before. Usually, I was the one escaping the awkward, post-coital touchy-feely.

I'd never seen him move so fast.

"Jay?"

"Yeah?"

"You okay?"

"Huh?" He turned to look at me, pulling his shorts up his incredibly lickable, hard-muscled thighs and over his bare ass. Oh, that ass. I could bounce a quarter off of it or take a bite out of it. "Whatcha mean?"

"I mean, where's the fire?" I sat up in the bed, wrapping the stiff, ugly floral-patterned bedspread around my breasts.

"What?"

"Is there a reason you're trying to flee ten seconds after you blew inside me? I can't believe I'm gonna ask this, but did I do something wrong? It's usually me doing the running."

"What? No. I'm not runnin'. But we're done. Right? I mean, did you want me to do somethin' else? I could—" He took a step back toward the bed, his arms outstretched, his dick still wrapped in the condom, wet and semi-hard. To do what, I didn't know.

"No. No, stop. Did you—did you sleep with me because you thought that's what I wanted?"

"Well, yeah. Didn't you? Billie, you wanted it right? Did I do somethin' wrong?"

"No." I shook my head. "No, that's not what I meant. I instigated it. Of course I wanted it. I meant, didn't *you* want it? I thought you did. Seemed like you liked—"

"No, I did. I did want it, 'course I did. It's just—I dunno. Guess I'm not much of a snuggler. Sorry. I could, if you want." He shook his head a little, and I had the feeling he wasn't saying what he really wanted to.

"No." I laughed. *I mean, like, seriously, dude, the moment's gone.* "No. Never mind."

"Was it—was it bad? I've never been with someone like you. I mean, you're beautiful. You probably got a lotta expectations. Sorry," he mumbled, walking into the bathroom. "Sorry if I… you know, if I bombed."

I heard water splashing in the sink, and then he reemerged, and he'd shucked his shorts for a pair of jeans. He grabbed his shirt from the floor and pulled it over his head.

Really? He doubted his sexual prowess? Had he seen his dick? It was fucking magnificent. And the look on his face when he came, all pained and sexy and wanton. I wished I had a picture of it so I could masturbate to it for the rest of time. And the way he filled me up? I'd never felt anything like it. The second he came, I was already masterminding a way to get him back inside me.

"No, Jay. It was good. Um, thanks, I guess. I'm gonna take a shower and get to work. You wanna run, get some coffee? I could use the caffeine."

Damn it. See? This. This right here. This was what I had been afraid of. He was acting weird. Skittish. Like he instantly regretted what we'd done. The insecurity roared in my head, and for the first time in years, I felt the urge to cry.

"Yeah, sure. The usual?"

"Yeah, thanks."

"No problem. Be right back," he said, grabbing the Jeep's key from the desk and yanking the motel room door open, spilling blasted early morning sunshine everywhere. How considerate.

What in the actual fuck?

CHAPTER ELEVEN

JAY

WE DROVE. For hours. We knew we couldn't sit on our butts all day, lettin' Theo get so far away. We took the PCH. The 101 seemed like the more practical route—more places to stop for food or gas—but Billie thought Theo would've chosen the opposite to throw off whoever was after him. Or whoever he was chasing. We still weren't sure which.

It hadn't mattered anyway, 'cause both routes ended up in the same place. We drove all the way to San Francisco without speakin' more than a short sentence or two. A grunt. An "mm hm." She was in her head and I was in mine. The only full sentences she'd uttered since we left the Sunset Coast Motel in Obispo had been, "Can't you drive any fucking faster? I swear to God, my Jewish bubbeh could make better time than you, and she's dead," and, "Stop. I have to pee."

Billie had made it clear she regretted what we'd done; things were tense and awkward between us. I didn't regret it. It had been the best sex of my life. Not just 'cause of the physical stuff, but I loved the way she'd felt—her skin against mine, her hair in my fingers, her breath mixed with mine. Her hands in my hair, on my body, my chest, my dick. The sounds she made, the way she moved. I was hard just rememberin', sittin' in the damn rental car on the highway in the middle of nowhere California. Beautiful as it was, all coastal magnificence and tall bridges hoverin' over cliffs that made my stomach drop into my boots, I couldn't be bothered with it.

'Cause more than the physical stuff, I loved bein' so close to her and seein' her so open and alive. All her masks had fallen away. There'd been no bad attitude, ornery moods, no hidin' behind clothes and makeup. She'd been just... Billie. And she'd never been more beautiful. I coulda stayed in that bed for days, just lookin' at her, holdin' her. I didn't think it was what she really wanted though.

She was an extraordinary woman, strong, confident, intelligent.

I knew I wasn't good enough for her.

Good enough—maybe that was wrong. There was nothin' bad about me. I had a good family. We had a good business. We were good people. We didn't go to church, but we helped the people in our community. We were honest.

But there was nothin' *special* about me. Not like Billie. Not like my brothers. I'd always been just a plain kinda person, and I'd never really fit in with my family. I loved 'em. I'd die for 'em, no matter the reason, but I'd always been different. Maybe it had to do with me bein' the baby, not havin' any time with our mama, or my dad, really.

Whatever. This whole line of thinkin' was so stupid. And none of it mattered anyway. I wasn't what Billie wanted. She'd probably just got caught up in the whole sharin' a motel room thing. Maybe she just woke up horny and I was there.

I ran so I wouldn't have to be there to see the look on her face when she realized she'd made a mistake.

I sighed. As stupid as it sounded, even just in my head, I'd wanted her from the first time I met her, and the longer we stayed stuck together, the worse it got, even as crabby and annoyin' as she'd been, and the more difficult it became to deny.

But it wasn't why we were in this situation, so I tried to focus on the task at hand.

It seemed Theo had run outta cash. He used his credit card increasingly, the last time in San Francisco, but by the time we pulled into The City by the Bay, he'd already come and gone and had used his card in Sacramento. We always found ourselves a city behind.

I wanted to stop for lunch. Billie needed to stretch her legs, get the blood flowin' again, but she nearly ripped my head off when I suggested it, so I kept drivin'. We stopped to fill up, and she complained about the subpar gas station coffee for miles, but at least she'd started talkin' again.

After another pee break, she set herself up in the back seat, MacGyverin' her smaller laptop to the back of my seat and her tablet to the back of hers. She seemed to have no end of good ideas. I was pretty impressed.

She fastened her ugly headphones to her ears, and that was the last I heard from her for a while, except for the continuous clickity-clack of her fingers on her keyboard, so I just drove, continuin' east on I-80 into the mountains toward Lake Tahoe. We didn't have exact coordinates for Theo, but our only option was to continue followin' his credit card purchases.

The clackin' died down after a while, and I figured she'd fallen asleep.

"I found the motherfucker!"

"Shit!" I jumped straight up outta my seat and swerved outta my lane a little. "Jeez, Billie. You scared the ever-lovin' crap outta me. I thought you were sleepin'."

"I know who's blackmailing Theo. It's that guy's son. The guy that screwed over Ace's parents. Remember I said he had a son?"

I took a big breath and released it slow, tryin' to calm my poundin' heart. "Uh, yeah, I think so."

"The guy's a douchebag," she said, climbin' over the center console and ploppin' down into the passenger seat. She elbowed me in the head on her way over.

"Ow. Jeez."

"Oh, did I hurt you? Poor baby," she cooed and pinched my arm, hard.

"You're a freakin' brat."

"Aww. It's like you know me. Anyway, Theo has paid this guy a total of three-hundred-thousand dollars from various bank accounts over the years. The guy used to have offshore accounts. He hid money everywhere!"

"That's a lotta money. Okay, so how do you know he's the one messin' with Theo?"

"Because I'm brilliant."

"Obviously," I said, archin' an eyebrow, "but in what way specifically?"

"I remembered seeing the email signature. Like, how the email was routed. I don't know why Theo needs this kind of secrecy, but I knew I'd seen this IP language before. And now I know where I've seen it.

"Hackers like to act like they hide in underground warehouses or super cool industrial complexes in Reykjavik and that they don't care about recognition, but it's all bullshit. Plus, we always want to be the best. So, we study each other's hacks. Try to outdo the guy before us. That's where

I've seen this before. Theo has his own hacker. Theo has hired Giovanni."

"Giovanni? Just Giovanni?"

"Yeah, dude thinks he's all that. He kind of is. He's good. And he's expensive." She stretched and yawned. "Whew. I think I need an ice cream cone."

"Huh? You wanna stop? For ice cream?"

"It was a joke, Jay. 'Cause I did a good job?" She shook her head and rolled her eyes. "But seriously, I do need to pee again."

"Okay. But where are they? And *why* is the guy black-mailin' Theo? And how many damn times a day you need to pee?"

"It's in direct correlation to how many cups of coffee you let me drink. You're supposed to stop me."

I snorted. "Like I could stop you from doin' anything."

"I need to call Carey."

"We'll stop for a minute. We need gas anyway. I wanna top off before we head up the mountain."

As I pulled into a gigantic truck stop somewhere in the vicinity of Auburn, California, Billie called Carey, and when we stopped, she jumped outta the Jeep, speedtalkin' into her phone.

"Carey, I figured it out! It's the son of that guy, the one who screwed over Aislinn's parents. His name is Blake Ormand and…"

She raced inside to use the restroom, so I followed her into the cavernous convenience shop to buy water, beef jerky, and a pint of mint chocolate chip ice cream. As I stepped up to the counter to pay, the sixty-somethin' lady behind the register with short salt-and-pepper hair and a whole lotta cleavage eyed me up and down and back again, smackin' a huge piece of gum in her mouth.

"Hey, baby. Find everything ya need?"

"Yes, ma'am, thank you."

"Ma'am." She huffed. "If I were even ten years younger, I'd have you out in my truck in no time, showin' you the time of your life."

I turned beet red and stared at my boots. Jeez.

"Oh, c'mon now. I'm only playin'. Besides, looks like you got your hands full with that one." She nodded out the big window beside her, toward where Billie paced back out by the rental car, practically vibratin' and performing feats of gymnastics as she explained to Carey what she'd found.

I chuckled. "Yes, ma'am, I do."

"You headed up to Tahoe?"

"Drivin' through."

"Road trip?"

I handed her a twenty, and she made my change. "Of sorts, I guess."

"Here ya go." She held a plastic bag out for me, but just before she passed it to me, she pulled it back. "Here, you'll need this too. Lake Tahoe can be romantic. Oh, and this… and these," she said, tossin' a few extra items in the bag.

"What—"

"You can thank me later." She winked.

I laid my change on the counter for whatever it was she'd thrown in the bag. "Thanks."

"Drive safe now."

"Yes, ma'am," I said, walkin' to the door.

"Ach, ma'am. My name is Sally."

I turned and nodded. "Thank ya, Sally."

"There you go, sweet talkin' me. Git on outta here."

Smilin', I pushed the door open with my hip, and the bell dinged. When I got outside, I looked in the bag. Sally had thrown in a pack of mint gum, one of those tree-shaped air fresheners—hibiscus scented—and a thin, discreet box of three "king-sized" condoms. I blushed and shoved the condoms into my back pocket.

Billie was still yammerin' on the phone to Carey, so I listened as I filled up. I washed the windows and checked the oil, just to give my hands somethin' to do, but I was pretty sure the brand-new Jeep Cherokee had plenty of clean oil. I finished up and lowered the hood, crossed my arms, and leaned against it.

"So, this guy, Blake, he's been creeping around Theo for a few years. Longer, I think. There's all kinds of secrecy surrounding Theo and Ace's dad. When he died in that car accident, of course he left everything to Theo and Aislinn. Except he didn't! He left money to Blake. But why?"

Billie listened to Carey for a minute, then rolled her eyes. "I'm getting there, Carey. Take a freakin' pill, man. Well, so Blake and Theo used to be friends growing up. Both families were buddy buddy. Joint vacations, cookouts in their matching Hamptons McMansions. You get the idea. But then Blake's dad ripped Theo's dad off. That was a whole messy thing. All kinds of legal mumbo jumbo that I'm still going through. Eventually, the two men went their separate ways, but I found payments years later from Theo's dad to Blake's.

"So, why? I don't know that yet. Then, when the Burroughs died, Theo's dad left a bunch of money to this Blake. But obviously, it wasn't enough for him because a few years later, he came sniffing around Theo. He has something on Theo or his family. He has to. Why else would Theo pay him? And why would it be a secret? Theo has paid someone to hide all this shit. I only found it because I recognized the IP routing from the email Aislinn received. I know who Theo hired. He's a hacker. But I know his style, so with a little more time, I'm sure I can find the rest."

She stopped to listen again and turned to face me. She stood ten feet away, starin' me down while she listened to Carey ask his questions. Her smokey eyes measured me, and I zoned out, imaginin' what it would feel like if she threw her phone to the ground and ran to me, jumpin' into my arms to kiss me.

Jesus, you're a sap.

"Jay?"

"Hmm?" Her voice dragged me back to reality, and I blushed, the heat crawlin' up my neck to my ears and cheeks. She glared at me suspiciously, narrowin' her eyes and bitin' her fingernail. "Ready then? I got your ice cream."

Clickin' her phone off, she said, "I told you, I was kidding about the ice cream."

"I know"—I held up the bag—"but it sounded good. I got mint chip. I stole some plastic spoons from next to the rollin' hot dogs and plastic melted cheese dispenser."

"How'd you know that's my favorite?"

"I didn't. It's my favorite too." I smiled. Stupid, I knew, but I liked that we had that tiny thing in common. It was probably the *only* thing we had in common. "So," I said when we'd both clicked our seatbelts back into place, "you still haven't said where this guy is."

"I don't know exactly where he is. When I said I found him, I meant I'd found *who* he is. Not where he is."

"I'm confused then. How do you know it's him?"

"Because back then, when the Burroughs died, the money Theo's dad left the guy was wired to his account. Easy as pie to trace and I just traced a couple of payments Theo made to the same account. Well, not the same exact account, but an account that used to be shared between father and son. But then it was all covered up. Now, the guy doesn't have any credit cards or even a bank account with more than fifty bucks in it, at least not that I can find. Yet." She paused and chewed on her thumbnail, like it was cotton candy flavored.

"But that makes me think he's after more. I can't find any communication between him and Theo recently though. But Carey just told me he spoke to a detective in Boston and get this—remember Aislinn telling Carey about her maid and driver back in Boston?"

"Yeah. She said she hadn't heard from 'em, right?"

"Yeah, well, she wouldn't have since they're both dead."

"What?"

"Carey says when Theo and Ace were out of town, someone broke into their house. The maid and this driver, Tim, were both killed. The detective in Boston thinks it was made to look like an accident. I'm pretty sure it wasn't, but they don't have any leads." She thought for a minute. "It's killing me that I haven't found any communication between Theo and Blake, but I know it's there. Unless he scribbled it on a scrap of paper and stuck it in Theo's locker during recess, I'll find it.

"But I think that's why Theo brought Ace to Wyoming. To get her away from the danger. Ace has no idea." Leanin' back against the seat, she sighed and closed her eyes. "I told Carey not to tell her about Louise and Tim. I'll tell her."

"Okay, so what's our plan?"

"Well, I need to think about what to say to her. It would be better coming from Theo, but obviously, he's not in a sharing mood. But right now, our plan is to keep following Theo's credit card and, if you can find it within yourself to drive faster than twelve miles an hour, catch up with him. Hopefully," she said, tightenin' her seatbelt strap.

"Then what?"

"No clue. Gimme that ice cream."

CHAPTER TWELVE

BILLIE

"YOU KNOW WHAT I THINK?" I mumbled, stuffing nearly the whole pint of generic but calorifically delicious mint chocolate chip ice cream into my mouth in one bite.

Jay laughed. "What's that?"

"I think—" I swallowed, giving myself mouth freeze and brain freeze. "Ow, ow, ow!"

"What's wrong?" He was all worried and cute as he flicked the turn signal on and began to pull off to the side of the road.

"It's fine. I'm fine. Brain freeze." Sucking my tongue to the roof of my mouth, I shook my head until my brain unfroze. A weird trick I remembered learning from my dad when he'd buy me slushies at the Zip Mart. Probably one of the only useful things I ever learned from him. I would've remembered those slushies with my dad with fondness if he hadn't used them to hide his drinking. Slushies mixed with vodka. Yuck.

"I think Theo is after Blake. Not the other way around. I think he's tired of being blackmailed, and he intends to put a stop to it. I think he's worried about what this Blake guy might do to get more money. I think Blake killed the maid and driver, and I think that's why Theo wanted Ace to go to the ranch."

"Did you tell Carey?"

"Of course I told Carey, and he's on the same page. Don't worry, you know the guys won't let her out of their sight. I think this guy is running from Theo. That's what my gut is telling me. But assuming that's all true, why did Theo's dad give this guy money in the first place? Why did he pay Blake's dad after they'd dissolved their business? What did they have on Theodore Burroughs, Sr.?"

"I've gotta find it. And why is he working with Giovanni? It makes no sense. That's why we need to catch up to Theo. I think he's on some kind of vigilante quest and... I don't know. I'm just getting a bad feeling."

"Yeah, me too," he said, and then we heard a big flopping *chugga-chugga-chugga* sound. We bumped and bounced on the road, then swerved into a ditch.

"Jay! What did you do?"

"Nothin', Billie." I could actually hear him roll his eyes. "We got a flat front tire. You okay?"

"Yeah, I'm fine. You?"

"I'm okay."

"How do you know it's the front tire?"

"'Cause we veered to the right, and our back end didn't swerve any. It's on your side."

Yep. When I stepped out of the Jeep, we had a very flat, front passenger-side tire. Huh. It never would have occurred to me which tire was flat by the way we'd swerved. It was kind of impressive he knew that. A little bit sexy, too, if I was being honest.

"Great. Now we'll have to wait for the rental company. Theo's getting further and further away." It wasn't like me at all, but I felt panicked. I really wanted to catch up to him. Ace needed him.

"Billie, it's okay." Jay walked around the front of the car. "There's no damage to the car. I'll change the tire, and we'll get back on the road. We'll call the rental company and explain that we had an emergency. Jeeps usually have a full-size spare. The nicer models come new with 'em."

"You can change the tire?"

"'Course."

"Even in a ditch?"

"It ain't much of a ditch. But yeah, as long as we have a jack, should be fine." Walking to the back of the Jeep, he lifted the rear door. "Yep, right here. Got everything we need."

"Okay." I chewed on my thumbnail. My stuffy mother would have swatted my hand if she'd seen me. "But can you hurry?"

"*Can* I hurry? Don'tcha mean 'hurry the fuck up' or somethin' equally as sweet?"

"Just hurry, okay? Please?"

"Hey," he said, walking toward me. He pulled my wrist gently, disconnecting my thumb and teeth. "What's wrong? We're gonna be fine. This won't take long. I promise."

"Okay. It's just, I mean, I promised Ace I'd find her brother. And when I take a job, I always finish it," I blustered, trying to sound tough, but he saw right through me.

"Billie," he said my name so softly, and I could feel the sound inside my head trying to pound down my defenses. "You care about Aislinn. It's okay to say so. You don't have to act so tough. Not with me."

"I barely know her," I tried again, but then I looked in his unbelievably blue eyes, and words rushed out of my mouth like a waterfall. "I promised her, Jay. I promised. She's all alone, and I know what that feels like. She's scared and sad and confused. She'll be devastated if anything happens to her brother. And then what will she do? Who will take care of her? Her parents are dead. Her friends are dead. She has no other family now. She's utterly pampered. She's never had to fend for herself. She can't take care of herself. She won't even leave the goddamn bedroom!" *Oh shit.* I clapped my hand over my mouth to stop the torrential spew of anxiety while Jay looked at me. He didn't say a word.

Goddamn him. And thank God.

He clenched his fists six times. I saw because I looked at the dirt. I didn't want him to see the vulnerability on my face.

"Okay then, let's get movin'." He turned away and walked back to the rear of the Jeep to pull a bunch of stuff out, dropping it all on the ground at his feet.

I'd just exposed myself. I had never, and I mean never fucking ever, allowed *anyone* to see my weaknesses. Not since I was a little girl, begging my daddy to stop drinking. Begging my mother to stay home with us. Begging my sister to breathe. That was what this was all about.

My sister.

Ace reminded me of Jessie. I hadn't allowed myself to talk about her in, oh, at least a decade. Probably longer. And since she'd died, I hadn't told a soul about her. The only time I'd come close was when Carey and I had worked the missing girl case because it brought up so many awful memories of Jessie. But Carey had known not to push me and that I probably would have maimed him if he had.

I stood rooted to the ground while my heart pounded, and I tried to assess just how much I'd given away. Did Jay know now how scared and sad I felt? Did he understand how I tried so hard to cover it all up?

He peeked at me a few times but never stopped working.

Rolling the spare tire next to me, he let it fall on the ground, then positioned the jack behind the flat tire and began to crank until the Jeep was lifted up like a cat frozen on a hot tin roof, one paw raised.

Watching him work calmed me. I watched his shoulders move and flex beneath his shirt while his hands turned black with grit and dirt when he removed the flat tire and replaced it with the spare and then used the lug nut thingie to tighten the lug nuts again. He finished and stood, rubbing his hands together.

When he turned to face me, little smudges of dirt streaked his face from swiping at the sweat dripping down his forehead.

"Can you grab the T-shirt you bought me in LA, please? I'm covered in grime. I think it's in my backpack. Grab me a clean button down too?" he called behind me as I opened the door and pulled his bag from the back seat.

When I came back around to hand him his shirt and backpack, he stood before me like Jason Momoa (admitted hot geek), only shorter and with shorter hair. And no beard. Okay, so maybe that was an extreme example, but jeez. His skin looked bronzed in the sun, and sweat glistened all over his chest like a mirage in the fucking Sahara. If I could have licked him from Levi's to lips—sweat, dirt, and all—without looking unhinged, I would have.

He noticed me staring and smiled.

Ughhh. It was so unfair when he did that. Only one side of his mouth curled up, and an adorable divot appeared below his lip. It taunted me every blasted time.

"Here," I said, shoving the cheap "California! The Golden State" T-shirt at him. He used it to wipe his hands, transforming the ugly eggshell color of the fabric to a nice brown-black mocha color, then pulled it inside out and used the fresh side to wipe the sweat from his face and neck. "Gimme that." Holding out one hand, I pushed the backpack at him with the other. He dropped the shirt into my waiting hand, took the backpack from me, and dug through it, looking for a clean shirt to wear while I watched every little tweak his body made. I held in a moan and squeezed my thighs tight as he pulled a shirt on and buttoned it, then rolled the sleeves up his hair-dusted forearms.

I wanted to lean into him and wrap those arms around me and never come out.

"See? That took no time at all. Ready?"

"How are you gonna get us out of the ditch?"

"Billie, it's not a ditch. It's a little dip in the dirt. We'll drive right out. It's a Jeep." He looked at me with a little pity in his eyes, like it was the most obvious conclusion anyone could come to and he felt bad for me that I hadn't.

The Tahoe National Forest was arresting, majestic, and alluring, and I'd never been much of a nature girl, usually preferring to view it on TV or on my computer screen, if I ever felt the urge, which I rarely did because it normally bored me.

We approached the mountains at sunset on the long, wide freeway, and I sat silently in awe of our surroundings while Jay drove. The peaks glowed, reflecting the western sky behind us, and the big pine and fir evergreens danced in the ethereal California light all around us. It turned from dusky, sparkling gold to a dreamy, orangey-pink color, then to lavender as the sun set behind us and night descended.

"I'm gonna stop here. We gotta eat."

"No, Jay, keep going. We have enough gas to get to Reno. Let's just drive through."

I'd been quiet since the flat tire. I felt so exposed after the word vomit explosion earlier, and I sat there in the dark of the rental car, terrified of Jay asking personal questions.

"Billie, we've had nothin' but fast food, beef jerky, and crappy ice cream all day. We can take it to go, but we need real food."

"Fine. Just—"

"I know. We'll be quick."

We stopped at a rustic family-owned diner kind of place, and they gave us meatloaf and mashed potatoes to go. Homemade sourdough rolls too. It was hearty, filling, and warm. Jay couldn't drive and eat, so I fed him with a plastic fork like he was the King of Sultan and I was his lowly hanger-on, harem junkie. He smirked and tried to hide it, and I rolled my eyes. Many times. But anything to keep us moving toward Theo. The panic inside my chest grew with each mile.

The temperature had dropped into the low fifties, and I didn't have a jacket. We had the heat on in the car, but still, I felt a chill. I rubbed my hands together as Jay pulled off the road again.

"Jay! This is the opposite of hurrying."

"I know, I know. One minute."

He ran across the mountain road to a small run-down souvenir shop, and I used the time alone to call Evvie to check on Ace.

Evvie whined into the phone. "Of course I'll help her, Billie. I've been trying, but sometimes, she doesn't make it very easy."

"Yeah, I know," I said. "But do it anyway. You just have to force her outside."

"I'll try. I promise."

"Good. I have some bad news for her, and when I tell her, it'll be better if she's exhausted so she'll be able to sleep."

"What? What happened?"

"I can't tell you yet. I need to tell Ace first. But promise you'll be there for her after I tell her?"

"Of course I will." Evvie took a deep breath. "Well, how's California? That's one state I've never been to."

"It's good. Pretty, I guess. We had a flat tire earlier, and the weather is so much colder in the mountains, but we're getting closer to Theo. He just used his credit card in Reno. We're almost there. Jay just ran into the store for something. I don't know how we're gonna find Theo once we get there since I can't track his phone, but I'll figure it out. If we get close enough, when he uses his card again, I can search city traffic cams."

"And how are you and Jay getting along?"

"Fine," I clipped.

"Fine?"

"Yes, Evvie. Fine."

"That's all you have to say? Fine?"

"Yes, and before you ask again, have I ever told you I can drain your bank account with a couple easy keystrokes? Don't forget, I can do that from anywhere, for any reason."

"Okay, Billie. Whatever you say." She laughed. "But if you're cold, I can think of one surefire way to warm up."

"Funny." I rolled my eyes and hung up on her.

Jay came back out a minute later with an eco-friendly tote bag in his hands. When he climbed back into the car, he pulled two huge, black sweatshirts from the bag that said, "Lake Tahoe, California," with a white outline of a bear loping across the chest with mountains and a rainbow-striped round sunset in the background.

"Here. Put this on. Your teeth are chatterin'."

"Thanks. Now hurry the fuck up," I said, turning my head to smile out the window. It was the sweetest, most romantic thing any man had ever done for me. For him to think of my comfort, even as we raced toward our destination in this weird situation we'd found ourselves in—well, it... I felt the urge to cry again.

Thankfully, my phone pinged with an alert because Theo had used his credit card again.

Score! I would be distracted from all my freaking feels, and we'd get closer to finding Theo Burroughs.

CHAPTER THIRTEEN

JAY

WE ROLLED INTO RENO, Nevada, The Biggest Little City in the World, late. The buildin's downtown were lit up like flashin' neon candy, and even though I'd driven through Reno before, it was a little disorientin' comin' from the browns and greens of the trees and dark mountain roads through Lake Tahoe.

Billie said Theo had used his credit card again on the east side of town, so we headed in the same direction, stoppin' and parkin' a block away from the gas station she'd tracked him to. He wasn't there, of course, so she propped her heavy, boxy laptop onto the hood of the rental and dove in, and I stretched and walked circles around her while she worked, tryin' to get blood flowin' through my legs again. She wore the sweatshirt I'd bought her. I'd seen the smile she'd tried to hide.

When she came up for air some fifteen minutes later, she slammed her laptop closed and kicked a tire. "Owwwa! Damn it! He's already gone. Why can't this guy stay in one place for five freaking minutes? Doesn't he need to sleep?"

"Where'd he go?"

"I have no clue. Look, here's his credit card char—wait a minute." She typed furiously, clickin' back and forth between a few different programs and websites on her laptop. "Ooo, fucking Giovanni. He's covering Theo's tracks! The credit card charge just disappeared."

"Billie." I waited for her to look at me. She didn't, just kept clickin' and typin'. "Billie, there's a motel down the road. Let's get another room. You need sleep. I need sleep."

"No."

"Billie, c'mon. We can't just drive all night."

"Look! It happened again. Theo used the credit card at an outdoor store. You know the kind with the big, dead, stuffed animals all over the place? I saw the charge, but now it's gone. Like it never existed." She stopped and looked at me. "What do you wanna bet he bought a gun? Or ammo? Jay, Theo is going after this guy. Like, to kill him. We have to find him."

"You really think so? We need to call Carey."

"Yes, I really think so, and no, we're not calling Carey. He'll tell us to stop looking. I can't do that."

I sighed. "Okay. Which way did he go?

"East. I think I just watched him drive out of town on I-80. He's driving a light-colored car. A sedan, four doors. Maybe silver or gray. It could be dirty white. I couldn't tell for sure 'cause the gas station's cameras are barely functional, and the traffic cams suck, but I caught a glimpse of the car turning onto the on-ramp to the freeway. I saw his face clear enough at the gas station though. It was definitely him. I was right. He buzzed all his hair off. Giovanni's good, but he's got sausages for fingers. I'm faster. Now that I know his game, he won't get by me again."

"Okay, well then, we head east."

"Here, look at the map." She pulled her phone from her

back pocket, and I stepped next to her, feelin' the hum of her skin against mine even though we didn't touch. "If he keeps heading east, he'll end up right where he started." She pinched her fingers, zoomin' out, and little ol' Wisper, Wyoming popped up onto the screen. "Why? Why would he go back?"

"Dunno. Maybe he wants to get back to Aislinn."

"Yeah. Or maybe Blake wants to get to Aislinn. But why? And Jay, we've been on his tail all day. There's no way he had time to deal with Blake. Wouldn't that take time? If he managed to catch the guy or, I don't know, shove him off a cliff, that would take at least a few minutes. And if he did find the guy, wouldn't he then stop? He's been on the road for days. He has to be running on empty."

"I have no idea. It doesn't make sense, but let's just go. I think I got a few more hours in me." I jumped up and down a couple times, tryin' to convince my body.

"I'll drive and you can take a nap."

I laughed. No way was I lettin' her drive again. "How 'bout I drive and you talk to me to keep me awake? We can play one of those I Spy games."

"In the dark? In the middle of nowhere Nevada? It'll be a really quick game. 'I spy something brown.' 'What's that, Billie?' 'The desert, Jay.'" She rolled her eyes.

"Just get in the car, woman. We're wastin' time." The exhaustion made me feel wonky, and I felt like I had a good second wind brewin'. "By the way, you keep rollin' your eyes like that, they're gonna get stuck upside down."

"Yeah, okay. That totally made sense." She rolled 'em again. "Fine. You can drive for now, but I'll take over in a while when you inevitably zonk out. But first, I'm hungry again. Take me to a drive-through. And Jay?"

"Yeah?"

"If you ever call me 'woman' again, I'll knock your teeth out." She didn't want me to see it, but she smiled.

Chucklin', I climbed back into the Jeep, and we headed out into the dark, dusty, barren desert after stoppin' again to hit up another In-and-Out, of course, for burgers, string fries, and gargantuan-sized caffeinated sodas.

"I need to call Ace," Billie said as we left Reno city limits.

"Okay."

"I-I don't know how to tell her that the person she was closest to in the world—probably the only parental figure she's had in years—is dead." She squeezed her eyes shut. "But I feel like I have to tell her, Jay. She deserves to know. She was right. Theo does treat her like a child. He should've told her when it happened. This guy is so messed up."

"I know it'll be hard, but you can do it. You're her friend."

"I barely know her."

"Maybe so, but you care for her. And she's comfortable around you. I noticed it the first night at the ranch."

She looked at me, searchin' my eyes, then took a deep breath, nodded, and clicked a number on her phone.

"Evvie, it's Billie. Can you put Ace on the phone, please?"

I heard Evvie at the end of the line, but not her normal happy chirpy voice. She must've recognized the doom in Billie's.

"Hi, Ace. Everything going okay back there? Did you get outside? Do something?" She smiled, listenin' to Aislinn talk about her day, and at that moment, she reminded me of Finn. He was my brother, but he was also my best friend. No matter how bad I felt about myself, how insecure I felt, how awkward the conversation, he was always there for me.

"That's cool. Yeah, I've never actually ridden a horse. I didn't mean for you to go all out equine princess." She laughed, but the look on her face was sad.

"Oh. No, we're not with Theo. But I need to talk to you. I-I need to tell you something." She took a deep breath again and interrupted Aislinn's questions. "No, no. Theo's fine. Last we saw him, he was driving near Reno. No, he didn't meet us. He took off again. But Ace, that's why I'm calling. I found something. Carey and I did. I don't know why, but Theo's been hiding something from you. I'm sure he has a good reason, but I thought you deserved to know what's going on.

"Ace, please, just listen. Um, your... your friend? Louise? And Theo's driver, Tim? Ace, I'm so sorry—they're dead." Billie clutched her chest, and tears dripped from her eyes. She sobbed silently, listenin' to Aislinn cry and freak out on the other end of the phone call. I heard it loud and clear, too, and I grabbed Billie's hand.

———

"What's your favorite color?"

"I don't know." She shrugged. "Don't really have one. Gray, I guess."

I tried to pull Billie out of the sadness she'd fallen into after the phone call. I'd asked all sorts of questions, but she just wasn't in the mood.

"Okay, last question. I looked at your website. I saw the sticker on your laptop case. What does bbtatb.com stand for?"

Finally, she smiled, a slow, smug smirk. "Billie's-better-than-all-those-bitches-dot-com."

I laughed, and finally, she did too.

"Is there a better name for my website? If you can think of one, I'll buy the domain and change it." She turned toward me. "Admit it, it's perfect."

"Yep, I admit it."

"Okay, it's my turn, Mr. Twenty Questions. What's your middle name?"

"William."

"Jonathan William Cade? Jonathan *Billy* Cade?" She giggled like a little girl.

"Yep. What's yours? Wait, didn't you see my full name when you looked me up online?" I tried, but I couldn't stop my lips from curvin' into a smile thinkin' about it.

"I only looked for your pic," she admitted, grinnin', then she sighed. "Okay, do you promise never to tell your brothers what I am about to divulge? Especially Kevin?"

"Yes. Scout's honor."

"Were you a boy scout?"

"Uh, definitely not." I shook my head. "My dad wasn't the boy scout leader type. And quit stallin'."

"Fine. My middle name is… Anne."

"What's so bad about that? Billie Anne Acker. I like it."

"Well, first of all, Billie Anne? It sounds so Tennessee trailer park. But that's not the embarrassing part. Trust me, I revel in the white trash street cred it gives me."

"Okay then, what is?" I laughed, takin' a big sip of soda, lovin' the cold sting of the carbonation slidin' down my throat. The caffeine was an added bonus. The change in Billie's mood was too.

"My first name. Billie is a nickname."

"Ha! I knew it… but what's Billie short for?"

She sighed, which turned into an embarrassed groan. "I am *so* gonna regret this." Coverin' her face with her hands and peekin' at me between her fingers, she said, "My name is… Wilhelmina."

I tried not to sputter my response. It was the last name I'd expected to hear. "Um. That's… unusual. But I like it. How come nobody calls you Willow?"

"I don't know. My mother never allowed nicknames. My sis—" She caught herself mid-sentence, and the followin' silence hung in the air like an anvil.

"You have a sister?"

Clenchin' her fists tight, she squeezed her eyes shut and faced the window, hopin' I wouldn't see.

"It's okay, Billie. You don't have to tell me."

She didn't say anything more and I kept quiet. I could feel the pain radiatin' off her body, and I wished I could rewind the last minute to erase the whole conversation. I wanted to stop the car and pull her into my arms.

Finally, she spoke. When the headlights from an oncomin' car illuminated her beautiful face, she whispered, "I *had* a sister. She was older than me. Her name was Jessie. Jesamin. She called me Billie. She took her own life when I was thirteen."

I knew she would argue or, well, maybe she'd try to pummel me, but I couldn't keep drivin' like she hadn't said it. I pulled the Jeep off to the side of the highway and clicked off the headlights. The road was empty and lonely.

I stepped out and walked around to open her door.

"Jay. Don't." She looked at me, and I saw a war brewin' in her eyes. "What are you doing?"

"I'm sorry, Billie," I whispered, reachin' into the Jeep and wrappin' her up in my arms, holdin' on tight. She resisted for a few seconds but then melted against me, lettin' me hold her up. She didn't make a sound and held her breath, but I felt the tears soak through my shirt, and her whole body trembled even though she tried hard as hell to make it stop.

I had no idea how long we stayed like that, but it felt like time stopped and sped up to forever all at once. I ached for her. I couldn't imagine losin' one of my brothers, and I wanted desperately to take her pain away. Eventually though, she stiffened and pulled away from me.

"This is stupid," she said, turnin' her body, facin' forward in her seat again.

But I felt brave. I was humbled and honored that she'd shared such a private and painful thing with me. I was pretty sure she didn't share things about herself very often, and it gave me the confidence I needed to say what I'd wanted to say for days.

"Billie, don't do that. Don't hide from me. Please? We don't have to talk about Jessie if you don't want to, but don't cover yourself up again. I've been desperate to know you since that first day last year when you came to the ranch to help Evvie. Remember?" She turned her head a little but kept her eyes away from mine. "Didn't you notice? God, all I could do was stare at you. Every time you came out to the house, I—"

"Oh please. Don't be such a bitch. This is so stupid. You already got laid. You don't have to put on the whole doe-eyed cowboy act. If you wanna fuck again, just say so."

Ahh. That hurt. I'd known there was a pretty good chance she'd push me away, but damn. It felt like she'd sliced a knife right through my heart. It stuttered and squeezed and *ached* inside my chest, and I dropped my hands. I still held 'em up in front of me, still reachin' for her.

At least now I had some inklin' as to where her pain and the rude mask she always wore might have come from.

I didn't say anything more, but I didn't look away till,

finally, she crossed her arms over her chest and tilted her chin away from me.

End of conversation. Or end of everything between us, if there ever had been anything to begin with. I thought there had been, or I'd hoped, but now… Guess I was wrong.

I shut her door quietly and walked behind the car. I took a minute to collect myself but then gulped down a deep breath and released it slow, climbed back in beside her, and drove.

After ten painful and silent minutes, she started back in on me. "And why did you say that this morning?"

"What? What'd I say?" I kept my voice low and even. She'd become a captive tiger, and I was not about to open the cage door.

"You said, 'I've never been with *someone like you*.' What the fuck did you mean? What, am I not blonde enough? I certainly don't look like your usual church-goin', pie-bakin', cowgirl Barbie," she spat in a bad imitation of what I assumed was my accent. "My nose a little too Jewish? Ass too big? Or maybe I'm just a little too smart. Make too much money? You roughnecks like to be the boss in the bank account *and* the bed, right?"

"What? Billie." I sighed and shook my head.

Now she was just lookin' to start an argument. Anything to distract me from the intimacy we'd shared. It made the fatigue I'd been tryin' to hold off come at me full force, and my body felt like it weighed four-hundred pounds. My shoulders slumped, and I watched her outta the corner of my eye, hopin' she'd back down, but she didn't. She held her body rigid as a lamp post, bitin' her lip and huffin' her breath.

"What I said was, 'I've never been with someone like you. You're beautiful.'"

"No, you didn't."

"Yeah, I did. Don't you put hurtful words in my mouth to

suit your attempt to push me away. You remember it wrong. You're the most beautiful woman I've ever seen."

She scoffed. "Bullshit."

"So now you're callin' me a liar? Nice. How 'bout we go back to not talkin'. I get that this is hard for you and you're hurtin', but your words are hurtin' me, too, Billie."

Her breathin' hitched and I knew she was cryin', but she faced the window, thinkin' I couldn't tell. I could. I could almost smell her tears. She tried so hard to act tough, but her armor was crumblin' down around her like overripe apples fallin' from an apple tree, with somebody standin' underneath, shakin' the trunk and laughin' as they all came thuddin' down to the ground, the smell sweet and rotten.

I pulled over again and sat in silence with my hands folded in my lap while she tried to control the storm threatenin' to break free from inside her.

"Fuck you, Jay! Why are you doing this to me? I thought you were a nice guy. But what? You think you're gonna pull a power trip on me? For what? Just to make yourself feel bigger? Fuck you." She threw her door open and escaped the Jeep, stompin' out into the black of the desert, and I followed but didn't say a word.

When she'd gone about a hundred feet into the rocks and brush, she rounded on me. "Stop following me! I'm not some scared little girl you can put over your shoulder. I'm not Evvie. I don't need your help, *baby* Jay." I stopped walkin' and sat on a big boulder. "I knew fucking you was a mistake. You're just like your brothers. You think this whole macho thing is a pussy magnet."

Now she was purposely bein' mean, and I wanted to stop her from sayin' somethin' more she'd regret. "Billie, let's just go, okay? Theo's gettin' further away. We're losin' our lead."

I hoped remindin' her of her quest to find her friend's brother might redirect her energy.

"Fuck Theo. And fuck Aislinn." She winced when she said it but kept goin'. "I don't need this shit. I could've taken three paying jobs just in the last day alone, but I was trying to be nice. In fact, I have a job right now, and I've been neglecting it for you. Look where it got me. I won't make that mistake again." She stomped toward me and tried to yank the key fob outta my hand, but I closed my fist around it tight. "Give it to me. It's my fucking rental car. I paid for it."

"No. You ain't driving when you're this upset."

"Oh, I *ain't*?"

"No."

She laughed. It sounded cruel and petulant, and then she pulled the sweatshirt I'd bought for her off. And her tank top. She unzipped her jeans but I stopped her. I placed my hand over hers. "Billie, stop."

She yanked her hands away from mine. "No, this is what you want, right? You wanna fuck me? And then we can go. But you're getting off the Billie express in the next town. You can find your own way back. I'm going home."

I got angry then. How dare she accuse me of wantin' to take advantage of her? I'd done nothin' but be overly respectful of her since we landed in LA, all the while she mocked and joked and treated me like shit. I picked her clothes up from the desert floor and marched back to the rental car with her followin' behind.

"Uh oh. Did I hurt poor baby Jay's feelings?"

"Yeah!" I shouted, throwin' her clothes in the open door, then turned to face her. "Yeah, Billie, you did. This, whatever this is, this mask you wear all the time—fuck you. You've pretty much done nothin' but hurt my feelin's since LA. I am *not* my brothers. If you'd paid any attention at all, you woulda noticed that. And I know you're not Evvie.

"'Scuse me for fallin' for you. How stupid am I? You practically glow with a big neon sign sayin', 'Stay away.' Guess I don't know how to read, you know, what with bein' a big, ignorant, macho cowboy. 'Don'tcha worry, little lady. I surely won't make that mistake agin'. Don't pay me no nevermind. I beg yer pardon.'" I pointed to her door. "Get in the fuckin' car."

Her eyes went wide as golf balls. "Jay, I—"

"Don't bother, Billie. This is fine. At least it's honest. At least now I know how you really feel, and I can stop deludin' myself that we could ever have somethin'," I shook my head and laughed. "I have no idea what I was thinkin'. Put your goddamn clothes on, and let's get the fuck outta here. Drop me in the next town, and I'll call the guys. One of 'em will come get me, and we'll keep lookin' for Theo."

"Jay." She stepped toward me with her arms still crossed over her bra. "I-I'm…" Takin' the last two steps, she stood an inch away.

"Stop. You're right. This is stupid."

She reached up, touchin' her fingers to my face, but I turned my head and looked out at nothin', holdin' my breath.

"I'm sorry."

I turned my head further. I wasn't gonna fall for her shit. She'd let me in for a minute and then push me away again, and I didn't think I could handle watchin' her pull that mask back into place one more time.

But then she nuzzled her nose into my neck and inhaled me into her body. I couldn't help it. *Dammit.* I was so turned on. Sayin' what I'd wanted to say for three days, my hands shook to touch her, but I shoved 'em in my pockets to stop myself.

With the exception of yellin' at Kev or Finn, I didn't think I'd ever talked to anyone the way I'd just barked at Billie. It felt good to get it out, and I was not about to let her take that away by seducin' me. Now she knew the power she held over me.

"Jay," she whispered, kissin' up my neck and jaw, tryin' to reach my lips.

"Billie, cut it out." I had that feelin' again—the feelin' that I might not know what I'd do. I felt wild.

"I'm sorry. I'm falling for you, too, and it scares the crap out of me. I've never told anyone about my sister." She kissed my chin so softly and reached up on her toes to lean her forehead against my cheek. "I don't know how to do this. I panicked, okay?"

"Billie, please," I said through gritted teeth, clenchin' and unclenchin' my fists to stop myself from grabbin' her. "You're breakin' my fuckin' heart here."

"Please forgive me, Jonathan. Please?" she begged, pullin' back to look at me.

I turned to her, finally, and we stood there silent, lookin' at each other. She wound her arms through mine and pushed her hands under my sweatshirt to find my skin, clutchin' at it.

"Please? I'm sorry."

The pinch from her fingers on my back caused somethin' in me to snap.

I pushed her away and ripped my sweatshirt over my head, unbuttoned my jeans, and pulled her back to me, my hands on her ribs, then lifted her up and turned to set her on the seat in the open door of the Jeep. She spread her legs to let me closer, and we just breathed.

Knockin' her flip flops off her feet, I pulled her jeans down real slow, never breakin' eye contact, and she shimmied her underwear down her legs and pushed my jeans down my hips.

I couldn't catch my breath. Every rasp I dragged into my lungs felt empty and too thin, and my chest pumped with the effort of tryin' to find any oxygen it could. I wanted her bad, and this time, I wasn't gonna let either one of us pull away again.

She reached for me, and I wrapped my arms around her back to pull her close, and she grasped my hips with her thighs, lockin' her feet together behind me.

"Kiss me," I demanded, but she didn't argue. She touched her lips to mine, and her soft moan filled the air all around us. The urge I felt to fuck into her was overwhelmin', but at the last second, I remembered the condoms in my pocket.

I didn't say anything, just pulled the box from my jeans and handed it to her. She opened it, unwrapped a packet, and rolled it on. My dick jumped, and my whole body bowed toward her when she touched it, and all too soon, the condom was in place. I pushed her hands away, lifted her up into my arms, kissed her hard, and lowered her down, penetratin' her body with mine.

CHAPTER FOURTEEN

BILLIE

HE RAMMED into me and I gasped. No one had ever been so open and raw with me before. It was a side to Jay I'd never seen. Barely imagined he had. And beside all that, he looked so cute and sweet, even as mad as he was. And so sexy with his dark curls, almost black in the deep, desert night, falling over his forehead and surrounding his neck like an adorable little-boy halo.

"I dunno about your nose bein' Jewish," he breathed, "but whatever it is, I like it. And your ass? It's fuckin' perfection." Digging his fingers into my hips, he stumbled sideways, pushing me against the back door of the Jeep and pressing me against it, bending his knees and pulling his cock out of me, but then, very slowly pushing back in. "Your lips haunt my dreams, Billie."

He groaned, resting his forehead against mine while the rest of his body struggled to hold me up. If I unlocked my legs behind him, I would've fallen on my ass in the dirt.

"I've wanted you from the very first moment you popped outta Carey's truck and stormed up my front porch stairs." Kissing my mouth at the very edge of my lips, he hugged me even closer to him, forcing me to feel him, his whole body, which was hard and straining everywhere, and buried his nose in my neck.

"But I'm not gonna let you intimidate me anymore. Enough with the rude commentary. And as far as money goes?" He pulled out again and stabbed back in, and I moaned. "You can make as much money as you want. You can buy me a boat if it makes you happy. I don't give a fuck. I'll help you make *more* money if you want." He thrusted again and again, faster.

Holding me still against the Jeep with his hips, he held my head in his hands, tangling his fingers into my hair, caressing my cheeks with his thumbs, and placed his lips against mine. With his mouth open, he inhaled, literally stealing my breath away.

He kissed me then and tried, with whole success, to dismantle my hard-earned intelligence by killing my brain cells again with his wicked, pleasure-driven tongue. He groaned, and liquid arousal gushed out of me, which he totally felt because he moaned, pumping faster.

Sweat bleeding out of every pore, my whole body trembled with an almost exhaustive need to be even closer to him than I already was. If I could've crawled under his skin, I would have.

"Billie," he moaned, "this feels so good. It's never felt so good before. Feel that?"

"Yes," I breathed, hiding my face in his neck, embarrassed to admit it. I lived nowhere near virginhood, but I'd never felt such a connection. I thought, if I let him, he could—

"Look at me? Don't hide. Be in this with me. Don't run from it. Please?"

I pulled my head back, peeking at him. I wanted to be

vulnerable, but I felt so self-conscious, so raw and bare before him. He was asking me to connect with him, to submit to this thing between us, to open myself to him, every fault, every insecurity, every flaw and weakness visible for him to see and judge. I closed my eyes against the shame.

I'd never been beautiful. Not even close. I wasn't unattractive, but I was a dork. A geek. Always had been, and a chubby one at that. I'd been made fun of by the "pretty girls" my whole life. And the pain I felt inside, hid from the world for the last thirteen years—the fear I felt at exposing all of *that* to him made me want to cry.

He'd guessed correctly when he accused me of using clothes and makeup as armor. That was exactly what they were. And a weapon. If aimed correctly, they had the capability to blow everyone just far enough away. So no one could see the broken, naive little girl I'd been most of my life. The stupid girl who always let people in. Bad people. People who meant to take and steal from me. Push me down. Tear me up. Like my mother. I hadn't let anyone see inside me for years. And I was so afraid to open myself to Jay.

But, oh, how I wanted to.

"Billie, I know you're scared to let me in, but don't think about it like that. I'm open for you too. Look at me and see *me*. Look at me vulnerable and nervous. I'm just as scared as you. I haven't ever been with a woman this way before. I dunno what it means. What to expect. But I know I want you. I want you to see me. No one ever has before. Will you look?"

I thought he was shy, but now he seemed so certain of himself, so self-possessed. But maybe that had been a mask just like my armor? I opened my eyes and slowly raised my head.

"God, you're so beautiful. See? See my fear?" He

moaned, slowing his hips. "Feel how much more powerful this is between us when you look inside me?"

I nodded. I did feel it. There were threads, invisible and figurative, but real, connecting him to me. Our minds. Our souls. Joining us where our bodies weren't touching. They scared the shit out of me.

He thrusted harder inside me, using the truck to hold me up with his hands under my thighs. I was naked except for my bra in the middle of the freeway, but I didn't care.

Feeling him push and pull in and out of my body, that hard, slow, creamy, velvety slide, while he devoured me with his eyes—oh, it felt so good. *So good.* I couldn't think anymore. I just existed with him, letting my body do what it wanted, needed, to do.

I tilted my hips a little, allowing him to push into me further, and we both moaned and gasped for air. I could feel his ass hardening and flexing under my legs behind him, and I wanted those perfect muscles in my hands, so I reached for them, clawed them, pulling his whole body closer to mine. His arms strained and shook with the effort of holding me up, but he'd never let me fall.

"Billie," he begged, "kiss me." He waited for me to take his mouth, but I still felt so shy. "Please. I need it. I need you."

Kissing him slowly, just soft touches of my lips to his, I felt his breath on my skin, and it was intoxicating. His chemistry mixed with mine as I breathed into him too. I felt braver and braver by the second, looking at him, tilting my head and slowly sliding my tongue into his mouth.

As soon as my tongue touched his, an electrical current ran from my mouth to my core, zapping me through my veins. It punched through my breasts to the tips of my nipples, causing my muscles below to grip and pull him further inside me, and his eyebrows arched in surprise when he felt the physical proof of our connection. He moaned and growled, plowing into me, knocking me against the truck, the metal groaning and complaining behind us.

"Jay... I-I'm—oh God. I'm—Jonathan!"

"Yeah. You... oh fuck," he breathed into my mouth, panting and kissing me, never looking away. "Ohh, Billie, come. Please," he begged, "make me come."

His words were my undoing, him begging me, giving me the power to control his body. His pleasure. I didn't think I deserved that power, but I took it. I'd never wanted anything more. This beautiful man wanted me, wanted my thick thighs and jiggling boobs and belly. He wanted my bad attitude and my smartass remarks. And it wasn't just that he wanted me— I made him wild!

My body clamped down hard on his dick, stopping him from moving inside me, and he came, a wild growl huffing from his throat, and the sound sent me soaring. I drowned in his obnoxiously beautiful blue eyes, our mouths open but still connected, as he stole my breath again and fed me his.

He pulled out of me, and my thighs released the death grip they had on his hips as headlights from another vehicle flashed across the side of his face when it pulled to the side of the road, illuminating his wet, swollen, kissed lips. He licked them and looked into my eyes, lowering my legs to the ground.

"Shit."

"Oh my God, Jay." I whispered, shaking from the mind-blowing... thing that had just happened between us. Thankfully, the angle of the Jeep was probably hiding most of the good bits from the driver.

Retrieving my clothes from the front seat, he handed them to me as the car parked in front of ours, probably to check to make sure we weren't stranded. I dressed as quickly as I could, and Jay pulled a "Lake Tahoe" sweatshirt over his head and yanked his jeans up.

A man stepped out of the car while I threw my clothes on behind the open door, hoping no stray body parts hung out.

"Hey there, you guys okay? Engine trouble or something?" he asked. The taillights from his car reflected off the Jeep and lit his face. He looked to be in his sixties, and he looked tired.

"Ah, no, sir. We just stopped for a little air. Been drivin' a while," Jay said, grabbing my hand. I stared at him but didn't say anything. The simple action felt comfortable and completely uncomfortable at the same time. He glanced at me to make sure I looked presentable, then dragged me with him to shake the man's hand.

"Well now, that doesn't seem like a good idea. There's no lights out here. If I hadn't seen your interior light, I might've run right into you."

"Sorry, yeah, wasn't thinkin'."

The old man eyed Jay up and down, then peered at me with suspicious eyes. "You okay, young lady? You need help?"

"Help?" Huh? Yeah, maybe he could help me by leaving so I could screw Jay again.

"Uh, well, yeah. It's late, you're alone with a man who's holding on to you, and you're awful quiet. This isn't some kinda hostage situation, is it?"

I lost it, couldn't help it, and bent over, laughing and

holding my stomach. "Hostage? Dude, we just screwed our brains out!" I laughed so hard, I couldn't breathe.

"Billie!" Jay berated me under his breath, squeezing the crap out of my hand.

"Oh, well, I, uh—"

"Richard, what's taking so long?" A gray-haired woman stepped out of the passenger side of Richard's new beige sedan, stomped her foot, and glared at him. "It's late and you know I'm missing my shows. I want to go home."

I laughed harder. "His name is Dick!"

"Yes, dear. Well, uh, you kids be safe. I'm glad somebody's answering the call of the desert." He nodded once, winked at Jay, and walked over to help his wife back into the car, but she stopped to give us the evil eye. "Jeanie, get in the damn car. They're fine. We'll be on our way." She hmphed and folded herself into the seat, and I could've died.

"She's not drunk, is she?" Dick whispered, walking back around the car.

"No, sir. Just rude. Sorry," Jay said, trying to hold in his own laughter.

I choked, hiccupping and snorting.

"Alright, well, night then. And get off the side of the road." Dick shook his head, and just before he climbed in, another car sped past us. "That's the third or fourth time I've seen that man. He's been zipping back and forth on this highway. We saw him earlier on our way to dinner, and now again. Looked to be chasing after another car earlier. You kids be careful. And turn on your damn headlights so that guy doesn't come plowing into you. I don't know if he's racing or just joy riding, but you never know with people."

Dick got into his car, slammed his door, and drove away. A puff of dust spat back at us when his tires touched the pavement.

I collapsed down into the dirt, pulling Jay with me since he was still holding my hand.

"What's the matter with you?" He chuckled. "He was a nice guy."

Tears streamed down my face as I relaxed back on the ground.

"Billie, you're layin' in the dirt."

I took a deep breath, trying to stop laughing. "You live on a horse ranch, and you're worried about a little dirt?"

"Well, no. I guess not." He hooked his fingertip under a thick strand of hair covering my eyes and lifted it, then let it fall into the dirt too.

"I'm sorry, but that situation was a little messed up. If Dick had pulled up a minute earlier, he would've gotten a show."

"Yeah." He breathed a laugh. "A good show."

"Maybe we inspired him. Maybe he'll go home and boff Jeanie's brains out." I sniggered.

"Kinda doubt it. Did you see her? She couldn't be any more uptight."

"He thought I was your hostage!" I laughed again, kicking my feet like an eight-year-old. I felt so free laughing like that, not worrying about what anybody thought of me in the moment, because Jay liked me for me, even when I acted like a jerk.

I felt like a different person, and I'd never felt more beautiful.

He smiled and dipped his head to kiss me. The moment his lips touched mine, dusty and gritty, I released some kind of girly, breathy sigh, and he climbed over me, straddling me. He reached for my arms and kissed each wrist, then held them in his hands. "You make me feel brave, Billie."

"I do?"

"Yeah," he whispered, and he kissed me again, but he stopped abruptly, pulling his head back. "Wait a minute. Did you hear what Dick said about that car?"

"No, I was laughing too hard about the fact that his name is Dick."

"He said he'd seen that car a buncha times tonight, and he thought the car had been followin' after another car..."

I sat up, pushing him off of me.

"It couldn't be... could it?"

"Only one way to find out. Let's go."

Jumping to his feet, he held his hand out for me, and I grabbed it, pulling myself up out of the dirt. He dusted me off and grinned, his face a portrait of innocent perfection, and I kissed him. Just a quick peck on the lips, but it felt so liberating to do it.

"C'mon."

Oh my God. What just happened?

We hopped back into the Jeep after he took a private interlude in the desert, probably to dispose of the condom he still wore, and then we took off, hopefully much closer to finding Theo.

CHAPTER FIFTEEN

JAY

"CAN I just tell you how turned on I am by the way you're driving right now?"

I huffed a laugh. "Thanks?"

"I'm so proud of you. You're going faster than the eighty-miles-an-hour speed limit."

"Hush up, woman," I said, smilin' and not even tryin' to hide the ridiculous grin stuck to my face.

We'd been drivin' down I-80, pullin' in and out of all the little towns along the way, lookin' for Theo, Theo's car, or, I didn't know, anything suspicious.

I held Billie's hand for a little while, but she fidgeted, and I got the feelin' she didn't like it, so I let go. She was playful with me, and she talked nonstop actually, so in that way, she finally seemed comfortable with me. I wasn't sure why holdin' hands would cause such a reaction after what we'd just done, but I knew it wasn't the time to delve into a long "get to know ya" conversation about it, so I didn't push.

I wished we coulda stayed on the road forever, talkin' and jokin' and existin' inside this thing we'd created together, but eventually, we needed gas again, so we pulled into a run-down old 76 station near Battle Mountain, Nevada.

The service station looked like somethin' from the 1980s, but it still had fuel and the pumps worked. We climbed outta the Jeep into the flickerin', too-bright lights under an old metal canopy, and I began the mundane task of fillin' up.

Billie walked around the SUV with an almost-skip in her step. "I'm gonna use the restroom and see if they have anything good to snack on. Want anything?"

I groaned. "No. I don't think I can eat anymore junk tonight. I'm actually startin' to crave lettuce."

"Really? I thought you macho cowboys only ate ribs and raw hamburgers," she said, and she scrunched her nose and stuck her pink tongue out at me. I wanted to kiss that scrunch, but she backed away, headin' to the store.

"Grab me a raw burger then," I called over my shoulder. "Eighty-six the lettuce." I turned to watch her walk away, but just as she reached for the bar to pull the heavy, dirty, glass door open, we heard a commotion comin' from behind the store. There were voices shoutin', grunts, and some kinda loud, echoin', bangin' sounds. Billie froze, listenin'.

I knew there was no way we'd get so lucky and it would be Theo behind the gas station, but somethin' told me to follow the noise. I left the nozzle hangin' from the gas tank and jogged toward the back of the buildin'. Billie saw me runnin' and followed behind, her flip flops flappin' against the unforgivin' cement.

When we were on the west side, I grabbed her hand and slowed our pace as we crept to the corner. There was only one light on at the back of the buildin', but it was enough to see by, and when I peeked around the corner, I saw a struggle goin' on between two grown men.

"I warned you! What? Your dead fucking maid wasn't a

clear enough message? And now you hunt me down like you think you're Jason fucking Bourne?"

A really tall, extremely built man with light-colored hair was beatin' and pummelin' a shorter, thinner, dark-haired man, shoutin' at him and knockin' him down onto the hard gravel next to a big green dumpster. A pistol was tucked into the waistband of the bigger guy's pants, and then I got my first good look at the man on the ground when the bigger man stepped to his side.

Holy shit. Theo!

Theo wheezed. "What are you doing out here? What are you looking for?"

Blake grunted, "Fuck you," kickin' Theo in the head.

I could see him now, clear as day, lyin' in a fetal position on the ground. My heart pounded in my ears, and I turned to run back to get Jack's shotgun from under the seat in the —*damn*.

"What are you doing?" Billie whispered.

"I don't have a gun."

"Jay, a gun?"

I whispered back, "It's him. It's Blake Ormand. He has Theo and he's armed. And he's huge!"

"I'm calling the police." She felt in her back pocket for her phone, but she'd left it in the Jeep.

I winced. "Okay, but I don't think we can wait." We peeked around the corner again to see the big guy kickin' Theo in the ribs. He'd covered his bloody head with his arms, and I couldn't tell if he was conscious. I looked around for anything I could use as a weapon.

Blake shook with rage, standin' over Theo like an ogre. "You thought you could stop paying me? Nobody fucks with my money!"

"Jay, no," Billie whispered next to me. "You are not going up against that guy."

"Billie, he's gonna beat Theo to death. Maybe... maybe I can distract him long enough for Theo to run," I said when I spied a pile of long-forgotten two-by-fours layin' in the overgrown weeds on the property next to the gas station.

Billie squeezed my hand hard, followin' my line of sight. "No. He won't kill him. He needs Theo. He wants more money. Besides, then the hulk will come after you!"

"Well, I'll just have to—"

We heard a vehicle pull up in the gravel and the croak of a heavy, old car door openin', so we peeked around the corner again, Billie crouchin' down in front of me. We probably looked like some kinda alien with only our heads visible, floatin' in the air, one on top of the other.

A third man, skinny and also tall, but young, younger than all of us, stepped outta the car. He walked to Blake and stood there, waitin' for somethin'.

"Well?" Blake planted his hands on his hips.

"What?" The younger guy—he couldn't have been more than twenty-one or two—backed up a couple steps. The kid was seriously skinny, and he looked malnourished.

"Open the fucking trunk, idiot!"

"Oh, okay. You're not gonna put him in there, are you?" The kid walked to the back of his old, rusted, light-blue sedan and unlocked the trunk with shakin' hands. Blake lifted Theo, hoistin' him over his shoulder with way too much ease. Theo was unconscious. *Shit*. "Oh, you are. Look, man. I-I don't—I mean, I don't wanna kill anybody."

"Did I ask you to kill him? No. I asked you to pop the fucking trunk." Blake dumped Theo into it. "You want your money? Looks to me like you're jonesin' a little. Do what I say, don't fucking argue, and you'll get what you're owed. Now, get in and drive."

"Billie, we gotta follow 'em, or we might never see Theo again."

"Get the license plate, and I'll go get the Jeep. I need that number!" she whispered, takin' off her flip flops. I handed her the key fob and she ran.

Blake slammed the trunk closed, and my heart fell into my boots. The men took off, headin' east, and Billie pulled up twenty feet behind me. She hopped over to the passenger seat as I climbed in, and we followed Theo and his captors. I recited the license plate number over and over in my head so I wouldn't forget.

"Where do you think they're taking him?"

"XOT997. XOT997. Get a pen. XOT997."

"Oh. Right." She dug in her backpack, and I recited the plate number again as she wrote it on her hand with a permanent marker.

While she called the cops and tried to explain the bizarre situation, I watched the car ahead of us at the next stoplight. The streets were silent and empty, no cars or people millin' around in the dark desert night, so they were easy to follow, and the kid drove carefully, not speedin' or swervin'. Probably didn't wanna draw attention to themselves.

I slowed the Jeep and turned off into a neighborhood. All the adobe houses had thick cement walls around 'em, and they made me feel claustrophobic. I knew it was weird to think about it at a time like this, but those confinin' walls made me glad for the ranch, for the wide, open meadows and fields, and the mountains in the distance, powerful, free, and wild.

Billie disconnected her call with a press of her finger. "What are you doing? We'll lose them!"

"I know, but we can't follow too close or they'll know we're after 'em. There's no one else around. They'll see us. What did 911 say?"

"She said she's sending someone. I gave her the plate number." She groaned. "They could go anywhere." Climbin' up onto her knees, she reached between our seats to pull her laptop from the back seat, then flopped back around and opened it. "Maybe I can find something about the driver. That was a Nevada plate, so maybe he's from around here." She typed like crazy, and I found my way back to the main road. I saw the junker turnin' east onto I-80, so I followed, but slowly.

Billie mumbled, worryin', "What is Theo hiding? Damn it. Why can't I find it?"

When I merged onto the highway, it was empty. Nothin' but lonely road, silence, and darkness for miles in every direction. Blake and the kid were nowhere. The mountains in the distance trapped us in a well, like the bottom of a deep, empty pool, with no way up to the surface.

"Dammit. They're gone."

"Hold on. The kid lives here. Blake's probably paying him to help since he's not from around here." She typed furiously for a few more minutes while I drove twenty miles an hour, goin' absolutely nowhere. Not one car passed us. "Damn it. My hotspot's dropping its signal... Wait. Here! He lives here. The car is registered to Imelda and Joseph Daniels. The kid got a ticket in that car last year."

"Jeez, Billie, that was fast."

"Please, the DMV is the easiest thing in the whole world to crack, but I won't have a signal much longer. I'm guessing wi-fi is a luxury out here. Um, so, his name is... Daniel Daniels? Okay, that's just unoriginal. They live out in the middle of nowhere. He has the same address as Imelda and Joseph. Probably his parents.

No, maybe grandparents. They're in their early seventies. Off of highway 305. Go there! Turn south." Pointin' to a road sign we were about to pass, she looked at me. "It cannot be that easy."

I snorted. "It ain't that easy. Even if they went to this kid's house, Blake is still armed and still huge. We have nothin', no weapons. Our phones probably won't work out there. If you're already losin' wi-fi, I doubt 5G is a thing here either. What was Theo thinkin'? The guy is literally twice his size."

"Damn, I should've brought a satellite phone."

"You have one of those?"

"Yeah, at my apartment."

"Well, here's the next problem. It's dark as hell out here," I said, turnin' right off the freeway onto Highway 305, "but we're gonna need to turn our headlights off. They'll definitely see us comin' if we leave 'em on, and there's no streetlights out here. I don't see their lights, but that's an old car, so it probably doesn't have runnin' lights. See if you can't figure a way to turn ours off in that fancy touch screen." I nodded to the Jeep's dashboard computer.

She clicked on the screen a few times. "Easy peasy. Our running lights are off."

"Good job."

"Told ya, I'm brilliant." She smirked at me. "Okay, so we'll park somewhere and walk to the house or whatever."

"Billie, in your flip flops? It's the desert."

"Oh. I have boots," she said, crawlin' over the seat to find 'em. "Here." Ploppin' back over, she huffed out a grunt with a pair of "boots" in her hands. They were soft leather, and she'd folded 'em together to fit 'em in her backpack. She blew her hair outta her face with a big puff from her pink cheeks.

"Those are boots?"

"Well, yeah. I mean, I didn't say they were heavy-duty boots, but they're better than flip flops," she said, slippin' 'em onto her dainty feet without socks.

"Ever worn those before?"

"No. They're new."

"Put socks on, two pair. Double up or you'll get blisters. What is that, like a three-inch heel?" Pullin' her bag up from the floor, she dug through it for socks.

"Yeah. They're sexy. They go almost up to my knees, and they make me taller." She smirked at me. "Also, added bonus, they make my ass look like a million bucks."

"Your ass doesn't need any help. When we get home, I'm buyin' you some real boots." At least the heels were square and not sticks, but what was I sayin'? Her home wasn't anywhere near mine. We practically lived on different planets.

"They are real boots. I only have one pair of socks." She held up the tiniest pair of ankle socks.

"They're girly boots. Look in my bag, I've got an extra pair."

"Maybe you haven't noticed yet, Jay. I'm a girl." She rolled her eyes but climbed over the seats for my bag, then climbed back and slipped my socks on.

"I noticed," I mumbled, blushin'.

She laughed at me. "Jonathan, how can you be so shy? After what we did two hours ago? You fucked my brains out."

"I did not."

"Yes, you did, and I loved every single second of it. I want you to do it again. Not right now, obviously."

I blushed more. She thought I was embarrassed to talk about sex, but that wasn't why my face was hot as the desert in the noon sun. I blushed 'cause I didn't think of what we'd done as "fucking."

Changin' the subject, I asked, "How much further?"

"Um, I think about thirty miles or so. I don't want to, but I'll call Carey. Maybe he can call in the cavalry, a helicopter or something. They could meet us out there."

It took Billie twenty-five of those thirty or so miles to get ahold of Carey on her phone 'cause I'd been right and our cell signal was spotty as hell. Her phone kept droppin' the calls, and she couldn't leave a message on Carey's phone. And apparently, there'd been some kinda local brawl at Manny's Bar back in Wisper, so he'd been busy dealin' with that, but finally, he called back and said he'd get in touch with Nevada law enforcement.

Billie had also been right. Carey told us to go back to Battle Mountain, but I couldn't do it. If Blake Ormand got away or took Theo somewhere other than this Daniel kid's house, if that was even where they were goin', we'd need to keep lookin'. We didn't know enough about Blake, and Aislinn wouldn't be safe if this guy was out roamin' around.

And what if Theo needed immediate medical attention? I didn't have a ton of first aid experience, but I'd learned enough at the ranch—injuries and basic lifesavin' skills. I'd taken the free CPR class at the Jackson YMCA. Jack and Dean made Kevin, Finn, and me take the course.

Billie agreed with my decision to keep goin'. I thought I woulda had to physically fight her to get her to let me turn back for Battle Mountain.

Finally, I flipped the headlights off, and the eerie darkness and stillness in the car creeped me out.

"We still have a few miles to go," she said.

"I know, but this is a wasteland. There's no trees or buildin's to block our approach. If they're lookin', they'll see us. They may have seen us already, but it's so dark out here. I couldn't drive without headlights."

"Right. It's just a little… creepy."

I laughed. "Took the words right outta my mouth."

"What is that?"

Billie pointed through our windshield to somethin' standin' in the middle of the highway ahead of us. I squinted and leaned forward in my seat, tryin' to see.

"Dunno. Is that… is it a horse? Maybe it's a wild one. There's probably a herd around here."

"Ooo, let's ride a horse to the house. They wouldn't see us coming then."

"You can't just ride a wild horse. It'll knock you silly, or worse, before it lets you mount it, *if* you could even get close enough. Suckers are fast, and horses are prey animals so they spook easy. I'm surprised he hasn't run yet."

I slowed the Jeep as we came nearer to the horse. He stood alone on the highway, and as we passed him, he looked at me through my open window, watchin' me and turnin' his body as we crept alongside him. It felt like he was tryin' to tell me somethin' as he stared into my eyes, noddin' his big head.

We were close enough to him that I coulda reached out my window and touched my fingertips to his nose. What the hell? We'd had plenty of experience back home with wild horses, but none of 'em had ever let us get so close, not without a long length of rope and a lotta fight. He was a Paint with chestnut, black, and white splotches all over and a white face with a multicolored mane and tail. Jack woulda gone nuts for this horse. He looked like he came straight from a 1960s Western.

His deep brown eyes stared me down, and I just knew he

was tryin' to communicate somethin' to me, but I had no idea what.

Billie gasped. "He's beautiful."

I pulled the Jeep over and parked on the side of the highway.

"Why are you stopping? We still have a mile or two to go."

"I think he wants us to stop."

"Who?"

"The horse."

"What? Are you for real right now? The wild horse prefers us to park here? Did he communicate that to you tele-pathically through your equine mind meld?" She scoffed. "Jay, come on. Don't be ridiculous."

"It's just a feelin'."

"What? What kind of feeling?"

"Dunno. Never had one before. C'mon. My gut's tellin' me we need to stop here." I opened my door and stepped out into the dry air, and I was sweatin'.

Somethin' was gnawin' at me. It felt like if we kept drivin', we'd lose Theo. My heart sped up, and I yanked my sweatshirt over my head and tied it around my waist, then looked around at absolutely nothin'. There were no land-marks around for miles, except for rocks, dirt, and empty desert, and the horse still hadn't moved.

Billie came up beside me and caught my eye. "Well? What does your alien radar tell you now?"

"My what?"

"Your alien radar. Obviously, you have an alien communi-cation device implanted into your brain. How else would you be able to know what that horse is thinking?"

"Funny."

"I kinda wasn't kidding. There are crop circles all over

this desert, and isn't Area 51 around here somewhere?" She slung her backpack over her shoulder. "Seriously, what now?"

"Dunno," I said, turnin' to face her. She looked about as outta place as she could in the desert with her fancy boots, tight jeans, and shiny hair. But I still wanted to kiss her. "What side of the road is the Daniels' house on?"

"On the right. About two miles up the road, I think. Maybe a mile and a half."

"Okay. Let's head that way then."

"You want me to walk two miles? In these shoes?"

"Thought you said they were good boots?"

"Well, yeah, but I don't actually ever leave my apartment. The distance from my desk to the fridge is about as far as I go on a daily basis."

I laughed, grabbin' her hand and pullin' her down the road. "C'mon, lazy bones."

"Do you have, like, a hand-holding thing?" she asked, stumblin' and trippin' to keep up.

"No." I dropped her hand and slowed my pace a bit. "Do you have, like, a hand-holdin' aversion?"

"No, but why do you always want to hold my hand?"

"No reason. I like bein' close to you."

"Oh." She watched me as we walked. I felt her gaze on the side of my face, and it heated up again. Tentatively, she reached over and placed her hand back in mine, and I tried not to smile. "Wipe that grin off your face, cowboy. This means nothing," she scolded, but I heard the smile in her voice too.

I heard shouting and we froze. It came from far away, and maybe it had been some kinda animal, but it sounded like a person yellin'.

"Did you hear that?"

"Yeah, but maybe it was just a coyote or a wolf. Or a bear! Are there bears around here?"

"No bears in the desert. It sounded like a man. Get down!" I crouched and yanked Billie down to the ground with me when a light flashed out in the middle of the open emptiness in front of us. I thought at first it had been a gun, but there'd been no sound to follow the light.

"What was that?"

"No idea." We snuck to the side of the road, hidin' behind some sagebrush. "Billie, I need to go over there. There's no chance you'd just agree to stay here, is there?"

"Yeah, sure. I'll stay," she whispered. "Did you fuck *your* brain cells away too?"

"What?"

"Oh, nothing. That was more of an inner monologue kind of comment. Sorry. I didn't mean to say it out loud."

"Okay, you're gonna have to explain that later." I shook my head. "There's somethin' out there between the Daniels' house and us. C'mon. Don't let go of my hand." I looked into her eyes. "And try to stay down."

"Have you ever heard the expression 'you can't keep a good woman down'?" she whispered, squeezin' my hand tight. "Well, I'm great. But okay."

CHAPTER SIXTEEN

BILLIE

WE WALKED, well, more like crouch-walked, for freaking ever. It was almost impossible to see where we were going, the only light coming from the partly cloud-obscured moon above us, but Jay wouldn't let me use my phone as a flashlight. He said Blake would see us coming for sure if I did.

I tripped twice and banged my shins and knees on rocks, but Jay caught me both times. He offered to carry me piggyback, but I knew it would slow him down, and I had no intention of being a "save me, carry me" Barbie.

Although, I was pretty freaked out about possible scorpion infestations circling my every step. Or rattlesnakes. Jay had explained snakes were another reason he'd been relieved I had boots to wear. Apparently, that was why you wore heavy boots when you were "out on the range." Rattlesnakes bit your ankles. Fucking great.

I kept thinking I heard something behind us, but when I looked, I saw nothing but air and dirt. The sound of my breathing seemed to echo all around us, so I'd probably just heard myself. Except then, I heard a snort, and I *knew* I hadn't snorted, and Jay had been quiet as a mouse. I whipped my head around to see the horse, the one from the highway, following us.

"Jay!"

"Shh, Billie. What? You okay?" He stopped yanking me in the direction of danger to see what I'd been whisper-yelling about.

"Look, the horse is stalking us." I pointed behind my shoulder.

"What the hell?"

"Maybe he's not truly wild?"

"I don't—" Jay froze when we heard another shout. He pulled me behind him, jogging toward the sound, and I tried not to fall on my ass. An old rickety structure stood in the middle of the nowhere desert, partly hidden by a few tall, prickly bushes, and we crept up to it.

"Here, come in here." He dragged me into the shelter, and I looked up and all around for man-eating spiders and packs of iguanas. "Stay in the lean-to while I look around, okay? Just don't stick your hands in any holes or, you know, touch anything. And don't sit down."

"Jonathan William Cade!"

"Shh, Billie. What? What's wrong?"

"Um, just so you know," I whispered, "I am a fully capable woman, and I don't need your help."

"Yeah." He breathed a laugh. "I'm well aware."

"But where are you going? And how long will you be gone? You're not leaving me here?"

"'Course not." He chuckled. "I'm just gonna slink up a little further, but I'm gonna get down in the dirt. I didn't think you'd wanna do that. The packs of tiny killer lizards might haul you off to feast off your flesh." He tried not to laugh at me, pressing his delectable lips into a line. "You grumble a lot. Don't worry. I'll be right back. I think I'll be able to see the house if I can get to that copse of trees up ahead. Maybe the police are already there."

I nodded. Okay. That sounded like a good plan. "Okay. Just, Jay? Hurry."

"I will," he said, leaning in to kiss my cheek, and I swooned, but only on the inside so he couldn't see.

I waited. And waited. And waited.

I could have painted my fingernails and toenails in the time I waited even though I didn't own any nail polish. Maybe after this adventure, I'd take Ace, Evvie, and even that pregnant vet to the nail salon, and we could all sit around sipping champagne and juice and get mani/pedi's. There was a first time for everything. A manicure on my hands wouldn't last very long, though, since I bit my nails like there was a gourmet meal in the beds.

I tried to listen for voices or cars or Jay coming back to get me, but I heard nothing. And then anxiety took over. Had Jay been hurt? Did a thug-gang of rattlesnakes haul him off to their den to suck his bone marrow? Did I need to make a mad dash back to the Jeep to drive to the nearest veterinary clinic to find scorpion antivenom? *Ugh.*

I hadn't heard any more shouting, so I hoped Jay hadn't been caught spying on the criminals, but what if they'd come up behind him and knocked him out with chloroform on a dirty rag? He wouldn't have been able to scream to alert me. My heart tripped itself into a rhythm it had rarely before experienced, and I worried I might pass out. I chewed on my nails again until I realized they were covered in dirt.

Fuck this.

I refused to stay behind like a good little girl. He never

should have asked me to. In fact, how dare he ask me to wait? I had more experience with criminals than he did. Although, that was probably something I maybe shouldn't have been proud to admit. *Whatever.*

Inching out of the "lean-to," whatever a "lean-to" was, I looked the whole time for snakes and gigantic, deadly centipedes, but finally made my way around to the back of the shelter. I was terrified. My stomach felt like it was super-glued to my ribs.

I remembered Carey explaining to Ace that I could handle myself if I got into a sticky situation, but I was pretty sure he hadn't ever considered I might end up on a midnight trek through hostile cobra territory, alone, with only knee-high Freebird boots to protect me.

The moon had escaped its cloud jail, so I could see better than before. I did see the lights from the Daniels' house in the distance, but not well. The trees Jay had talked about were in the way, but I could see them clearly, so I crouch-walked my way over to them, grumbling and cursing under my breath the whole way, intending to give Jay a piece of my mind. Really, I focused on being mad at him because I was terrified to admit that something could've happened to him.

When I reached the trees—the very weird desert-y trees with tiny little leaves that fell like confetti from the sky—I looked everywhere for Jay. I crept up and down the line of oddly shaped, spindly trunks, whispering his name over and over, and each time I said it, my heart beat faster.

There was no answer.

I stopped walking and stood still and silent, searching inside myself for a zen I'd never before been able to find, listening for him. For any noise at all.

That was when I heard Blake's voice. He was talking on a phone. How did the prick have a signal and I didn't?

"Yeah, the asshole finally caught up to me, but he's a fucking toothpick. He had a gun, but the pussy was easy to disarm. I've got him in the trunk. I picked up some idiot outside the local bar to help me, but at least he's got a house out in the middle of nowhere. His old granny and gramps were home, but I took care of it. Did you find his sister yet?"

He listened to the person on the other end of the line for a minute. "No, but I will if I have to. You know what a big deal this guy is. His dad was a big deal. He's got all kinds of clout. I can't let him get ahead of me. If anyone finds out she's illegitimate, it'll kill Theodore Burroughs. All those rich mogul types care about is their reputation. I should know. I used to be one. The world finding out his dad wet his prick with some junkie who hasn't been seen since she gave birth would ruin Theodore Burroughs, and it would stop my steady stream of income."

What? Aislinn wasn't Theo's biologically full-blooded sister?

How could I have missed that? And Theo knew? I'd spent all this time looking for evidence of some kind of proof that Theo and Blake's dads had embezzled a shit-load of money or something. Ace's paternity never even crossed my mind.

I hid behind a tree, desperately hoping my body would be camouflaged behind the skinny trunk and Blake wouldn't spot me. I listened as hard as I could to try to hear every word he said while Blake paced fifteen feet away from me, and what little of his face I could see in the patchy moonlight became a mask of complete disgust and hatred.

"I don't give a shit what you think. Your conscience has no fucking bearing on my plans. She's got to be in Wyoming. If you want to find her, that's where you start."

So Blake had been blackmailing Theo with the threat of releasing the information of his father's infidelity and possible criminal activities to the media, with no intention of ever doing it, of course, because then his leverage would be dust. But then Theo had stopped paying, and the psycho killed his employees. Theo had taken it upon himself to hunt Blake down, but he hadn't accounted for Blake's strength, size, and general all-around white-trashery.

And if Blake and whoever was on the other end of that phone call knew Aislinn was in Wyoming, it wouldn't be long until they found her. Giovanni must've been working to hide Ace, disabling her phone and covering up any online activities. Theo would want her to be able to continue to live her life without noticing anything was going on.

Blake listened for a minute more and shook his head. "No. He'd want proof. He won't just believe me. And since I have no proof, it's not going to work. Why don't you just leave the planning to me and focus on finding her. That was the deal. You help me get my money and I help you locate the brat. And find me a new place to take Theo. I'll get rid of the kid and old people, and then I expect to hear back from you. Got it?" The other person on the call screamed into their phone as Blake slammed his satellite flip phone shut. Damn it! Why hadn't I thought to bring mine? From now on, the stupid thing would go everywhere with me.

He mumbled, "If she's freaking out now, the cunt will really be surprised when I shoot that spoiled-rotten bitch right between her blind fucking eyes," and stomped off toward the old, ramshackle farmhouse I could now see clearly.

I exhaled, feeling like I might throw up, but a hand wrapped around my mouth and pulled me backward. My knees collapsed and I tried to scream.

"Billie! Billie, it's me," Jay whispered, catching me and holding me up.

"Oh my God!" I turned and wrapped my whole body around his, squeezing the breath out of him.

"Shh, shh. You okay?" he breathed, nuzzling his face into my hair. "Why didn't you stay in the lean-to? I was freakin' out."

"You were gone forever. I thought Blake found you. Or you'd been killed by snakes."

He smiled and kissed my lips. "C'mon, we need to call the cops again. They're not here yet, and Blake has the grandparents tied to a fence."

"Jay." I pulled him back when he turned to walk away. "I know why Theo ran. Blake's blackmailing him because Ace isn't his sister. Well, she is, but not his full sister. Their dad had an affair. He's gonna kill the Daniels. I heard him talking on his phone to someone. He's gonna kill Ace! We have to do something."

"Shit. Okay, um… here, gimme your backpack." I pulled my backpack off and around me, and Jay searched with his fingers for the zipper. When he found it, he tugged it down really fast, and it made such a loud noise. We both froze, listening for Blake, but we didn't hear any movement or voices, so Jay dug through all my stuff. "Where's the phone? Never mind, I got it."

When he looked up, his face morphed from relief to horror, and someone grabbed both of my upper arms and yanked me backward. Jay reached for me, but it was too late.

"I knew I heard something." Blake held me, his fingers digging into my arms like bear claws. He let go with one hand, and two seconds later, I felt something digging into my ribs—his gun. "Stay right there or I'll shoot her."

Anger and fear clouded my eyes, and I watched Jay hold his hands up in surrender, dropping my backpack and the phone to the ground. His eyes flicked back and forth between Blake's tall height and my face.

"Who are you? Just some jolly do-gooders? I thought I saw a car following us in town. You really stepped in it now. C'mon, walk ahead of me so I can keep my eye on you. Don't turn around or I'll shoot." Blake growled next to my ear, "And don't *you* say a fucking word." Pressing his lips to my temple, he rubbed his scratchy beard against my face. "Ooh, you smell good. Too bad I don't have time for you tonight, girl. Later. I'm about to be filthy fucking rich." He lifted his head and barked at Jay, "Move it!"

Jay took two steps to walk past us.

"Mister? You there? Listen, this wasn't part of the deal…" We heard Daniel Daniels' voice from the other end of the trees, and Blake turned his head toward it, but it was just enough time for me to kick him in the shin with my overpriced-but-oh-so-sexy boot heel and for Jay to slam into him. Blake lost his grip on my arm, and I jumped away from him.

"Billie! Get the phone. Run!"

Blake and Jay struggled, and I watched in absolute horror as Blake beat and kicked Jay. He towered over Jay and had at least sixty pounds on him. I fumbled and stumbled to find the phone, but finally, I did and I ran.

I didn't want to leave Jay, but I knew if I didn't find a place to hide, Blake would kill us both. I needed to call the police. Everyone's lives depended on me getting the police: Jay's, Theo's, Aislinn's, the kid's, his grandparents', and mine.

I ran for what felt like forever and no time at all in the direction of the lean-to, or so I thought, but couldn't find it. I stopped by a huge boulder and tried to catch my breath.

My whole body shook, and I couldn't get my fingers to

work. I dropped the phone, and when I picked it up, as I stood, a big horse face came nose to nose with mine.

"Oh, fuck!"

He snorted and stomped his foot.

"What? Are you trying to talk to me now? I don't speak horse! What? What do you want?" Oh my God. I *so* did not have time for this. I tried again and again to dial the police. Finally, I got through, and this time, a male dispatcher answered.

"Please, send help!" I recited the Daniels' address and tried to explain, but the horse kept nudging me, and I couldn't focus.

"Please, ma'am, stay on the line. The police have been dispatched."

"They already should have been dispatched! Tell them to fucking hurry! He's gonna kill Jay!" I tried to whisper and hung up, then shoved the phone into my back pocket.

Ohmygodohmygodohmygod. I crept back toward the trees, my heart absolutely pounding, but Jay was gone. I couldn't see him anywhere. The stupid horse nudged my shoulder and pushed me, and I whipped around to push him back, and most likely lose my mind because, duh, I was arguing with a fucking horse, but he'd turned to the side, and it looked like he was… offering me a ride?

The horse lowered himself, bending his front knees and resting them in the dirt. Okay. This alien/horse mind meld really was a thing.

Oh! I had an idea. I looked around for anything I could use as a weapon. A battering ram to be exact. I saw a piece of sun-bleached wood lying on the ground—a tree limb, but there were no trees around that it could've fallen from. Whatever. I picked it up and tested its weight, trying my hardest to ignore thoughts of scorpions living inside of it or, yeah, tiny killer lizards. It was heavy. Good. Okay, now, how to climb onto a horse with no ladder? He didn't even have a seat for me. *Ohmygodohmygod.*

Hoisting myself up, I positioned myself onto the horse's back, hefting my "stick" up with me, and he stood. Oh shit! I grabbed for his hair and fumbled my stick, almost dropping it, but caught it at the last second.

And then the damn horse began to walk. *OMFG.* Okay. No big deal. I could ride a horse. But my plan depended on the horse going fast. How hard could it be? I tried to remember any movies I'd seen about people riding horses. Something about keeping your heels down and then you were supposed to use them to nudge the horse? I tried it (very gently, I didn't want to hurt him), and he loped into a jog.

Oh, matza balls!

It took every muscle in my body—and some I was certain I didn't even possess—to stay on top of the damn horse, but I accidentally nudged him again, and he went even faster. His quicker pace evened out some of the up-and-down-bouncy-boobs routine—small and jiggle-free were not words often associated with my gazongas—and that helped a lot. I tightened my grip on my weapon and hoped the horse knew where I wanted to go. He seemed to. He headed straight for the Daniels' house.

No one in the whole world would ever believe this if I told them.

Not one person.

CHAPTER SEVENTEEN

JAY

LYIN' in the dirt, I tried to breathe. I was pretty sure I had some broken ribs, bruised at least. Each drag of air through my lungs was torture. I'd fought Blake off as long as I could. Billie had gotten away, though, and that had been the point. The guy was a beast. If he'd gotten his hands on her again... Hopefully, she'd made contact with the police and they'd arrive any minute. I just had to stay alive till they did.

The kid had followed our fight, or more like my attempt at a fight but what was really just Blake draggin' me by my hair through the dirt, the whole time tryin' to convince him to stop tryin' to kill me and to leave. Blake wasn't havin' any of it. He pushed Daniel down, and I hadn't heard anything from him since. I hoped he'd just stayed down and hadn't hit his head on a rock or somethin'.

His grandparents were still tied to the fence by their cattle barn. I could hear 'em cryin' and beggin' to be let go, and when I twisted my head to get a look at 'em, the grandpa tried to clutch at his chest, but his hands were bound too tight. I hoped to God he wasn't havin' a heart attack.

Where were the cops? All I could think about was Billie.

If this Blake guy decided to use his gun to "take care" of the Daniels, he'd use it on me too. Billie would be alone, and I knew she couldn't fight him off, no matter how gutsy she was. Goddamn, what I wouldn't have given for my brothers' help.

I tried so hard to focus. I needed to keep Blake's attention on me so he wouldn't go after her.

Lookin' around again, I noticed a pitchfork stickin' outta a bale of hay about a hundred feet away from me, between me and the grandparents. If I could reach it, I'd have a fightin' chance against him.

It became my mission to reach it.

Drawin' in as much breath as I could without puncturin' a lung, I rolled onto my stomach. My ankle had been broken for sure. I knew the second it happened. Blake had stomped on it, then lifted himself up as I lay face down in the dirt, tryin' to muster the strength to get up to go at him again. He hopped a little and came back down on my ankle with his big foot, and I heard and felt it snap in half.

I'd stopped myself from screamin' 'cause I knew if Billie heard me yellin', she woulda come back for me, and that was the last thing I wanted. I moaned and bit my lip hard, and I could still feel blood dribblin' down my chin.

The blood dripped into the dirt as I crawled and dragged myself toward the pitchfork. Grandma Daniels caught my eye and shook her head. She had about as much confidence in my plan as I did, knowin' how big and how pissed off Blake was. Apparently, havin' a couple "do-gooders" show up had irritated him.

I had no clue where he'd got off to. I'd been too dizzy and too busy tryin' my hardest to hold in vomit when he'd broken my ankle to watch which direction he'd stomped off in. No matter. He'd gone somewhere, and I had to seize the opportunity. I prayed to God he hadn't gone after Billie.

I tried to crawl faster.

I had about ten feet left to go when I realized he'd come back and was standin' behind me, watchin' my pathetic attempt at escape. I heard him breathin'.

The defeat I felt debilitated me. It was heavy and hollow in the pit of my stomach, and my heart seized inside my chest. I'd gone my whole life feelin' unimportant and unexceptional, but I knew I could be good at lovin' Billie. Finally, I'd found somethin' special to me—someone—and now, I'd lose it all, in the middle of nowhere, alone, lyin' in the dirt like a loser.

No fuckin' way.

Rollin' as fast as I could, I tried to launch myself upright, but the pain from my ribs stabbed into my chest, stoppin' me cold. I coughed and choked on the pain, spittin' more blood into the dirt.

Blake laughed and placed his boot on my stomach, pushin' me back down. "Where do you think you're going? Thought you'd try to be the hero, did you? Sorry, man. Tonight, I win."

The look in my executioner's eyes sent chills down my spine; he looked scared and uncertain but resolute. He drew his gun slowly with shakin' hands, aimin' at my head, and I froze in place.

Grandma Daniels begged for my life. I heard it, but her voice sounded muffled and far away, and there was a ringin' in my ears as my eyes focused on the hollow barrel of the pistol.

My mind raced, thinkin' of anything it could to get us outta the situation, but the gun pointed between my eyes was a final nail in the coffin of possibilities.

"Don't think I won't do it. I crossed that line weeks ago. And now, you're just in my way. Theodore Burroughs has way too big a piece of the pie, man. How's that fair? His sister is the perfect motivation for him to share a piece." He nodded toward Daniel's car. "That asshole walks around like he owns the world. But he's not perfect. Far from it. He's a lying fucking cheat, and if he won't pay willingly"—he ran his hand through his hair and straightened, steppin' closer to me, aimin' the gun more squarely at my head—"I'll make him. But you showin' up here? I can't take the risk that some-body isn't helping you, that you're not going to get in my way."

I hoped Billie had made it far away and wouldn't see me die. I hoped my brothers would be okay, that they'd know I'd fought hard to get back to my family.

Billie. I'm sorry. I think I really love you. I sent the thought out into the ether and wished with everything left in me she'd hear it.

Watchin' Blake's finger on the trigger intently, I fixed an image of Billie's face in front of my eyes and counted down the seconds I still had left to see her beautiful scowl.

"I've come too far to—"

I heard a bang, but I was confused. Blake's finger hadn't twitched at all. He looked away from me, toward the Daniels' car, and then I heard the most beautiful sound in the world.

A fuckin' war cry!

Blake spun around, sendin' a cloud of dirt into my face, and I tried to blink the gritty dust from my battered and swollen eyes to see what the hell was happenin'. He let loose a bullet, aimin' at somethin' comin' at him fast, and I snapped my eyes open and closed to try to see.

Steppin' to the side to get a better shot at whatever it was, he fired again, and I sucked in a breath so fast, my ribs stabbed my lungs, and for a suspended minute, no oxygen entered or exited my body.

I watched as a beautiful, dark-haired, pale-skinned angel of death came racin' toward us on a horse—the horse from the highway. She rode bareback, and she carried a big ol' piece of wood in her hands.

She swung as she approached, and I heard the thwack as it made contact with Blake's skull. He fell in the next second, and Billie leapt from the horse, half fallin', half jumpin', and she scrambled up from the ground to stand over Blake, hittin' him over and over and over with her tree branch. She screamed and yelled the whole time. I couldn't understand all of what she said, but I heard some of it.

"Don't." *Thwack.* "You." *Thump.* Grunt. "Ever touch." *Thwack. Thwack.* "Him." *Thump.* Grunt. "Again!"

Somehow, I managed to sit up and saw Blake, bloodied and unconscious, in the dirt while Billie lifted her branch to hit him again.

"Billie. He's out. Billie! It's okay." She dropped her weapon when she heard my voice, and she turned and stepped over to me, droppin' down onto her knees. Tears streamed down her face, makin' little tracks through the dirt on her cheeks. She cried and then sobbed.

"Hey, hey, it's okay. Everything's okay. Are you okay?"

Through more tears, she nodded, her inky dark hair fallin' into her eyes. I pushed it away with my fingers, and she launched herself at me, wrappin' both her arms around my shoulders and holdin' on tight. She pressed herself against me, and the pain from my ribs made me almost pass out. I fell back, but she caught me.

"Jay! What's wrong? What can I do?"

"I'm okay. My ribs might be broken and my ankle. Just don't squeeze so hard." I winced and tried to laugh it off, but that hurt too.

"Oh my God. I'm so sorry. Here, lie back."

"No, help me up. I think Mr. Daniels might be havin' a heart attack. Do you know CPR?" I held my right arm out, and she crawled under it, liftin' me up when I attempted to stand. My head spun from the pain movin' caused, and I swayed on my good foot. Billie steadied me and retrieved her branch from next to Blake, handin' it to me to use as a crutch. We turned and hobbled toward Mr. and Mrs. Daniels, but someone was already helpin' 'em.

Theo.

The trunk of the car he'd been stuffed into had been opened somehow, and he'd found his way out. It must've been the bang I'd heard. It was open still in front of the Daniels' dilapidated, old farmhouse.

"Theo?"

"Jay, is that you? Are you okay?" His voice sounded clipped, gritty, and pained, but he kneeled next to Mr. Daniels and cut through the rope bindin's holdin' the old guy to the fence, and an unconscious Mr. Daniels slumped to the ground. Theo adjusted him so he lay flat and began CPR with one hand. He held the other up against his chest.

Billie deposited me next to Mrs. Daniels, and Theo tossed her a pocketknife.

"Cut her ropes," he said, noddin' to Mrs. Daniels as he continued pumpin' his hand up and down on Mr. Daniels chest. Mrs. Daniels hadn't said a word, but tears flowed down her face, and she looked so small and scared.

"Is he dead?" she cried. "Joseph? Joseph, wake up!" Billie cut her ropes, and she got up onto her knees next to her husband.

"Oh, thank God." Theo groaned, and we all looked down. Mr. Daniels' had opened his eyes and reached for his wife.

"Joseph!" She wrapped him up in her arms, and all of our heads turned when we heard the first signs of help arrivin' in the Daniels' driveway. And just like that, the property became overrun with police, firemen, and paramedics.

"It's about fucking time."

"Watch your mouth, young lady," Grandma Daniels scolded.

I tried not to laugh 'cause I knew how much it would hurt, but Mrs. Daniels sounded just like Ma when she used to yell at Finn or Kevin for cursin'.

"Are you for real right now, Granny?" Billie said, her eyebrows archin' up underneath the thick curtain of hair over her eyes.

Theo stood, holdin' out his hand to try to help me up. "I hoped me disappearing might influence you to give up chasing me, but thank God you didn't. I'm sorry. I had to protect my sister." All the color drained from his face, and suddenly, he wasn't standin' upright anymore. He collapsed on the ground, and his chest didn't move with breath.

Two paramedics rushed over to start CPR on Theo. They stuck a tube down his throat and hooked a bag to it to force air into his lungs.

Jesus.

The paramedics took Theo and Mr. Daniels in the first two ambulances that had arrived at the Nevada cattle farm, and Billie and I waited on another while they patched me up and attended to Blake. Eight cops stood around him, guns drawn and handcuffs at the ready, as he roused, moanin' and groanin'. Like I said, the guy was a beast.

We were questioned, Carey had been called, and two state police were in the process of tryin' to get ahold of the detective in Boston workin' on the case concernin' the death of Theo's driver and Aislinn's maid.

Daniel Daniels was nowhere to be found, but Mrs. Daniels said it had been him who'd sprung Theo from the trunk.

"What took so damn long?" Billie said. She stood in front of a police officer with her hands on her hips. "We called 911 hours ago! Why didn't you come then? He was gonna kill us. All of us! The old guy would have died!"

The local Battle Mountain officer stared down at the dirt. "Well, the 911 operator who took your first call is Daniel's ex-girlfriend, Macie. She knew if he got in trouble again, he'd most likely end up in jail. She was trying to protect him."

"Are you shitting me?"

"She's been fired, ma'am, and there will be an investigation. We didn't know anything was wrong until you called again. But luckily, your friend, Sheriff Michaels, also called the Nevada state police, and they were already on their way. It just took a while for them to get out here."

Billie stalked off, mumblin' somethin' about "stupid lovesick women."

"Is the horse gonna be okay?" I asked, and the officer looked behind him at the local veterinarian working on the savior of the day.

"Yeah, the vet said he was hit by a bullet in his flank, but it just grazed the muscle a little. A few stitches and he should be good as new. His name's Buster. He's been Joe's number one work horse for years, but the Daniels are getting up in age, and they've sold the last of their cattle stock, so the horse has become a bit of a pest. He gets in almost as much trouble as their grandson does. He keeps escaping his paddock and stall. I think he's bored."

The whole situation sounded like a murky mess, but it didn't much matter to me at that point. All I cared about was Billie, my knight in gothic armor.

"You saved my life," I said, holdin' Billie's hand and lookin' into her eyes. They reflected the blue and red lights from all the cop cars. We sat propped against the fence while the police walked around, markin' spots here and there with little flags.

"That horse saved your life. I just went along for the ride."

"No, it was all you. Billie, how in the world did you convince him to let you ride him? I didn't think you knew how to ride."

She turned her head, then angled her body toward me. "I don't. He knew what he was doing. He practically forced me to do it." She bit her lip and hid her eyes from me, lookin' down at the dirt.

"Hey." Pushin' her hair away from her face, I brushed my hand over her cheek, and she leaned in. "Seriously, thank you. He was gonna shoot me."

She shivered and looked down at her legs. "That was not fun. Let's never do it again." She smiled, but fear and exhaustion cracked in her voice, and she sat back, leanin' her head against my shoulder. "Oh! Does this hurt? I'm sorry." She pulled away.

"No, it doesn't hurt." I guided her head back down and held it with my hand, rubbin' with my fingers through her hair. "Sure you're okay? Nothin's broken? Nothin' hurts?"

"My whole body hurts. I'll be miserable tomorrow, but no, nothing's broken. I had no idea the muscle it takes to ride a horse."

"And you did it without a saddle. That takes some serious core muscles."

"Yeah, muscles I don't have."

"I'll kiss 'em and make 'em feel better tomorrow when they're sore."

She snorted. "Yeah, right. You're a bloody mess. You won't be able to move tomorrow. I hate to tell you this, but you looked like a little kid going up against Blake."

"Ow, ow, ow."

"What?" She gasped, sittin' up. "What did I do?"

"You punched a hole in my ego."

"Ha ha. Funny, Jay."

"You got away. It's all that mattered to me."

She scooted away a little and looked at me for a minute, her eyes full of… somethin'.

"Billie, hey. Everything's okay. You did good." I tried to turn to face her. I put my hand on my ribs to hold 'em in place as I moved, but it didn't help, and I hissed and growled at the sharp pain.

"Stop, Jay. Don't try to move." She got up onto her knees, gently pushin' me back against the fence, then held her breath and stood. "Thank you for helping me find Theo, but… I-I don't think—" She released her breath. "I think it's time for me to… go my own way."

"What? What're you talkin' about? Billie?" She shook her head, backin' away from me, and she stepped to the side as a paramedic walked over to us.

"Mr. Cade? Your ride is here. We'll get you loaded up and be on our way here in just a sec." I didn't look at the woman. I couldn't see anything but Billie's face. A tear fell from her eye when she turned away from me.

"Yeah, thanks," Billie griped at the woman, flickin' the tear away with her finger. "The ambulance only took two days."

When I woke in the mornin' in the hospital, I looked down the line of people standin' by my bed and saw Billie, Carey, Dean, and... Isaac? The smart-aleck teenage ranch hand?

He shrugged and said, "I just came for the road trip aspect. My dad thought it was the coolest thing that I'd been invited by the sheriff of all people." He rolled his eyes and Carey chuckled.

"How ya feelin', brother?" Dean asked.

"Besides the poundin' heartbeat tryin' to break through the skin on my ankle, I'm fine. Just sore," I said, lookin' down at my casted foot. I reached for Billie's hand, but as soon as I touched it, she backed away.

"I'm gonna go check on Aislinn and Theo. He's still unconscious and she's alone."

"I just checked on her," Carey said. "She's fine."

"Yeah, that's super helpful, Carey. She hates you, numb-nuts. She wouldn't tell you if she wasn't fine. I'll be back."

And there it was again. The mask. She'd slipped it back on, and somethin' in the pit of my stomach told me it might never come off again.

CHAPTER EIGHTEEN

BILLIE

"ACE?"

She gasped and turned when I opened the door to Theo's room. Carey had driven her out to be with her brother after he'd gotten word from the Nevada State Police that Theo had been transported to the hospital in Battle Mountain.

I needed to tell her what I'd learned. I'd confirmed it all this morning through all kinds of documentation. I was so pissed at myself for not finding it earlier, but once I knew what to look for, I found it quickly, though there hadn't been much to find. Her father had hidden it quite well, and really, back then, people got away with keeping things offline much easier than they could today. And then Theo had continued the tradition, hiring Giovanni.

There was more to it. There had to be. What had happened to Ace's real mom, and who had been the other person on Blake's phone call?

But now I knew that Aislinn was the product of an affair her father had had with a young woman who worked for his and David Ormand's investment company. Aislinn's real mother had disappeared in what had been deemed suspicious circumstances, but Burroughs Sr. had good lawyers and had been saved by them from any serious legal or criminal scrutiny.

And after, Aislinn had been raised by Theo's mom like her birth mom had never existed, but there were no death records. There was nothing to find about the woman. Theo's dad was a white guy, but his mom was Black like Ace's mom must've been, so Ace would've never realized the difference.

Blake's dad had known all about it and had extorted money from the Burroughs, but he must've told his son because after he died, Blake also followed in his father's footsteps, taking up the blackmailing tradition.

Aislinn was not who she'd always believed herself to be.

"Oh, Billie. I'm so glad you're here."

"How's Theo doing?"

"I don't know. The doctor said he'll be okay, but I can't tell. What if they're lying to me?" She cried silently, tears falling down her cheeks. "All I can hear are these awful machines. His skin feels cold and strange. I feel so helpless."

"Ace, chill, it's okay. He *is* going to be okay." Pulling a plastic chair away from the wall, I sat beside her, holding her hand in mine. Her other hand hovered over Theo's forearm above an IV line. "He looks better than he did last night. He has more color in his cheeks. I think his skin feels weird to you because it's bruised and swollen. Also, your hand is right above an IV, so maybe what you're feeling are the fluids going in."

"Oh. Where can I touch, Billie? I'm so afraid to dislodge an IV or a tube or something. I don't want to hurt him."

Theo had suffered a pneumothorax, and the doctor needed to insert a chest tube to relieve pressure from the air surrounding his lung, but his oxygen levels were good again, and his heartbeat sounded steady and healthy. He remained unconscious from a concussion, and he had broken ribs, a broken orbital bone, a fractured wrist, and a body full of bruises and cuts, but he would heal. It might take a while but…

I saw an unbruised patch of skin on Theo's upper arm, so I stood and moved Aislinn's hand there. "You can hold this hand, too, if you want. It's a little scraped up but not so bad. The other one is in a cast."

"It's funny. I rarely touched my brother before this, unless he was guiding me." She sighed but squeezed Theo's arm. "I've been so angry since the accident. I blamed Theo. I knew it wasn't his fault, but I took my anger out on him anyway. I'm so ashamed of the way I've been behaving."

"I'm sure he knows you don't really blame him."

"He lost his parents too. He lost the life he had before the accident, before our whole world changed. He was happy, and all of that fell apart because of me."

"Ace, you were a teenager. Neither of you knew how to cope. Why are you thinking about all this now? You just need to focus on taking care of yourself so you can take care of Theo. Have you eaten?"

"The sheriff made me eat on the way here."

"That was hours ago."

"I'm not very hungry. I'm so tired, but I don't want to sleep because Theo might wake up, and I don't want him to feel alone."

"Okay, I'm gonna go get you something to eat. I'll bring it back here. You can eat and rest, and I'll stay with Theo."

"Please don't leave me here alone, Billie!" she begged, squeezing my hand like she was lost in the ocean and I was her only way back to shore.

"Okay, okay. I'll text Carey. He can send the kid for food, okay?"

"Okay."

I sighed and slumped in my chair. "Okay."

"Are you all right? You sound… sad."

"No, I-I'm just tired." I texted Carey and stuck my phone back in my pocket. *Now, Billie. Just tell her.*

"Billie, you're lying."

I froze. "What?"

"I'm sure you are tired, but there's something else in your voice. What is it?"

"It's nothing. I'm fine." I couldn't do it. I wanted to. I wanted to be worthy of her friendship, but I just couldn't do it. My sister—my family—had been ripped away from me. I couldn't do that to Ace too.

She didn't say anything more, and we both sat there listening to Theo's heartbeat. The doctor had already removed his breathing tube.

After a few minutes, she squeezed my hand again. "Have I told you how much I like when you call me Ace? I hated you for it at first but only because my father used to call me that. I feel like we've known each other for a long time, Billie. You don't see my disability, or well, maybe you see it, but you don't care about it.

"You don't think of me any differently than you would anyone else. You have no idea how much I appreciate that. How much I love it. You listen when I whine and complain, and you're so supportive and helpful and encouraging." She turned in her chair to face me. "Talk to me. Tell me what's wrong. Let me help you this time."

She looked right at me, and even though I knew she couldn't see me, it felt like she could. Something in her beautiful and strange light-jade eyes comforted me, and I wanted to talk to her. I wanted to be honest, but I couldn't hurt her. And I wanted to tell her about Jay, about how I fell in love with him but now felt so fucking scared. All morning, I'd been fighting the urge to run away, like a coward.

"Billie?"

I gasped in a big breath and it all came out.

"I love him, Ace. I'm so in love with him. How is that possible? It's only been a few days. I'm not—I am not that woman!"

"What woman?"

"The stupid one. The one that should run away from the axe murderer but invites him in for coffee instead. The one who swoons when the big alpha cowboy smiles at her and flexes his stupid biceps. I don't want to be that woman. I don't want to change. If I let myself love him, I will. I'll become different. I won't be me anymore."

"You feel like you can't be yourself around him? Why not?"

"Because I don't *like* who I am around him. I'm an introvert. A dork. I only go outside when forced. He needs someone better suited to ranch life. And I feel like an asshole all the time. His stupid beautiful eyes are always watching me. And every time I open my mouth, I feel like… I feel like all I do is hurt him. But I've been this person for so long. I don't know how to be anyone else."

She laughed.

"Thanks, Ace. Thanks so much. You're a fucking gem. You said I could talk to you, and now you're laughing at me."

"Billie, no, I'm sorry. But which is it? You can't be yourself or you don't want to be?"

"I don't know." I scoffed and crossed my arms.

"Who are you, Billie?"

I whined, "What do you mean?"

"I mean, tell me what makes you… you."

"I don't know." I crossed my legs and uncrossed them

again, then sat straighter in my chair and kicked Theo's bed with my boot but immediately felt awful for doing it and winced. Thankfully, he didn't wake and he looked peaceful still. "I'm smart. I'm loud. And obnoxious. And sarcastic. I hate most people, but the ones I do like, I'd do anything for them. I like helping. I think I'm a good person. I try to be. Maybe no one can tell, but I do. And I want him, Ace. I want to love him. I want him to love me. I want a family. I want… a home."

"And you think he would make you stop doing those things, wanting those things? You think he doesn't like your sarcasm or your intelligence?"

"No." I sniffled, wiping my eyes with my fingers. At some point during my confused confession, tears had leaked out. Stupid traitor tears. "It's the opposite. He seems to like *all* of me. Even when all I do is bash him and torment him. He doesn't care that I'm chubby. I don't even think he sees it. But I guess, *I* want to change. I don't want to be a jerk all the time, but it's just who I've been for so long. It protected me from stupid people. It protected me from me, so I could hide," I sighed, "from myself."

"Billie, you're not a jerk. You're the kindest person I've ever met. I love being around you. You're hilarious and so honest. I bet he loves that about you too."

"Maybe, but he says I'm hiding behind a mask."

"But maybe that's about you opening up to him about how you feel and who you are, not about how you look and how you act. You wouldn't be you if you weren't sarcastic, but you can still be a smartass and be open and vulnerable with him at the same time."

I thought about it. It would feel so weird to expose myself to him on purpose. But maybe, if I could just try… maybe I could do it. I wanted to.

"Billie?"

But no. I wouldn't. I drew in a deep breath through my nose. "Yeah?"

"You're leaving, aren't you?"

"Ace, I was so scared. I saw that douchebag pointing a gun at Jay and—I've never felt anything like that before. It was like my life, my future, flashed before my eyes. If Jay had died—I just couldn't—I want him so much. I don't know what to do with this feeling. It's overwhelming, and it scares the shit out of me."

And if I loved him and lost him, like Jessie? I wasn't sure I could survive that.

"Billie, it's okay to be scared, but I think you need to say all of this to Jay. You'll feel better if you do. Just be honest."

Right, like I am now?

"Yeah, 'cause I'm such an expert at sharing," I said, sarcasm oozing out of my mouth.

"Well, there's a first time for everything," she said.

She reminded me of my mani/pedi plan, but I wouldn't be around for that. I was leaving.

I wasn't brave at all.

I was a coward. I should've told my friend the truth so I could've been there to help her cope. But I couldn't do it.

We talked more. I tried to convince myself she would be okay before I left to try to ease the guilt I felt about not telling her the most important thing anyone would ever tell her.

But I failed.

We ate disgusting veggie soup and crackers from the cafeteria, and instead, I told Aislinn all about my daring equine rescue, and how I beat the crap out of Blake Ormand with a tree branch, and about my "road trip" with Jay, how pretty California had been, and how we'd had sex up against the Jeep in the middle of the freaking highway.

But the whole time, a nagging, burning feeling grew in my chest and in my hands.

"Billie, I'm okay now. Go. Go talk to him."

"What?"

"Come on. I can feel your nervous energy. I've been talking nonstop for five minutes, and you haven't responded once."

"He's probably resting."

"Billie."

"What?"

"You don't strike me as a scaredy cat. I know you're nervous to talk to him, but I know you'll do it anyway because you are the strongest, most independent woman I've ever known. And so brave. Just do it."

I held my breath, then pushed it out, and with it went all the hope I'd felt over the last few days, all the dreams of Jay being my person, of him loving me and being my family. I pushed until all that was left was the old Billie. The Billie who was alone. The Billie who was furious with her sister for leaving her, furious with her mother for living instead. The Billie who was so fucking angry at herself for letting all of that keep her separate from the rest of the world. I pushed until I was safe again behind my mask.

"Okay, okay. Jeez, Ace, take a pill," I lied, but instead, I left her and walked in the opposite direction of Jay's hospital room. I climbed into the Jeep outside and drove all the way to Oregon, leaving behind the best friend I'd ever had and the man I loved.

CHAPTER NINETEEN

BILLIE

WHEN I FINALLY MADE IT home, after the most miserable drive ever with several side-of-the-highway pitstops to cry uncontrollably, there were several messages waiting for me on my jurassic answering machine.

The jilted wife had left a few. I'd kinda blown her off, so I quickly located her husband and sent her a report. He was in Aruba—classic—with someone named Wendi, another housewife from their small town who'd left her husband and two small kids for the jerk, Marc Carnahan. I returned her money. It literally took me less than twenty minutes to find the idiot.

I couldn't help her with what to do once she knew where he was. I couldn't help anyone with anything.

I couldn't help myself.

Carey had left two messages. He didn't yell at me for taking off like a thief in the night. He'd just wanted to check on me. To make sure I was okay and didn't need anything. He said Jay was home and fine, and Theo was being transferred to the hospital in Jackson, Wyoming near Wisper, but he would be okay, too, and Ace would stay with the Cades until he could go home.

Carey also wanted me to call him because he had one of his gut feelings that the Blake Ormand thing wasn't over. He wanted me to keep digging. I hadn't told Carey what I'd learned about Aislinn, and Blake hadn't blabbed, probably hoping he could still use the information somehow. And I doubted Jay even remembered. So much had happened that night.

I felt like a total schmuck for leaving Ace like that, but I just couldn't face her.

Or Jay.

He'd reached deep down into my soul in one weekend and I just… I didn't know what to do with that. I didn't know how to give him that. Everyone wanted something from me, needed something from me, but I didn't have shit to give.

I knew he was okay and home. I broke through the Battle Mountain hospital's server and hacked Jay's file, and I hacked Finn's computer in Jay's bedroom. He stupidly left it on and connected to wi-fi after a pathetic game of Spider Solitaire, and it was nothing to break through the Cades' system; I had been the one to bulk it up back in October.

I watched him for a few minutes through the camera in Finn's monitor. He lay in bed looking up at the ceiling with his ankle propped up on a stack of pillows, clenching his fists over and over. He was so angry. When he rolled onto his side, I cut my connection.

It hurt to look at him. To know that I'd walked out on him without a word after all he'd given me, after what we'd shared.

I felt like my mother.

Funny enough, the last message on my answering machine was from my mother. She said she wanted to check on me, but she probably just wanted to ask for more money to buy a new wardrobe to impress some fat-cat banker from Switzerland or some half-rate baron from the UK.

She called again, and I was too depressed to screen the call before I answered. I hadn't showered in three days, and all I'd been able to force myself to do was stare at the TV while shoving stale bread and crackers into my mouth until I ran out, then I ate the freezer-burned contents of my freezer, one package at a time. I was too depressed to even order groceries, so I ordered fast food from two blocks down the road and paid a fortune to have it delivered.

I picked up my phone intending to just hang up on whoever bothered to call me. "Yeah?"

"Wilhelmina?"

Rolling my eyes, I sighed. "What? What is it now, Patricia? I'm busy, and I'm not sending you money to buy a fur coat made from poor, defenseless, rare Afghani foxes. Buy your own murder jackets." My terrible joke was greeted with silence. "I can hear you breathing. What do you want?"

"I just wanted to check on you, darling. You do know what day it is?"

"No, I—" Standing, I padded over to my laptop sitting open on my desk. I looked at the date. "That's why you're calling? Yet again, you feel the need to remind me of my sister's death? Don't you think I know when she died? I was there! I'll never fucking forget. I don't need you to remind me every year."

"I-I know. I'm sorry. I just wanted to hear your voice. I miss you. I wanted to make sure you're okay... Are you okay?"

I snorted. "Right. 'Cause you're mother of the year. I did forget that." I almost hung up on her, but something kept nagging at me while I chewed my nails down to the quick, drawing blood, but the rip and sting didn't distract me like it usually did.

I was so tired of being alone in the world. For once, I wanted it to be true that she missed me. I wanted her to be my mother instead of just some overpriced nuisance. The feeling grew and festered until I couldn't stop the words from exploding out of me.

"No. I'm not okay! I'm alone. I'm always alone, and it's your fault. If you'd been a better mother, Jessie would still be alive and I wouldn't feel like this. I wouldn't be angry with her, and there would be someone in the world I could call. There would be someone to love me. The only person I have is you, and all you ever do is remind me that I'm not good enough. Not smart enough, successful enough, pretty enough, skinny enough! Fuck you. Fuck you, *Patty, darling*." I hoped my grandmother's pet name for her made her seethe.

"Wilhelmina, I-I'm... Please—"

"No! Why didn't you do something? Why didn't you fight for her? Why didn't you protect us? How could you not know what was happening to your own daughters? And then you did, and still, you did nothing! All you ever cared about was your image and money. All those sorry housewives you spent your life trying to impress—where are they now, Patricia? Do they call to ask you how you're doing on the day your daughter took her own life? Do they even know you exist?

"Well, I found someone who does care. In this awful fucking world, I'm the one he wants. He cares what I think, how I feel. *He* doesn't berate me for not being perfect. He thinks what I do is cool. Noble even. I think he loves me, and it's your fault I can't love him back. It's your fault. It's your fault she's dead. So don't you call me to remind me. I know. I'll never fucking forget!"

CHAPTER TWENTY

JAY

"UH, JAY? YOU EXPECTIN' a delivery?" Kev asked. "A big one? Jack's been tryin' to text you."

"My phone's dead. No. I'm not expectin' anything," I said, proppin' my ankle up on the coffee table and grabbin' the TV remote.

"Okay, well, he says to get your ass outside. Somethin' just arrived for you."

"Just tell me what it is. I don't feel like trudgin' out there."

"Uhh, nope, this you gotta see."

"I'll look at it later."

"Get your ass movin'." My brother walked in front of me with his hands on his hips, blockin' my view of some bland nineties sitcom.

I looked around him, wishin' I could see right through him. "No. Go away."

"Okay. Be like that." He walked away, and I settled in for mindless, unentertainin' entertainment and annoyin' laugh tracks.

It had been a week since Billie left me in Nevada.

She hadn't even said goodbye.

I was pissed off and so… disappointed. And maybe my heart was broken just a little.

Maybe a lot.

My equine therapy project was all but dust. Theo was a mess. He wouldn't talk to anyone. Not even his sister. As soon as he could, he'd leave Wyoming and probably never come back. After what he'd been through, could I blame him?

And now, everything I'd worked so hard for seemed so pointless. I'd failed and let so many people down. My brothers. All those people we could be helpin'… And I'd wanted so bad to prove myself.

I proved myself alright. Proved myself unnecessary.

Turnin' up the volume, I shut my mind off, but it wasn't another three minutes till my annoyin' brothers were there again.

"Up you go, baby Jay." Arms lifted me from behind, and I heard the deep rumble of Dean's voice as Kevin walked around the couch to hoist my legs over his shoulder.

"What the fuck are you doin'? Put me down. I ain't a two-by-four."

"C'mon," Dean said, gruntin' and adjustin' my weight in his arms. "We're goin' outside to see what Santa brought for you." I tried to struggle out of their hold, but the movement hurt my ribs, and I didn't wanna jack my ankle up any worse, so I sighed and gave in, lettin' my stupid brothers haul me outta the house and down to the barn like a kayak.

Dean sat me in the ratty, old computer chair from the tack room and turned me to face Jack, who stood in the middle of our barn, facin' me with his hands on his hips and annoyance clear on his face.

"Here," he said, and he handed me a thin white envelope.

"What is it?"

"Dunno. The man who delivered your package left it for you."

"What package? I didn't order anything."

"Just open the damn thing."

"Fine." I opened it and pulled out a letter addressed to me written on wide-ruled notebook paper with the little ripped fringes on the edge still attached. The handwritin' was messy scrawl.

"This is—what is this?"

Dear Mr. Jay Cade,

I want to thank you. The police explained what happened and how you, Mr. Burroughs, and Ms. Acker ended up at our farm that night. I'm feeling much better, so you know. But I also wanted you to know that your courage and bravery have inspired our grandson Daniel to get help. He checked himself into an addiction treatment center two days later, and I have just come from visiting him. I feel hopeful for the first time in a long time.

Buster has long been my friend and companion, but I believe he is meant to be yours. He's a hard worker, and I know he will be the same for you on your family's horse ranch. I hope you and Ms. Acker will enjoy him. He's still got good life left in him, as do we all, old or young.

I have included his papers, though he is just an ordinary horse. He has no special bloodlines or history. But he is the most exceptional horse I have ever known, and I want you to have him.

Thank you all for what you did for us. And please, if there is ever anything I can do for you, Ms. Acker, or Mr. Burroughs, all you need do is call.

Sincerely,

Joe Daniels

"What?" I looked up when I heard hooves clompin' on the dusty ground, and my brother Kevin walked the horse from the highway, Buster, into the barn. He stomped his foot, nodded his big head at me, and chuffed a breath in my direction. "Seriously? He gave me his horse? What—why? Why would he do that?"

"From what Carey says, sounds like it was the only thing he had to give," Jack said. "A man don't give his horse to just anyone, Jay. It's his way of thankin' you. He's a fine horse. Beautiful."

I stood, and since I didn't have my crutches 'cause I'd been carried outta the house like a hog on a spit, ready to roast, Dean gave me his arm and helped me hobble to Buster. Jack pushed the computer chair behind me while Kevin hooked Buster to the crossties on either side of the aisle, and then my brothers left me alone with my new friend.

"Hey, Buster. You okay? How's your—" I looked down at his flank to where he'd been grazed by Blake Ormand's bullet. "Looks good. It's healin'." I patted his back and he swung his head toward me. "Yeah, guess I'm healin' too. My body is but… Billie's gone. You remember her, right?" He chuffed, pointin' his ears toward my voice.

"It was only a few days, but I guess I thought… I thought she was meant for me. God, Buster, I'm pretty sure I've loved that woman since the first time I saw her. Love at first sight. You probably think that's stupid, huh? I mean, who does that? But you shoulda seen her. Back in October when she first came to the ranch? I dunno. She just—she took my breath away. I feel like I haven't been able to breathe since." I rubbed my hands down his back, then leaned against him, listenin' to him breathe.

I thought back over the last couple weeks. The last several months, actually. I'd been so excited to finally have a plan.

To know what I was doin' with my life. For the first time since I was probably five years old, I wanted to be on the ranch. I wanted to use my skills to make it better. To make a difference in the world. But now, the defeat I felt was just like that night when Blake aimed a gun at my head.

And I knew everybody would think it was stupid, but I did love Billie. I didn't wanna hide it or be ashamed of it. I wanted to scream it to the world. Unfortunately, she didn't wanna hear it, so what would be the point?

I was pissed at myself. She had made me brave, but it'd all seemed to disappear when she did.

"It doesn't matter. She doesn't love me. Why would she? I'm just baby Jay. Unimportant. Unremarkable. Unsuccessful."

"JJ, you are not any of those things."

I whipped my head up to see my mama standin' in the barn door, holdin' some books in her hands.

"What are you—?"

"I'm sorry. I didn't mean to eavesdrop. I just came to check on you. Kevin said you were in here." She walked over and stood next to me, lookin' at Buster. "What a cool horse. I've never seen one with markings like these. What kind is he?"

"He's a Paint."

She patted Buster's nose and looked at me. "Can we sit for a minute?"

"Sure," I said, lookin' around for another chair.

"Here, you sit." She pulled the computer chair closer, and I sunk into it. "I'll grab a chair from the tack room."

"Okay."

When she returned, she flipped a feed bucket upside down and sat in front of me. "How are you feeling, sweetheart? You've been through so much."

"I'm fine," I lied. I wasn't fine. I was utterly crushed.

"So, I wanted to show you this," she said, settin' one of the books on the ground at my feet so I couldn't see it, but she held the other a little higher in front of her chest. "It's something I made for you when you were a baby. I don't know. It's nothing fancy. Just a little scrapbook of thoughts and memories, a few pictures. I hid it in the attic years ago, before I left."

"I don't mean to be rude, but I'm not really in the mood for—"

"Please? Just for a minute?"

Lookin' in her hopeful eyes, I sighed. "Okay."

She dropped her head, starin' at the barn floor. "I knew when you were born that something was wrong with me." When she looked up again, she had tears in her eyes. "I didn't know what postpartum depression was back then. I only knew that I loved you so much and that I didn't ever want to hurt you. But every day, the depression got worse, and I became more and more detached from all you boys. I didn't know how to fix it. So, I made this for you because I didn't ever want you to think I didn't love you. Or that you weren't special enough. Because you were. You *are*.

"Look." She opened the book and showed me a picture of myself I'd never seen from when I wasn't even three feet tall. "Did you know you walked at eight months old? I couldn't believe it. I think Jack walked at a year. Dean too. Kevin was a little sooner, and Finn," she laughed, "he took his time. He didn't walk till a year and half. He could have, but he just didn't feel like it, and now he can't sit still.

"But you? One day, there was a toy horse on the kitchen table. Funny enough, it kind of looked like this horse." She motioned toward Buster. "You were in the living room, and you kept looking at it. And then Kevin picked it up, and I watched you follow it with your eyes. You stood for the first time with no help, walked right over, and took that horse out of Kevin's hands.

"He cried and stomped his feet, and he pushed you and you fell on your little bottom, but you held that horse with all your strength and smiled at Kevin." She laughed. "You did things like that all the time. You spoke early—really early, actually. It scared me 'cause I couldn't figure out where the voice was coming from. But I looked at you, and you pointed to another toy and said, 'I want.'

"You were gutsy and determined. Whatever you wanted, you figured out how to get it, and then you just took it." She cocked her head to the side, grabbin' hold of my hand. "But I think, when I left, maybe you packed that away? Maybe it was me who made you feel unimportant because I wasn't here to tell you every day how special you were. How important you were to *me*.

"JJ, you were. You are. Every day I was gone, when I'd wake up in the morning and go to sleep at night, I would say out loud, 'I love you, JJ. Mama's so sorry.' I missed you so much. Every damn day, but I thought—no, I *believed*—I was hurting you. I thought the sadness and despair I felt was infecting you all. It became a physical thing, like some dark creature, following me around, lurking and trying to pound you down too. For years, I thought that made me a bad person. A bad mama."

She sniffled, wipin' her tears away with her sleeve. "But you have been exceptional since before you were born. You are the reason I'm alive. Without you, I don't think I would have made it. Some days, you were the only person I talked to. Thank you for being there for me. You didn't know that was what you were doing, but you were.

"Now, I don't know Billie very well, but I do know it isn't

you. Whatever's going on with her that's keeping her away from you—it's not 'cause you aren't important or exceptional. Because you are. I know I'm your mama, so maybe my opinion doesn't hold much weight, but to me, you are the most exceptional person on the planet."

She sniffled again, stood, and handed the book from the floor to me—an old and withered copy of *The Chronicles of Narnia*. The memories of her holdin' me while UJ read to us rushed at me, and I felt so warm inside. She handed me her blue scrapbook too. "Here. Look through it when you feel like it. When you need to be reminded of just how special you are. There are lots of examples for you in there." She leaned down to kiss my forehead, then walked away.

"Mama?" I stood, leanin' on my good leg, and set the books on the chair.

She turned back toward me. "Yeah?"

"Thank you," I said, and I opened my arms.

"Oh, JJ." She rushed at me, threw her arms around me, almost knockin' me over, and held on. "I love you."

CHAPTER TWENTY-ONE

JAY

"THANKS FOR COMING, Jay. How are you doing? How's your—" Theo motioned to my ankle with a wave of his casted wrist from his hospital bed. He'd been moved to the hospital in Jackson and was healin' well, but he had a long way to go. And not just physically.

He'd called and asked to meet with me, and I couldn't help the feelin' of dread in the pit of my stomach when I thought about him tellin' me he'd decided against investin' in Cade Ranch. What would I tell my brothers?

But I wouldn't give up. I'd find another way.

"Yeah, I'm doin' good. Can I—is there anything I can get for you? Do for you?"

He shook his head. "You and your family have already done so much. Thank you for taking care of my sister. I knew she'd be safe at the ranch. I... I'm so sorry for everything. I dragged your family into my mess. I'm just so sorry. I don't know what I was thinking. I could've gotten us all killed." He looked out the window at the gray and dismal early fall day, and it reminded me of the glarin' difference between warm, sunny California and Wyoming. It reminded me of the glarin' absence of Billie.

His stare went on for so long that I thought maybe I should just leave.

"Theo?"

He didn't look at me.

"I, um, I know this isn't easy for you. I'm sorry for what you went through. I wanted to say, if there's anything I can do to help, I hope you'll let me know. And Ace—Aislinn can stay at the ranch for as long as you need. It's not a problem."

"Actually, there is something. Can you look into setting your ranch up as a nonprofit?"

"A nonprofit? I don't understand. Why would I do that? The ranch is how my family makes its money. We have to make a profit."

"Not if you were to receive a yearly donation." He turned his head toward me and smiled, but it didn't reach his eyes. "Normally, I would be more involved with the project, but I-I don't know that I'm going to be available for that. I don't know how long I'll be here in the hospital, and then when I leave here… I can't go back to Boston. My—" He took a deep breath. "The man, Tim, my driver. He was—" He turned toward the window again, but I didn't think he saw anything beyond it. "He was more than just my driver. He'd become more to me than just that. And I," he sighed, "I can't go back there."

Squeezin' his eyes shut, he took a deep breath and adjusted himself, anglin' his battered body toward me, and he opened his eyes. "But I've contacted a local lawyer, and he's coming here at the end of the week so we can set something up for your project. I would put the funds into a trust so that if anything ever happened to me, you would still receive the money every year. It would be separate from your breeding program, of course, so you could continue to make a profit from that. This lawyer has experience with corporate and trust law, and he's from Wisper, so he might even know your ranch and your family. His name is Brady Douglas."

"Yeah, I know him. Well, I know of him. My brother's boyfriend knows him. They're friends, I think."

He cocked his head. "Your brother's gay?"

"Uh, yeah. Kevin."

"Oh, so he came out." He smiled a little and nodded. "Good for him."

"You knew?"

"I might've had a hint." He laughed a little under his breath. "Well, you can use Mr. Douglas for the ranch, too, if you'd like, or find someone else. But I'd like you to be here for the meeting. That way you can make sure you get everything you need. I don't want to hold you back any further."

"Theo, you don't have to do this for us because you feel bad about what happened." I said the words, but I could feel all my brothers telepathically thumpin' me on the head, sayin', "Shut the fuck up, Jay! Take the money!"

"I know that, Jay. I'm not. I'm doing it because you have a good plan. Let's be honest, you weren't ever going to make millions with an equine therapy business. This way, you'll have the funds you need to help people. I think that's what your family is meant to do.

"And you can still run your breeding program, build it out even. You'll have more room once the renovations are completed. I think you'll find some messages in your inbox over the next few weeks and months, people looking for good, strong horses. I hope I've helped.

"I suppose maybe it does have a little to do with how grateful I am to you for taking care of Aislinn." He sighed. "I haven't been honest with her. She deserves that. Maybe she can handle it now. She's almost like a different person. She's found some strength. She has a lot more fight inside her than she did a month ago."

"Uh, yeah." I winced. "That might be 'cause of Billie. Sorry."

"Sorry? I love it. Seeing my sister with confidence and a desire to live her life? I can't even tell you how happy that makes me."

"I guess Billie has that effect on people. She did on me too."

"Well, then she's meant to be a part of all of this too. My mom would say, 'The girl that should have you, hold tight to her.'"

"That's my plan. She just doesn't know it yet." I decided right then and there: I was goin' after Billie. I just had one more thing to take care of first.

I cleared my throat.

Three of my brothers sat around the old kitchen table that had been dragged out to the arena office years ago. It was faded, dinged, wobbly, and ugly. Finn was on my laptop, grinnin' at me through Zoom. I stood at the head of the table while they joked and argued and made fun of Finn's tiny head on the screen. Finally, I cleared my throat again, louder this time, and Jack looked up.

"Shut up, y'all. Jay's got somethin' to say."

Noddin' to Jack, I took a deep breath. "So... Theo has offered to donate his money for our program. We'd have to designate the new business as a nonprofit. It would, of course, exclude our breedin' program, and we would still run that as a separate, profit-based company. He's hired

Brady Douglas to set it up. Anybody object to that? Free money?"

Nobody said anything. They all just stared up at me.

"It would make it possible for us to help a lotta people without havin' to worry about the ranch turnin' a profit. And Theo pointed out that, with the renovations we've planned for the arena, we'll have more room for our breedin' program. We could grow that too."

I looked at each of my brothers. "But it's gonna mean big changes real quick. We won't have to start slowly. While the reno's happenin', we can start lookin' for horses to train. We'll all need some trainin' ourselves so we know what to expect. There are a lot of things to consider. I've found a large equine therapy barn in Montana. Pas Edgemont over at Wild Heart Ranch used to work there. They've had a great deal of success, and we're gonna go up there to learn from 'em. I've already spoken to the owner. We just have to set up some dates.

"And there's gonna be a lotta new people on the ranch every day." I looked at Jack and raised my eyebrows.

"Okay," he said.

"Okay. Good. Also"—I took a deep breath, as if I could inhale more confidence—"I'm takin' over. I want all the bills and accounts for the ranch. All that stuff can be done online. It all needs to be streamlined. We need a better website and online presence, so I'll need all the account information and passwords for those.

"Jack, you'll still deal with our breedin' customers since you've already cultivated those relationships over the years. But everything else goes through me. If you need supplies, if you have questions, unless they pertain to the actual trainin' of the horses, come to me.

"Oh, and Kev? You're the official Cade Ranch photographer. You're gonna be donatin' your services." I smirked at him, and he rolled his eyes but nodded and smiled. "We need all new pics of our current stock, and then when the new horses get here, pics of them. I want photos of the property, the barns, the house. And once we're up and runnin', I want you to take candids of the clients with our horses, as long as they or their parents sign off on their images bein' used. Just take pics of everything. It's all gonna be used online and for brochures we can send out to area doctors and therapist offices. Dean, you'll take those to the Veteran's Center."

There was about a minute of silence, and eyebrows all around the table raised. All eyes were on Jack. Baby Jay orderin' Big Jack around didn't happen every day. In fact, it never had before. I planted my feet, gritted my teeth, and waited for the argument.

"Thank God," Jack said, and he slapped his hand on the tabletop so hard that I jumped a little. "I hate doin' all that shit. Finn's supposed to help me"—Jack eyed the little square box on my computer's screen with Finn's face in it, and Finn grimaced—"but he's got about a four-second attention span. I wanna be outside in the sunshine. I want my nose filled with heated dirt again. I'm tired of sittin' behind that stupid desk. It feels like a prison. I been waitin' on you, Jay. What took so damn long?"

All I could do was laugh. "Wha—ah, you... What?"

"Alright then," Dean said. "Let's get to work."

"Uh, wait," I said. "Throw this stupid table out. I ordered a new table. I ordered all new office furniture. We're gonna have to keep this place up, guys. The house needs paintin', inside and out. Oh, and by the way, I'm done shovelin' shit. It's time we found more volunteers for that crap. Literally."

Kev laughed. "How long you been waitin' to say that out loud?"

Heavin' a sigh, I said, "You have no idea, brother."

Everybody stood, and each one of my brothers walked over to slap me on the back. Finn smooched at me, cooin', "I wuv you, baby Jay. Good job, little dude," and I smirked and slammed my laptop closed.

Jack stayed behind as our brothers all filed out the door. When they were gone, he flipped his green baseball cap backward, wrapped his arm around my shoulders, and said, "I'm proud of you, Jay. And thank you."

"But I tried to get you to—"

"Yeah, but back then, I wasn't ready. And then you weren't. I been waitin' on you to figure this out for yourself. If I'd ordered you to do it, would you feel the same pride you do now?" A slow smile spread across his face.

Chucklin', I shook my head. "No, brother, I reckon not."

"Alright, well, all I gotta say is… have fun bein' Finn and Kevin's boss." He snorted. "They're all yours."

CHAPTER TWENTY-TWO

BILLIE

"CEDAR HILL CEMETERY, PLEASE," I said, scooting into the back of a taxi at the airport in Hartford, Connecticut, my hometown.

I hadn't been there since I left for MIT after high school. When I quit college, all I wanted to do was get as far away from my past and my mother as I could. Oregon was on the opposite side of the country, but still, it never felt far enough.

The memories and images flew at me, and it felt like I had to try to swim through them to the surface so I could breathe. We hadn't lived by the airport or the cemetery, so I didn't see my old stomping grounds, but just being back there, smelling the river, feeling the familiar crisp fall air, it all brought me back.

I was so ensconced in my memories of Jessie that I didn't even hear the cabbie trying to get my attention.

"Miss? Miss. Miss!"

"Oh, sorry."

The guy rolled his eyes in the rearview, and it reminded me of Jay telling me my eyes would get stuck upside down. I smiled despite my gloom and doom.

"We're here."

I nodded, tossing fifty bucks through the little plexiglass window between the seats. "Thanks."

Taking a deep breath as he drove away, I slung my backpack over my shoulder, and then I just walked. I remembered where Jessie's grave was, but I had to work my way up to it. I stalked the cemetery grounds like some creepy emo chick trying to find inspiration for her super-gothic, angsty makeup tutorial on pinstagrambook.

The architecture of the buildings and grave markers were kind of cool though. Old and new world-y. I laughed out loud when it occurred to me it had probably been the reason my mother had chosen the cemetery—because it felt rich. It would've impressed her pompous friends, the Jewish who's who of Hartford.

Finally, when I approached Jessie's grave marker, I read her name out loud. "Jesamin Anastasia Acker. Beloved daughter." I snorted. "What was our mother smoking when she named us? Seriously. We sound like spoiled two-bit princesses twice removed from some tiny European country no one can ever remember the name of."

Dropping my backpack, I sat on it next to Jessie's headstone. "Hey, Jes. How ya doin'?" I sighed and my whole body slumped. "I know you're not really here, but Matilda the Money Hungry Hun called last week to remind me you were dead." I scoffed and shook my head. "Like I could forget? I guess I just—I needed to be somewhere connected to you. I couldn't go home. The house is gone now, replaced by a Stepford wives development. There's no one there.

"I miss you so much," I whispered, and the tears literally poured out of my eyes. "Every single day. I miss your laugh. I miss your optimism. I don't have any, and sometimes, I think it's because you took all mine with you when you left. I miss your strength. God, you never got mad when she tried to manage you. When she made you change your hair or your clothes to fit the image she wanted everyone to see when they looked at the perfect Acker family. How did it not make you furious? I hate her for it.

"How did her constant berating and picking and judging not drag you down? I still can't get up. I still look in the mirror every day and see... less than. Ugly. Fat. Unappealing. Remember? She always used to say that. 'You look so unappealing. Do better.'

"And then, when she found out what had been happening, she did nothing. She wouldn't because her brother held all her cards. The *money*. He should be in jail, Jessie, for what he did to you. He should be dead. I will never forgive her. Never.

"My friend Carey wouldn't let me kill him, but I did, maybe, redirect Uncle Ray's, um, funds to a sexual abuse charity. They even sent him a thank you card and a T-shirt with their logo, and on the back, it said, 'Stop the abuse.'"

I laughed through my tears. "Think he wears it?"

Picking at the strands of grass growing up the sides of Jessie's grave, I was still trying to avoid what I needed to say. What I came to say.

I needed my sister. I needed her advice.

"It looks like someone keeps up your grave. It can't be Matilda, so I guess it must be the groundskeepers here. I wonder if they know how lucky they are to see your name every day. You know, I hadn't said your name out loud until recently. I just—I couldn't. It hurt too much. But...

"But then Jay—Jonathan. He just waltzed right in and—it's so stupid. I barely know him." Huffing a breath, I flicked my tears away with my fingers. "But I *know* him, you know? I know the doubt he feels about himself because I feel that way too. But don't you let him fool you. He wears a mask too. Only his isn't made of smudgy makeup and short skirts or sarcasm. His is made of shyness and quiet.

"But what am I supposed to do, Jes? Tell me what to do. I love him and I know you think it's stupid, but I do. I want to. But what if he really does see past all of this, past my masks? What if he doesn't like what's there? What if *he* thinks I'm unappealing?"

I could hear Jessie in my head. She said, "He won't."

And even though I knew I was hallucinating, I answered, "But what if he does? How do you know? 'Cause then I'll be left standing there, exposed for all the world to see, alone again. I don't know if I can handle that. It took years to build this mask. How did he rip it down so fast? Damn him."

"Wilhelmina?"

Jumping straight up off the ground, I squeaked, "Shit!" My mother was standing right behind me. "What are you doing here?"

"I'm sorry. I didn't mean to scare you. I-I moved home. I've been coming here a lot."

"Oh." I exhaled slowly, trying to slow my heart.

"I heard what you said."

"You heard me? Which part?"

"Most of it, I think. You were right. You *are* right." She closed her eyes, whispering, "I'm so sorry," but then, taking a deep breath, she opened them again and stared right at me. "I let you both down in the most awful way. I failed to protect you and Jesamin. And, what's worse, after she died, I abandoned you. I left you to fend for yourself. There's no excuse."

Realizing I was posted in front of Jessie's grave like a guard, I relaxed my shoulders and stepped to the side, and my mother looked at the headstone and cried.

I didn't know what to do, what to say, so I just stood there.

I'd figured living in the lap of luxury with rich men all over the world would have kept her young, but she looked old. I hadn't seen her in more than five years, and that time hadn't been kind to her. Her hair was a lusterless mousy brown color, minus her patented chunky highlights, and she had dark circles under eyes.

The anger I'd felt for so long tried to surface, but something about the way her whole body shook with sobs pushed it down. But I didn't go to her.

I waited, breathing quietly. Wishing Jay was by my side. Wishing I could hold his hand.

"I'm sorry," she said when she could control it. "I promised myself I wouldn't cry when I finally spoke to you. But seeing you here, with Jes—Jessie. Oh, Billie. I know I don't deserve it, and you will probably never forgive me but —" She sniffled. "My therapist said I shouldn't ask for your forgiveness yet. That I should tell you how sorry I am, but that I shouldn't ask anything of you because your pain isn't about me."

She wiped her tears away with her coat sleeve. It looked like a regular old discount store coat, not designer, for sure, with its tacky vinyl sheen. And holy shit. She was seeing a therapist? "But, Billie, I'm here. I'm here now. For you. If you want me. If you need me. I found a job, and I've been saving money to pay you back for all the times you bailed me out."

I meant to be rude, but my words came out in a whisper, "I don't want your money."

"Still, I'm going to keep saving. And I have a lot of work to do… emotionally. I have a lot to learn about self-acceptance. I unloaded my own insecurities onto you and Jessie. I let you believe you weren't enough, weren't good enough. But, Billie, you are. You're more than enough. And I'm proud of the woman you have become. I'm proud that you help people."

For some reason, I couldn't stop blinking. Or swallowing. There was a huge lump in my throat, and I had no clue what to say.

"So, you have a young man?" She smiled apprehensively, like she thought I might rip her head off just for asking the question. A fair assumption, judging by our last phone conversation. "What's his name?"

"Jay. Jonathan. His name is Jonathan."

"That's a nice name." She reached her arm toward me. "Y-you said on the phone that I was getting in the way of you having a relationship with this man. So, I was wondering"— biting her lip, she pulled her hand back, clutching her fingers in a tight fist—"is there anything I can do? To help?"

I snorted at the absurdity. "Like what? You wanna come with me to Wyoming so you can explain to him why your awful parenting caused me to be a jerk to him?" I shook my head. "Thanks, but that's on me. It's not your fault. It's mine and I need to apologize. Even if he never forgives me, I have to try." The irony of the words did not escape me. "You can't help me with that." I shrugged. "But thanks. For offering. I guess."

"Okay," she said, laughing a little. "Yes, that makes sense. Good decision, not taking your mother with you to try to reconcile with your boyfriend." She smiled a little. "But would you maybe have time for coffee before you go to Wyoming?"

I looked back at Jessie's grave, imagining her ruffling my hair. She would say, "Go for it, Billie. Love them. Let them love you. You deserve it."

When I returned to the Jackson airport and stepped out onto the curb for a ride-share, wouldn't you know it, Marla, my five-star driver, rolled down her window and waved.

"Hi! Guess we made an impression on you last time you were here, huh? Hop in. So, you're headed back out to that ranch?"

"Yeah," I said, sliding into her backseat.

"Do you work out there?"

"No."

She glanced in the rearview. "Sorry, we don't have to chat."

I remembered my first drive with Marla and wanted to kick myself. "I'm sorry. I didn't mean to be rude to you last time. I have… issues."

"Oh." She smiled awkwardly, avoiding my eyes in the mirror. "S'okay. Not everybody likes small talk. I get it."

"Marla?" Pulling up to a red light, she turned to look at me. "I'm an ass. I'm really sorry. I'm just not good at it. I'm not good at talking to people. It's a defense mechanism, but I'm trying to be better." Great, I could tell by her nervous giggle that I was making things worse.

I tried again. "I-I was kind of working at the ranch. I'm a private detective. Well, kind of, but I'm good at finding people. Someone was missing, and my friend asked me to help."

"Really? That's so cool. Well, so, did you find them?"

I chuckled under my breath when she stepped on the gas but looked back at me expectantly in the mirror. She was smiling openly again. Seriously, that was all it took? A little honesty? Well, I could give her that. "I did. We did. Jay and me. He's—well, he's kind of my boyfriend. At least, I hope he still wants to be. That's why I'm going back…"

By the time Marla dropped me off, we'd exchanged cell numbers, and I'd promised to text her to let her know how it went with Jay. She was still a little too peppy for my taste, and I thought if I ever encountered her in the morning, I might be tempted to strangle her with her bouncy curls, but I grudgingly also thought maybe she could teach me how to relate and talk to people. I planned on trying to learn anyway.

She drove away, and I turned and was confronted with the sun setting over the mountain in the distance. It was orangey-pink, with little wisps of purple streaking through the clouds. Evvie waved from the pasture where she stood with Aislinn, petting a yellow horse. They looked friendly with each other, so I hoped Evvie had been a better friend to Ace than I had been. I would need to address that. But first…

Evvie pointed to the red barn, so I dropped my bags and headed in that direction.

I was so nervous. I was wearing boot-cut jeans, not the tight, organ-rearranging kind I usually had to paint on, and a plain old black tank top with my old MIT sweatshirt wrapped around my hips. There wasn't a stitch of makeup on my face. Not even eyeliner or mascara!

When I got to the open door, I gasped. Literally gasped. Jason Momoa had *nothing* on Jay Cade.

He stood, leaning on one crutch, brushing a horse—Buster!—and talking to him. "So, that's my plan. Whatcha think, B? You think she'll even talk to me? Knowin' her, she'll probably just yell at me for showin' up unannounced but—"

"She won't." I desperately hoped he was talking about me, otherwise this conversation had died before it had even begun.

"What?" He whipped around, dropping the weird oval comb in his hand.

I was breathless just looking at him. "Hi."

"Hi," he said, his apprehensive, ocean-blue eyes shaded in the waning afternoon light.

"Is that who I think it is?"

Glancing back at Buster, he said, "Uh, yeah. Mr. Daniels gave him to us." He bent to pick up the brush/comb thingie, balancing precariously on his good leg, holding himself up with his hand on a wobbling crutch. "Whatcha doin' here, Billie?"

"Jay, I—"

Buster pushed him with his big wet nose, and Jay stumbled a few steps toward me. "Ow. This damn horse."

I laughed but reached for Jay's hand, steadying him and holding on tight. "I'm sorry, Jonathan. I'm sorry for the way I treated you. I'm sorry for all the things I said, and I'm sorry I left. I lo—"

"Wait." He pursed his lips, narrowing his eyes. "Stay here."

Swallowing hard, feeling like a puppy with my tail between my legs, I waited. Jay limped on his cast, leading Buster to a stall. He pulled the door shut gently and stood there a minute, not moving.

When he turned and hobbled back to me, he stared at me. He didn't say a word.

"I-I have so much to tell you. But first I wanna tell you that I lo—"

"Stop. Come with me." Grabbing his other crutch from against another empty stall door, he made his way past me. When he was outside, he turned left, and I followed him to the last door at the end of the humungous barn, then back inside to a staircase. He was making me pay for leaving him,

I knew, but if he'd really been planning to come find me, then
I hoped he'd at least hear me out.

"Where are we going?"

"Just hold your horses."

"Yeah, but—"

Turning back toward me, he rolled his eyes. "You always
gotta be in control?"

I zipped my lips and shook my head.

"C'mon. Up here."

When we'd made it to a room at the top, after a harrowing
one-foot-at-a-time climb with him nearly falling backward
and knocking us both down the stairs, he held the door open
for me. I walked in and stood in the middle of the little room,
waiting for him while he closed the door, hobbled over, and
lowered himself onto the end of an old rickety twin bed. He
crossed his arms over his chest and looked up at me, raising
his eyebrows, which was my cue.

"Wait, before I start, are you okay? Your face is still so
bruised." Stepping forward, I touched the tips of two fingers
to a fading green and light-purple bruise on his cheek, and he
closed his eyes. "It's been two weeks. How's your ankle?
Your ribs?"

"I'm fine." He tried not to lean into my touch but didn't
quite succeed.

Just my two fingers feeling the warmth from his skin gave
me confidence. And the connection was immediate. I felt
centered. Nervous but grounded.

He opened his eyes. "My ankle's healin' well, I think. My
ribs weren't broken, just banged up. It looks a lot worse than
it is."

I nodded. "Yeah, I kind of hacked your hospital file, but
that's good to hear."

"You hacked my file instead of just callin' me?"

I didn't answer—it was a rhetorical question, right?—and backed up a few steps, and he tracked my every move with his eyes. Slowly inhaling a deep breath, I blew it out while my heart thudded in my chest. I had rehearsed what I wanted to say on the flight to Jackson like a lovesick fool, much to the annoyance of my aisle buddies, but now that he was in front of me, I was scared. But I was so past the point of return.

I realized there was nothing I wouldn't do for him—including embarrassing myself on a commercial flight and in the ride-share back to the ranch with poor Marla. Whatever I had to do to be with him, I would do it.

I would rip off my own mask and bare my soul because he deserved it, no matter how terrifying it was.

"Don't say anything, but I love you." He opened his mouth to say something, but I cut him off. "Please?"

His eyebrows hit the roof. I wasn't sure if he'd ever heard me say please, but he stayed quiet.

I sucked all the air in the room into my lungs. "I was just in Hartford, Connecticut. That's where I'm from. Where I grew up. It's where Jessie's buried, and I went to see her. Well, her grave. You asked before how I'd met Carey, and I told you that we worked that missing girl's case together. But what I didn't say was that I took that case with Carey *because* of Jessie."

"You did?" He scrunched his face in confusion. "How come?"

"Because the mom of the little girl had already lost one daughter. To suicide."

"Oh, I didn't know that. That's—"

"It was fucking awful. And I knew how much it hurt when Jessie took her life, and I couldn't imagine that little girl having to go through that all alone, or worse. And Jessie's

death was similar to this other girl's suicide. I was actually
the one to figure it out. It was connected to the little girl's
disappearance."

"How?"

"Carey's hunch was that the mother's step-brother had
been involved. So, I dug into their lives and found that the
step-uncle had"—I closed my eyes, squeezing my hands into
fists—"sexually abused the sister." Jay opened his mouth to
say something again. I heard his sharp intake of breath, but I
cut him off. I needed to get it all out.

"That's why she killed herself. The little girl had been
abused, too, by the uncle, and the uncle freaked, thinking the
girl would report him. He actually tried to sell her to a human
trafficking ring, but he lost his nerve. He didn't care about the
girl, of course, but he was scared the thugs would kill him
once they had her, so he just abandoned her on the highway
and took off. The feds caught him trying to cross into
Canada."

"So, Jessie was abused? Sexually? Billie, I'm so sorry."

"Yeah, well… we had an uncle too."

"We? You mean—"

"He tried. Jessie stopped him. Made herself more enticing
to him so he'd go after her."

Jay stood and slowly came to stand right in front of me.
"Billie."

"No, it's—I'm fine. It's fine." I shook my head.

He whispered, "You can stop. You don't have to say it."

My instinct was to stop. I didn't want to say it out loud.
But at the same time, I couldn't stop. I wanted to tell him
more than I'd ever wanted anything. How did that make
sense? I wanted him to know, but having him hug me and
console me seemed so… big. I'd worked so hard and for so
long to deny it, to deny that the attempted abuse had affected

me at all, but it had. And to deny that Jessie's death had been because of me.

But it was the truth.

My hands began to shake, and Jay inched closer to me, then took me in his arms. He hugged me to his body, holding me so tightly. His crutches fell on either side of us, and he surrounded me everywhere.

His body, his scent, and his heartbeat calmed me. It was probably just his soap or shampoo, but he smelled so good. He smelled like the earth, but sweet. Like safety and ground-edness. It must've hurt, the way he held me in the middle of the barn with me hugging the breath out of him, squeezing his bruised ribs, but he didn't complain and I couldn't stop.

But still, my knee-jerk reaction was to reject the intimacy. "I don't need you to coddle me, Jay," I said into his neck. "It was a long time ago."

"I'm not coddlin' you. I'm holdin' you. Besides, what if I need this?"

"Whatever." But I didn't push him away.

"Maybe you already dealt with this, but I just learned about it. It hurts me, too, Billie, to hear it. So, just shut up and hug me 'cause I need it."

It was a trap, I knew, but I wanted him to hold me so badly. I thought I'd feel physical pain if he didn't. After Jessie died, I remembered wanting my parents to hug me, to hold me like Jay was, but they didn't. They couldn't.

"I'm sorry," I said.

How? How had he broken down my defenses so fast?

"It's okay." He hugged me even closer, if it were even possible.

This was it. I knew it. All my tough talk, all my blustering and false airs had to come down. If they didn't, I'd lose Jay. This thing between us, which had become so important and beautiful, would crumble and the dust would scatter with the wind.

Since Jessie's death, I'd never faced anything harder.

But I heard her in my head, telling me I could do it. I could give myself to this man because he was good and special, and he loved me.

He hugged me so hard. No space existed between us, no air to carry pretense. No stops and starts. And I held onto him like I'd fall to the core of the earth if I didn't, then my hug turned into something visceral; I clutched and pulled at his back, digging my face into his neck. I couldn't get close enough.

"I love you," he said. He didn't whisper, and it sounded loud and strong in my ears, in my heart, and on my skin. "I can handle whatever you wanna tell me. I'm not gonna run or judge. I just wanna help you carry it. If you'll allow me the honor, Billie, I'll do anything for you."

In the smallest voice, I said, "It's my fault she's dead. It's my fault she went through that, and… and maybe, if she hadn't, she'd still be alive." I said the words, and I felt like I might throw up. The truth of them, the anger and guilt and shame I felt, wanted me to retreat. To superglue my mask to my face and run away. To never come back.

Jay didn't argue. He didn't say, "Don't say that, it's not your fault." I knew it wasn't my fault, logically, but in my heart, I couldn't help feeling like maybe there had been something more I could've done. Maybe there'd been some way for me to save Jessie like she'd saved me.

I told him everything then. I told him how I sat in my bedroom crying, knowing what had been happening in the room next to mine when my uncle had stayed with us when our parents had gone out of town. How Jessie begged me not to tell my dad about the abuse, and how I hadn't told at first because Jessie promised she could handle it. I thought she could handle anything. She was the strongest, bravest, most beautiful and alive person I'd ever known.

I told him all the bad stuff but all the good stuff, too, like how beautiful Jessie had been and so fun when she'd sneak into my room at night with a flashlight to read me the cheesy eighties romance novels our mother had loved, with the Fabio characters on the front and all the silly love scenes with "her heaving bosom and his throbbing member." How we'd giggle and fall out of my bed and then freeze, waiting for our parents to come in to yell at us and tell us to go back to sleep. And how, after that, she'd sing me to sleep while she wrote, "I love you, Billie Bean" on my back with her fingertip.

I told him how proud of Jessie I'd been when she was accepted to state college even though our mother had been so disappointed in her for not getting into Harvard or Stanford or wherever. I'd known Jessie would do amazing things no matter where she ended up. She'd been so happy and optimistic about everything that day. She could have done anything, and she would have been so good at it. Anything. She had the world in her hands.

He held me the whole time and let me talk, didn't interrupt once. We stood there, clutching each other in the middle of the weird, dark, ugly wood-paneled room forever.

When I finished and took several long, deep breaths, he limped, leading me by the hand to the little bed. We sat and he cradled my face, swiping at my tears with his thumbs. I tried to turn my head to hide them, but he held me in place.

"No. Don't move. You're perfect."

I rolled my eyes. "Jay." It had only been a day. I wasn't *that* well-adjusted yet.

"Thank you."

"For what? Blabbing for hours? Oh yeah, I'm sure you're *so* grateful about that."

"Thank you for tellin' me, for lettin' me carry some of it for you. I'll never put it down."

I scoffed and tried to look away.

"I'm serious. Thank you." He pulled my face back to look at him. "And I love you."

"You really do, don't you? Why, Jay? Why me? I'm all wrong for you. You need some earthy chick. Annie Oakley or whoever."

He chuckled, and he was so beautiful in that moment that my heart choked me. "Don't think I really ever had much choice. First time I saw you, it was like somebody sucked all the oxygen outta the world. I had to remind myself to breathe. And then you spoke. I loved your wit and your fight. And you're so smart. And clever. And sweet." I shook my head, scoffing again, and Jay held my hands. "Don't worry, I won't tell a soul. You agreed to help Evvie and Aislinn when Carey called you, no questions asked." He pursed his lips a little. "And can I tell you a secret?"

I nodded because I was so desperate to know his thoughts, I was breathless again.

"I hate bein' a horse rancher." He winced. "Don't get me wrong, I love our ranch. I love the horses. But if I have to shovel one more load of horse shit, I'm gonna lose my damn mind. And the horses don't like me. They never cooperate. I don't have that thing my brothers have. I've never had it."

"Seriously?"

"Yeah. Except Buster," he said, smiling, tucking loose strands of hair behind my ear. "Mr. Daniels gave him to you and me, so you're gonna have to help me take care of him. And I'm thinkin' you should probably learn how to ride properly.

"Billie, as hard as this has been, tellin' me all this about Jessie and your mama, you did it. I'm proud of you. And I'm in awe of you. Your strength. And the way you make me feel? It's like I could conquer the whole world as long as I have you by my side. Your courage gives me courage." He squeezed my hands. "Guess what I did?"

I couldn't guess. Arching my eyebrows, I shook my head.

"I sat the guys down and told 'em I'm takin' over. It's past time I stepped up. I've already got things movin'. I'm gonna make 'em believe in me 'cause *I* believe in me."

"I believe in you too."

"I know. Thank you." He pulled me closer, and I reached across the space between us to kiss him.

"Wait a minute. Help you take care of Buster?"

"Yep. You're stayin'. Carey needs you. So does Ace. But, Billie, I need you. I want you, and I'm not lettin' you push me away anymore." He ducked his head just a little. "I mean, if you want to."

"Okay," I said, nodding once. "Well then, there's one more thing."

"What?"

"Close your eyes."

CHAPTER TWENTY-THREE

JAY

"KEEP THEM CLOSED," she said, leanin' down to kiss me.

Listenin' to the rustlin' of her clothes as she removed 'em, I pictured her face. She'd shown up to profess her love for me and to apologize without her makeup—her mask—and her face was pale and perfect.

"Okay," she whispered, and I opened my eyes.

She stood before me like a goddess, naked and radiant. Lettin' her clothes fall from her fingers, they dropped and pooled on the floor around her bare feet, and her hair fell down around her shoulders like shiny, dark liquid sin.

"So, I-I want you to see the real me. Without my masks." She looked down at her body, fidgetin' a little. "I'm not perfect. Far from it." Takin' a deep breath, she stood her ground. "But I like my body. All my life, I've looked at it like it failed me. Like because it didn't look like everyone else's, it wasn't beautiful.

"But this body has held me up and carried me through so much, and I love it for that. My butt's too big. My boobs are floppy, my thighs—ugh." She rolled her eyes, and I couldn't help my smile. "But there must be something good about them if you like them because you're good. And honest.

"And I like food, damn it. What's wrong with that? Right? I'm not unhealthy, though I admit, after our wilderness trek through the desert, I realize I could probably do more to be stronger physically. But I don't want to change how I look. And since you said I'm beautiful—the most beautiful woman you've ever seen—I'm thinking maybe you don't want me to change either?"

"Never. Not one fuckin' thing." I growled the words, reachin' out to grip her hips. "Don't you dare."

"Lie back," she said, and I scooted up the bed. She knelt by my feet and untied my boot. "Wait."

Scootin' off the bed, she walked slowly to the door and locked it, then flicked the light switch on. The bare bulb zapped and flickered above me and the pull to look at her body was intense, but I couldn't look away from her eyes.

Plain as day, she said, "I don't want to hide from you anymore."

Crawlin' back over me, she straddled my legs, then pushed my shirt up, and I took it off. She pushed me a little, rollin' me to the side so she could pull my wallet out, smirkin' at me when she found a condom tucked into the little pocket inside. She dropped it on the bed next to me.

I watched her body while she removed my jeans and boxers. I remembered thinkin' her skin would be so soft, so I reached out, trailin' my fingers down one arm, and she shivered. We'd been together twice, but both times the light had been dim. Now I could see every part of her. Every inch, every curve, dip, bend, and beautiful dark hair.

Her breasts were large, but floppy was the *last* word on my mind. They were rounded and full and pale with nipples the color of dusted rose. I sat up, wrappin' my hands around her hips to pull her closer. They were wide and supple, and they fit my hands perfectly.

She moaned when I clutched 'em, and I sucked one peaked nipple into my mouth, lickin' and caressin' her breast with my tongue, gently pinchin' the hard bead between my teeth. With her legs spread wide above mine, I dragged my hands slowly, feelin' every inch of 'em, down as far as I could reach and back up the insides of her thighs till I felt the wet heat from her core on my hands, then slid my fingers through the slick and ready arousal just waitin' for me.

I looked up into her eyes, and she braced herself with her hands on my shoulders and rubbed herself against me. My other hand found its way around to her ass, and I held one cheek in my hand, usin' it to push her harder against my fingers still slidin' and glidin' her toward release.

"You are perfect, Billie. You're perfect for me. It hurt to be away from you."

When I pushed my fingers into her body and slowly pumped, she gasped. Her head fell back, and her long hair tickled my legs as I leaned forward, inhalin' and rubbin' my mouth between her breasts, soft and beautiful and flushed pink.

Pumpin' faster, I gripped her ass harder, then rubbed my thumb over her clit, and she moaned, a low, serious, husky sound. Her body squeezed my fingers, tryin' to pull me in deeper.

"Look at me. I wanna watch you come."

When she opened her eyes, she locked 'em onto mine, and there was uncertainty about her body, but there was also trust and love and so much need. Leanin' down, she rested her forehead against mine, and I gazed up at her above me, but she reached between us and pulled my fingers out, pushin' my hand away.

She retrieved the condom and rolled it over me, then positioned herself above my ready cock and sank down.

"I love you, Jonathan," she whispered. "I want to make love to you."

She did. We made love for hours, touchin' and explorin' every single inch of each other. I worshipped her body with mine, my hands, fingers, and mouth. I made love to every part of her body she doubted, to prove to her that every single inch of her was sexy and beautiful and perfect to me.

And she owned me with that body.

It was slow and quiet, and there was no shame or fear—no inhibition. No hidin'. No masks.

Only love and desire.

"Say my name again, Billie."

"Jonathan?"

"Yes. Say it again."

"Jonathan, Jonathan, Jonathan…"

EPILOGUE
JAY

"Seriously? You like this place? You don't have to make such a big decision so soon. You can stay at the ranch as long as you want."

Billie and I had been to three houses in and around Wisper, lookin' for a place for her to buy. She'd also bought the Jeep from our trip and named it Cali.

"Yeah, I know, but Carey wants me here for a while to work on this stuff with Theo. I'm afraid of what I'll find. That Blake guy eluded to Ace's birth mom being murdered." She sighed. "I don't want to have to tell her that, you know? Telling her that the mother she'd loved, who raised her, who she mourned, was not actually her real mother was the hardest conversation I've ever had. She's so hurt. And she's *so* mad at Theo. I'm not sure she'll ever forgive him."

I pushed her bangs away from her eyes so I could see 'em. "I know. You're a good friend."

She smiled. "But I figured we might need a place of our own. Or do you *like* Finn lurking around while we're having sex? And what's not to like?" We slowly walked through the empty, old, two-story farmhouse three miles from my ranch, and I trailed my hand over the woodwork. "Besides, I can work from anywhere."

She looked at me and plainly stated, "This is where my family is. It's where I wanna be." She shrugged and I kissed her lips. "My... mother wants to come out." She said the word like it made her nauseous. "And it's big enough for all of your overgrown brothers to hang out or eat dinner or whatever. And Ace can stay here while Theo recovers and they work out that whole thing. And we *definitely* need to separate Finn and Ace. They need to go to separate corners for time out." She giggled like a little girl, and man, how I loved the sound. "You noticed that right? It's not just me?"

"Oh, I noticed."

"Anyway, she says she wants to stay in Wisper. Surprised the crap out of me. She's a city girl through and through. But I think she feels safe here, you know? And since that Louise lady and Theo's driver were killed, they don't have any family left in Boston. No ties except for Theo's business." She shrugged again and opened a closet door to look in. "She wants me to help her create a vlog."

"Yeah. I can't blame her for wantin' to stay. Theo's doin' better, but he's still a mess. I think the whole thing took a toll on him. I mean, physically, he'll heal, but I think he was in love with his driver. I feel bad for him. He seems so lost." I looked in the closet, too, and out the window. The house faced south, so I could see the same mountain I looked at every day from the paddocks at the ranch. "But I guess I figured you for a modern kinda person. This place is almost a hundred years old."

"I like old shit. Have you seen my answering machine?"

I chuckled. "It's a lotta money though. Are you sure? You've only seen it once. It'll probably need some renovations."

She turned, blockin' me from exitin' the master bedroom as we were about to walk out. "Guess it's good then that my boyfriend and his brothers know how to fix shit"—she kissed my lips—"and that I have money if they don't feel like it. We could grow brussel sprouts in the front yard. I think the realtor said the property has two acres."

She smiled up at me, crossin' her eyes and makin' a goofy face. "Besides, I need space to spread out. I need more gear. I'd like to dedicate one whole bedroom to my searches. Ooo, I can picture it. Like a gigantic electronic perp board from some over-directed FBI TV show. Touch screens *everywhere*." She clapped her hands together in front of her voluptuous chest, fanned her face, and said, "I'm getting hot just thinking about it."

I smiled and shook my head. "You're a nerd."

"Damn straight. And no fair," she whined.

"What's not fair?"

"When you smile like that, I get wet." She pushed up on her toes to kiss me, slippin' her tongue in my mouth, and she grabbed my ass with both hands and squeezed.

"Billie," I whispered.

"What?" She leaned back, dipped her chin, and peered up at me with a seductive smile in her eyes. "Are you blushing?"

I flashed my eyes, droppin' 'em in embarrassment, and shook my head at her blatant attempt to seduce me in the middle of somebody else's house with the realtor just downstairs. "Yeah, but you could rent a place. Are you sure you wanna buy a house?"

"Are you planning on dumping me?"

"Nope. You're stuck with me. That freak you out?"

Her face lit up and she smiled big, then tilted her head to the side, listenin' for the realtor. She reached down the front of my jeans, wrappin' her fingers around my erection, the one that was permanently hard since she'd come back to me and settled in.

"Dammit, woman. You're trouble on two legs."

"Oh, come on," she whispered, slidin' her panties down, slippin' 'em off her legs under her short skirt and stuffin' 'em in her messenger bag, then dropped it to the floor with a soft thud. "The realtor's downstairs on the phone." She grabbed my hand, guidin' it between her legs. "Make me come. Quick. It'll be good luck. And then, after I buy it, we can christen every room in the house with your cock inside me."

"Billie!" I chastened, but I slid my fingers between her wet lips, rubbin' 'em over her clit, and she moaned as we shuffled back against a wall.

"Yes." She rocked against my hand, closin' her eyes and grindin' hard, and I bent my knees and pushed two fingers inside her. "Ohh," she breathed. "And we can have the wedding out back. There's a great view of the mountains past the field of wildflowers. Perfect for a girly wedding."

My eyebrows hit the roof and I froze, lookin' right in her pale gray eyes when she opened 'em, but they weren't surrounded by makeup. She really had shed her mask.

I sputtered, "Did you just ask me to marry you?"

"Well, I didn't ask, exactly. I planned to do it a little more smoothly, but I can't help myself when you touch me. But yeah, I did just ask you to marry me. You gonna argue?"

Through half-closed lids, I looked down upon her as she rode my hand to rapture, her mouth open, chest heavin' with breath. The look in those sultry eyes was pure sin, and I captured her mouth with mine, matchin' the rhythm of my tongue with the rhythm of my fingers below, and she gasped and moaned into my mouth.

Watchin' the pleasure on her face never got old, knowin' I did that to her. Made her feel so good.

But she made me brave.

When I felt her core start to squeeze and contract around my fingers, I dragged 'em from her body, slidin' 'em up the hot wet channel between her legs slowly, then unbuttoned my jeans and shoved 'em down my hips a little. My dick sprang free between our bodies, and I lifted her up, impalin' her on my cock, and she locked her ankles behind my ass. Thank the sweet Lord for birth control pills.

I rasped out, "No. I ain't arguin'."

I groaned and she yelped, "Yes!"

"Shh, Billie," I whispered, smilin' and thrustin' my hips hard. She grunted and panted and dug her fingers into my scalp as she kissed me. It was all so hot and hurried, and the exhibitionistic feelin' of the whole thing made me harder, made the ache in my dick worse.

Plus, she did just ask me to marry her.

I fucked her faster, and she rolled her hips against me as hard as she could.

"I'm gonna come, Jonathan. Please... oh please, make me come. I'm right there."

"Oh yeah," I grunted, "me too." She licked her fingers and reached between us to rub her clit. "Fuck."

"Oh my God. I love when you cuss."

Her eyes rolled back in her head when I slammed her hips down on mine. I lost my balance a little 'cause I still couldn't put much weight on my ankle, so I pushed her hard against the wall for support, and she banged her elbow.

"Ow!"

"Shit, sorry. You okay?"

Mrs. Brooks called up the stairs in chipper voice, "Miss Acker? Are you up there?"

"Yeah!"

"Billie," I begged, but I wasn't sure what for. I didn't wanna stop but—

"Don't stop. I'm coming," she whispered, and I kissed her, pushin' my tongue in her mouth, and she sucked it. I pounded my hips once more and we came. "Oh!"

Her body clamped down on mine and I saw stars.

"What do you think of the house?" Mrs. Brooks asked as she climbed the stairs. "It has a lovely feel, doesn't it? Perfect for a young couple."

Billie collapsed against me, pantin' and gigglin', then slid down to the floor, adjusted her skirt, zipped my jeans, and turned just as Mrs. Brooks stepped into the doorway.

I tripped over my cast and fell on my ass while she tried to hide her smile. "We love it! We'll take it."

BYTE ME

TTYL

END

;)

If you liked the book (or loved it, I hope), please leave a review—even just a few words would help—wherever you buy your books, Amazon, Goodreads, or Bookbub. Self-published indie authors rely heavily upon reviews to get our stories out to the masses. And thank you. I know it takes time to do this. I appreciate the time out of your day and the effort.

BLINDED

I was dreamin' of the ocean.

The waves lapped at my feet as I stood, facin' out to look at the big, wide expanse of the world, listenin' to the quiet water roll and push and pull.

The gentle crash of the surf was warm and frothy, and it calmed me from my toes up to the top of my head. I smiled, swayin' in the night air, inhalin' and drawin' a slow breath into my lungs, the soft scents of sand and salt water and… somethin' else relaxin' me. Somethin' tropical. No, somethin' sensual—sexy. Like what I imagined a woman's skin would smell like after she'd been swimmin' in the ocean. Salt and wet, sweet sweat and desire.

Funny, I could describe what desire looked like on the outside but not what it felt like inside my body. Not really. I couldn't describe what it felt like to touch a woman who wanted what was on the inside of my mind instead of on the outside of my skin—a woman who wanted me for how I made her feel and think, instead of just what I looked like.

Plenty of women thought that was what they felt for me, plenty had told me they desired me, but aside from the baser need to release, I'd never met a woman I desired that way either. Not one who turned me inside out with need and love and want. And, contrary to what everyone believed about me, I'd never met a woman who desired *me*. I wasn't sure anyone cared about the thoughts in my head.

But, even though I couldn't describe what it felt like to be really wanted, somehow, in my dream, I knew the scents I could smell all around me, taste on my tongue, feel like silk on my skin—I knew the woman I would be with, when I finally found the one I couldn't live without, I knew she'd smell like this.

Like the sea.

Drawin' the scent into my body one last time, I turned to walk away; it was a dream, but I still had a shit-ton of work to do in the mornin', so I figured I could hint to my dream self that it was time for a little uninterrupted REM.

But as I turned, somethin' grabbed and slapped at my feet. Hard. It stung my wet skin, tuggin' me backward gently, and instinctually, I kicked at it but it began to wind up my legs.

It felt like a wide scratchy rope, but when I looked down to see what had stung and scraped my skin, I gasped. An iridescent, incandescent ribbon of light that changed from ice blue to glowin' pale green with little sparks of yellow wound its way up my legs, flashin' and winkin' in the dark.

It scratched and crawled its way up my body quickly, trappin' my arms to my torso, and then it wrapped itself around my chest. It didn't hurt, not really, but it was uncomfortable.

Suddenly, it stopped its trailin' ascent, pullin' itself into a tight circle around my throat. I worried it would try to choke me, but it didn't. I wanted to rip it off, but the warm and irritating ribbon seemed sad. Lost... Okay, yeah, this was a dream, but come on. A sad fuckin' ribbon? What the hell was my subconscious up to?

Wrappin' itself around my eyes, the melancholy marauder blinded me, cuttin' off my last advantage. It pulled itself into a tight knot behind my head, tanglin' my hair in its clutches, and fell away from every other part of my body, hangin' loose, danglin' and swayin' in the ocean breeze next to me, pokin' me here and there. It ticked my skin.

The ribbon wanted to play, or so I thought.

But then those deceptive tendrils started hittin' me, pummelin' me in the face! They shoved themselves inside my mouth, chokin' and gaggin' me, and they dragged me back to the water, pushin' me down into it. The salt assaulted my nose and ears and burned my skin as I was dragged under.

I tried to call out for help, but really, what had I expected —I was still in la-la land—there wasn't anybody around to help me. And no sound came outta my mouth anyway. I couldn't move my arms or legs, and they felt like they weighed a thousand pounds apiece.

Somehow, in all my drownin' glory, it occurred to me that I wasn't even tryin' to fight. I didn't wanna die, 'course not, but I wanted my tiny, murderous ribbon to be happy, to feel free.

I heard Homer Simpson in my head—"D'oh!"

Had I, in about two minutes inside of some imaginary dreamscape, succumbed to some kinda kinky inanimate-object-focused Stockholm syndrome?

Fuck. My last thought was that I was about to die in two feet of water in an ocean I'd never actually seen, and I hadn't even had a chance to perfect my Mole sauce or Boeuf Bour-guignon!

Well.

Shit.

Pre-Order BLINDED: A Cade Ranch Novel, coming Spring 2022

WANT MORE?

Become a Wisperite!

Join my newsletter for exclusive stories, Wisper news, and The Cade Ranch Sexcapades—naughty little interludes for my subscribers ONLY!

Jack and Evvie's wedding scenes are there!

Sign up for your first FREE short story, Wild Heart: Welcome to Wisper

Sign up on my website!

gretarosewest.com

I would love to hear from you, email me at greta@gretarosewest.com.

I'll reply.

You can find me on the usual social sites, but I mostly hang out on Instagram, Facebook, and Goodreads.

Join my Team!

Receive an advanced review copy of my next book. Join my Street Team, a wonderful group of people who help get the word out when I release a new book!

Sign up on my website

gretarosewest.com

ABOUT THE AUTHOR

Greta Rose West was a floundering artsy flake until Jack showed up, knocking on the door of her brain, and then pounding on it, and then he just plain kicked it down. She lives in NW Indiana with her husband and her two precocious kitties, Geoff Trouble and Sally Mae Midnight. When she's not writing, she's reading and devouring music. She enjoys indie films no one else likes, and her favorite food is Aver's Veggie Revival pizza.

Made in the USA
Las Vegas, NV
20 February 2022

44247559R00163